DARK DATA

CONTROL, ALT, DELETE

For permission requests and subsidiary rights, contact
Plum Bay Publishing, LLC at the website below:
www.plumbaypublishing.com

Library of Congress Control number: 2019938584
ISBN: 978-1-7335253-3-6

Printed in the United States of America

Cover design by Lauren Harvey
Interior layout by Lance Buckley
Edited by Jeremy Townsend and Kate Petrella

DARK DATA

CONTROL, ALT, DELETE

DOUGLAS J. WOOD

PLUM BAY PUBLISHING, LLC

"CYBER WARFARE IS AS MUCH ABOUT PSYCHOLOGICAL STRATEGY AS TECHNICAL PROWESS."

—JAMES SCOTT,

SENIOR FELLOW, INSTITUTE FOR CRITICAL INFRASTRUCTURE TECHNOLOGY

PHASE ONE

PLANTING THE SEEDS

ONE

PIAZZA DELLA SIGNORIA, FLORENCE, ITALY
ONE YEAR FROM NOW

HASHIR RASHID SQUINTED AT THE BRIGHT SUN SHINING OVER THE PIAZZA DELLA SIGNORIA in Florence. It would soon reflect off of the blood that was about to flow. Tourists and locals alike gathered, as they did every afternoon, at the Caffe Rivoire for a cappuccino and biscotti. Some enjoyed the gelato and homemade chocolate or sipped beer and wine. Adjacent to the Piazza della Signoria, in the shadow of the Duomo, Rashid gazed at Florence's town hall and the office of its mayor. Then he turned his eyes up to the Duomo. Next to the Vatican, the Florence Duomo is Italy's second largest cathedral and is always crowded. He knew he could count on a big crowd, especially on such a beautiful day in early spring. The art- and history-filled Renaissance city, the birthplace of Michelangelo di Lodovico Buonarroti Simoni, Dante Alighieri, Leonardo da Vinci, and Filippo Brunelleschi, would be a great place to die.

No one paid much notice to twenty-two-year-old Rashid. His dark hair, olive complexion, and slight build helped him blend in to those crowding the piazza. He was dressed in jeans, and while his coat was bulky, nothing about him looked out of the ordinary. He was just another tourist.

Rashid calmly walked across the piazza as if he did not have a care in the world. The fact that he was about to die for Allah meant nothing to those around him. It could not. How could they know that Rashid was about to obliterate himself for the glory of his God, and murder or maim hundreds of infidels? No one knew how anxious Rashid was to meet his destiny. It meant everything to him.

He muttered the words of the Quran, 4:74: "Whoso fighteth in the way of Allah, be he slain or be he victorious, on him We shall bestow a vast reward." Rashid was born in Saudi Arabia, and was Sunni, but was radicalized from his early childhood. His father, Osama Rashid, a devout Muslim, was committed to the calls of the radical Sunni Salafi-Jihadis to annihilate anyone who did not bow to the Will of Allah. But Rashid now knew his father was a coward at heart, unwilling to give up his own life for the jihad. He did not, however, hesitate to offer his son for sacrifice. He gave him over to the radicals when Hashir was just four. The men not only offered to care for the boy but to see that he was properly educated in Islam and groomed for glory to Allah. What more could a father ask for? In the early days of his training, Hashir hated his father for abandoning him, but the more radicalized he became, the more he believed that while he may have been a coward, his father had done the right thing.

Rashid's training was a lot more than simply learning how to fire a gun or build a bomb. When he was fourteen, Rashid was sent to North Korea under a secret student-exchange program. He learned to speak Korean and became further indoctrinated against the United States and its allies. When his schooling in Korea was completed, he was next sent to England to study at the University of Oxford, where he was taught economics. During breaks, he returned to Saudi Arabia for more training. Radical groups like ISIS, al-Qaeda, Islamic State, the Taliban, Al-Shabaab, and Boko Haram realized in the twenty-first century that education in Western ways was essential to break down the institutions the infidels relied upon. Rashid was taught that the civil wars in the Middle East, and the flow of refugees into Europe, would make it all the easier to freely move radicals throughout the continent. By the time Rashid was prepared to meet his God, operating cells of terrorists were established throughout Europe.

So here he was at age twenty-two, a seasoned Islamic radical, thoroughly schooled in traditional academics and taught to hate democracy, America, and anyone who disagreed with the teachings in the Quran, prepared to die in a glorious conflagration.

Rashid's dedication to the Islamic cause was unquestioned. At just under six feet and weighing 190 pounds, he was physically fit and an expert in hand-to-hand combat and martial arts, earning a black belt when he was only eight. He was fearless and thoroughly indoctrinated to the Islamic cause. And he was ready to die.

As Rashid walked toward the Caffe Rivoire, he looked with deep disdain at those he passed, hiding his hatred behind his dark glasses. Most of the tourists with cameras appeared to be Asian. Rashid had no patience for Asians despite his months in North Korea. He saw them as infidels to be hated just as much as Christians and Jews. He reveled in the idea that they too would soon be dead. But they would not join him in the afterlife. Rashid would be with his harem of virgins enjoying the religious validation he so yearned to have. The infidels would burn in the Jahannam, hell where they belonged.

Rashid mumbled to himself, "I will cast terror into the hearts of those who disbelieve. Therefore strike off their heads and strike off every fingertip of them." Quran (8:12)

Rashid spotted a figure atop the Loggia dei Lanzi. He recognized Farid Humayun, his Mullah, his mentor. The night before, Farid had prepared Rashid, reciting the shahada with him. *La ilaha illa Allah wa-Muhammad rasul Allah* ("There is no god but God and Muhammad is the prophet of God"). They bathed in the purity of Zamzam, the holy water of the Sunni. They donned their ihraam, the sacred white robes Islamic worshippers wear to their pilgrimage to Mecca and as shrouds upon their death.

"Excuse me," asked an Asian tourist, stopping Rashid, and pulling his attention back to the piazza and the mingling doomed souls around him. "Would you mind taking a picture of my wife and me?"

Rashid first considered the request as an unwanted interruption. He wanted to tell them no, but thought it ironic that two people he was about to annihilate wanted a photograph for posterity.

He smiled at the idea of leaving such a photo in the rubble he was about to create.

"Do you know how to work this phone?" the tourist asked.

Do I know how to work this phone? Rashid wanted to respond. *You are about to die and you want to see if I can take a picture from your phone!*

"Yes, of course. I have the same phone," Rashid lied.

He took the picture and handed back the phone. When the couple suggested that they'd like to take a selfie with him in the photo, Rashid said no. He had no interest in being in any photograph with an infidel.

Rashid continued to the Caffe Rivoire, calmly looking to see how many people were gathered. It seemed to be more than enough. He was particularly happy to see two uniformed police officers within fifteen feet of him. They were the local Carabinieri, Italy's military police, assigned to the piazza, and patrolled as they always did, oblivious of the tourists and just trying to get through the day to the end of their shifts. They showed no interest in confronting anyone, much less some young Muslim wandering among the crowd. Knowing they were also about to die only made Rashid feel more fulfilled.

It was time. Rashid screamed, "Allahu Akbar!" and pressed the button on his detonator.

Click.

Nothing.

Rashid repeated his scream and clicked the button again. The plastic explosives, nails, and ball bearings wrapped tightly around his chest and back should have vaporized him and the infidels around him. But nothing happened.

Click, click, click.

Nothing.

Within seconds, the two Carabinieri tackled Rashid to the ground. The piazza visitors ran in panic. Chaos erupted.

Rashid was docile and in shock, unable to understand his failure. He caught sight of Humayun. Farid appeared to be talking on his phone. That was all the more confusing to Rashid.

Humayun watched from atop the Loggia dei Lanzi and made a call to his liaison at the United States Central Intelligence Agency, pleased to report that everything had worked according to his plan.

TWO

GORGONA, TUSCAN ARCHIPELAGO

GORGONA ISLAND IS LOCATED TWENTY-TWO MILES WEST OF LIVORNO ON ITALY'S WEST coast. While little more than an hour from Livorno by ferry over calm seas, access is forbidden without permission from the Italian Ministry of Justice. Some supervised tours are allowed, but cameras are strictly prohibited. If a private boat is foolish enough to cruise closer than a quarter mile, it is swiftly met with police boats and chased away.

Security is very high because since 1869, the island has been a penal colony incarcerating some of Italy's most violent criminals. Although the prison is high-security, cells are relatively comfortable and there is significant space for group activities, including a full soccer field. What very few know, however, is that the island has been a dark site for the United States Central Intelligence Agency since the first terrorist bombing of New York's World Trade Center, in 1993.

What most sets the island apart in ironic contrast to its prison walls are the vineyards that cover the hills and provide the Vermentino and Ansonica grapes for a white wine produced under the watchful eyes of Marchesi de' Frescobaldi, one of Italy's most fabled vintners.

This prison's reformation to a vineyard began in 2008 when an inmate tried to cultivate some old vines on the island. While the wine he produced was considered awful, the warden seized on the idea and reached out to Frescobaldi for help. The association has been very successful. Since 2012,

Gorgona wine is among the most expensive and rarest in Italy. Annually, fewer than 4,000 bottles are produced.

Prisoners tend to the vines, raise animals needed to maintain the island's economy and grow tomatoes, eggplants, zucchini, fennel, and basil while producing cheese, bread, and honey as well. Being winemakers does the inmates well; their recidivism is one-fifth of what occurs among their counterparts incarcerated in the mainland prisons.

Gorgona was Rashid's new home.

Rashid's head was covered in a black hood so he could see nothing. But he knew he was not alone. He sensed others around him even though no one was talking.

What went wrong? he wondered silently.

He and Humayun were meticulous in preparing for his moment of glory. Everything was wired carefully and checked over again and again. All the prayers were recited with complete piety and reverence.

Why did Allah deny me? What did I do wrong?

Rashid felt someone's hand gently rest on his shoulder while the other grabbed the hood and removed it. The light was bright, but it took only a few seconds for Rashid to gain his focus. What he saw confused him further.

"Farid?" *What is my Mullah doing here?* he wondered. "Where am I?"

"Welcome to Gorgona, Hashir," Humayun said to him. "You are in the island prison of Italy, in the Mediterranean, much like Alcatraz is in the San Francisco Bay in the United States. You've probably heard of Alcatraz, yes? But you have never heard of Gorgona."

Rashid looked around. He was in a small room with no windows. The floors and walls were cement, painted a dull gray. A single fixture hung from the ceiling, giving the place a dark, threatening aura. With its musty smell, Rashid sensed he was in a basement or some other underground facility. The chair he sat on was metal and bolted to the floor. His hands were cuffed behind his back and his ankles were shackled to the legs of the chair.

Humayun sat on a chair about three feet in front of Rashid. Two men in guard uniforms flanked him. Humayun was dressed casually, as he was the night before, when he and Rashid prepared.

"I know this is all confusing for you, Hashir," Humayun began. "You were never destined to die today. That was not the plan. Instead, you were saved from a fate no one deserves. And no one in that piazza deserved to die, either. Not for the Will of Allah or any other God."

"I don't understand, Farid. You and I prepared together. I was ready. We prayed together for my salvation. What have you done?"

"What I have done, Hashir, is save your life so you can redeem your soul before it is lost forever. I have kept you from murdering countless innocent people for no purpose. I have given you a chance for true redemption."

Rashid shook his head. "How could you betray me? How could you betray Allah?"

"Hashir, listen to me. You need to pay attention to what I'm saying to you."

"Farid, I don't know what you've done, but you have forsaken our solemn obligations. The obligations you and I prayed for just a day ago. You're as condemned as the fools in the piazza who should have died with me!"

Rashid spat at Humayun.

Humayun waved away the guard who was about to slap Rashid.

"No, leave him alone," Humayun ordered. "Hashir, you will soon see the error of your ways. Just as I did. It will take time, but we are patient. For now, you will spend some time here. Then we'll talk about how you'll serve the true meaning of Islam."

Humayun stood and left the room.

The guard unshackled Rashid's hands and legs and led him down the hall to a staircase. As they walked up the steps, the guard shoved his baton into Rashid's ribs and said, "As far as I'm concerned, you're a piece of Muslim scum. Why we don't just cut your head off is a wonder to me. I hope you rot wherever they intend to send you."

Rashid said nothing despite the pain. He's experienced far greater pain before. He only felt anger and hatred.

The guard pushed him into a cell. It was tiny, with a cot, a soft mattress and pillow, a prayer rug, a desk, and a chair. A barred window along the ceiling's edge allowed light into the room.

Rashid, now alone, lay on the bed, cursing his life and praying that Allah would give him the opportunity to avenge Humayun's treachery.

THREE

GORGONA PRISON CELL

RASHID AWOKE THE NEXT MORNING TO THE HARSH METALLIC SOUND OF THE DOOR TO HIS cell opening. He wondered if that sound would wake him up every day for the rest of his life.

"Get up!" ordered one of the two guards who had greeted Rashid on his first day in Gorgona Prison. "We're taking you to the shower so you can clean up and rid yourself of your terrorist stench. Here's some breakfast. Eat."

I guess he doesn't like me, concluded Rashid. *I'll be sure he dies with great pain.*

The other guard appeared and placed the tray of food and a cup of black coffee on the desk. Rashid was hungry and wasted no time eating all of it. He mentally noted that the fork and spoon were metal, but he was not given a knife. He was inclined to hide the fork or spoon to later use as a weapon. But he concluded the guards, as stupid as they were, were not complete idiots and would realize something was missing. They at least knew how to count to two.

After eating, Rashid obeyed the order to follow the guards down a hallway bordered on both sides by cells. Like his cell, they were small but comfortable. Most of the dozen or so cells along the corridor were empty. Only two had inmates, both of whom were clearly Arabic.

As Rashid walked by, he greeted each prisoner with *As-Salam-u-Alaikum*, Arabic for "Peace be unto you." But neither responded. Neither looked up at Rashid as he passed. Each had the look of a defeated man. Rashid felt a shiver as the finality of what he was facing started to sink in.

The hot shower felt good. It had been nearly two days since Rashid last bathed. He was glad to get rid of the smell the guard complained about, although he hardly regarded it as the odor of a terrorist. Rashid saw himself as a servant of Allah, now wanting to believe he was spared in the piazza for a reason. He resolved to wait for his opportunity to kill as many of the infidels in Gorgona Prison as he could, including the traitor Humayun. Then he would free his other brothers from their cells.

Once Rashid was done with his shower, a guard threw him a towel and some prison garb like the clothes the prisoners in the other cells were wearing. Gray and drab but clean and comfortable.

As Rashid looked at himself in the mirror, he feared he was looking at a ghost. In his heart he felt he had failed, but Rashid told himself there had to be a reason Allah let him live. Surviving the bombing without taking out a single infidel could not have been worse. His only salvation, as he saw it, was Humayun causing the failure. And Rashid knew that Humayun would eventually pay for his sins.

"Stop staring at yourself and follow me," ordered a guard, snapping Rashid out of his daydream.

Down another hallway with empty cells on either side.

Are there only two other prisoners here? What is this place for?

The guard brought him into a windowless room with light-green walls and a six-foot wooden table in the center. One side had two armchairs and the other side had one. The chairs were like the ones you find in an office conference room, not in a prison interrogation room. An empty side table was against one wall. A long mirror hung above it. On the opposite wall was a large whiteboard, markers lying in its tray. Paintings of outdoor island landscapes of grapevines and livestock occupied the other two walls. The floor was carpeted. It was much more comfortable than Rashid expected.

The guard motioned him to sit at the table opposite the mirror. Instead, Rashid started to move to the other side of the table so he could sit with his back to the mirror.

The guard grabbed his arm tightly and led him to the side with the single chair.

"Sit down." Rashid obeyed, noting that the guard was not armed and knowing that if he wanted to, Rashid could kill the man in just seconds. Such abilities were all part of his training. But he also knew he needed to wait until he could kill more than only one. His real target was Humayun.

I must be patient. Allah will tell me when to kill and to die in his glory.

As far as Rashid was concerned, the guard's order confirmed his suspicion that the mirror was two-way so the room's activities could be observed from the other side of the wall. He was right.

Once Rashid sat, the guard positioned himself behind him. Rashid could see the guard in the mirror. He had as good a poker face as Rashid had ever seen. The other guard stood by the door.

As Rashid took in the surroundings, he took particular notice of the guard's uniforms. They looked military but had no insignia. Nor did they have names embroidered on the pockets or any way of identifying the unit to which they belonged. This was unlike Western thinking, which produced uniforms typically strewn with names, badges, flags, and any other insignia of perceived importance. In Rashid's world, uniforms were blank canvases.

This must be a secret prison. Stay strong.

Based on what he had observed, Rashid was convinced they were Americans. While only one guard spoke, and at that said very little, his accent gave him away. Rashid resolved to store that in his memory bank. He smiled at the prospect of killing two Americans.

The door opened, and Humayun walked in with another man.

"Good morning, Hashir," said Humayan in Arabic. "I trust your night was comfortable and you are feeling refreshed."

Rashid said nothing and gave Humayun a hateful stare. Humayun clearly understood.

"Hashir, you may hate me now and hold a fervent desire to kill me, but we're going to try to change that." Humayun's voice was calm, as it always was with Rashid. This time, however, Rashid derived no comfort from it.

"Let me introduce you to Richard Harris," Humayun said, switching to English as he gestured to the man next to him. "Mr. Harris is with the United States Central Intelligence Agency. And so am I."

Rashid was shocked at how frank and matter-of-fact Humayun was in admitting he was with the CIA. No organization in the world could have been more of an anathema to Islam.

"Good morning," offered Harris as he and Humayun sat opposite Rashid at the table. Within seconds, the door opened and two attendants came in as if on cue with coffee and some pastries. Rashid was happy to accept a cup of coffee but declined anything to eat. Harris took a cup of coffee while Humayun took bottled water. Neither opted for a pastry.

Richard Harris was obviously not a "by the book" CIA field operative. Rashid could sense that immediately. The man was tall, with a muscular build and imposing air. He was obviously in command. Humayun must report to him. Rashid wondered who else did, and just how high up Harris was in the hierarchy. He felt a slight glimmer of pride that he deserved such attention.

With double agents strewn throughout the world, including Humayun, Harris was as good as anyone can be at clandestine operations. An array of CIA black sites like Gorgona were under his command. He reported directly to the director of the CIA and his budget was unknown to all but the director, the U.S. president, and a handful of members of Congress. It had virtually no limits.

Only a small number of trusted colleagues knew the identities of his agents and informants. Quite often, even the Director of the CIA, Michael Hellriegel, was unaware of their names, operations, or locations. The director only wanted results. It was better for political appointees to be unaware of details, allowing plausible denial when needed and "eliminating" failed field agents easier.

Yet even with his imposing presence, Harris carried himself in such a way that no one would ever guess that the lives of so many depended upon his orders, and at times on his whims. If there ever was truth to the James Bond myth of possessing a license to kill, Harris had one—and he was not afraid to use it.

Harris's circle of influence included Senator Horace Simpson, Chair of the Intelligence Oversight Committee, and Congresswomen Beatrice Hue, Chair of the House Intelligence Committee. Both were key to funding what Harris needed for his covert operations. Like the legendary J. Edgar Hoover, former director of the FBI, Harris made sure he had dirt on each of them to be certain they remained beholden to him for more than political support. It wasn't hard to get it. As far as Harris was concerned, there wasn't an honest politician in Washington. You didn't get elected by being a choirboy. Some might call it blackmail. Harris saw it as the insurance a patriot needed to stay in the business of protecting America.

FOUR

GORGONA INTERROGATION ROOM

"MR. RASHID, MAY I CALL YOU HASHIR?" ASKED HARRIS.

Rashid did not respond.

"Please call me Richard. Formalities are not necessary here."

I'll call you the pig you are and one day piss on your entrails.

Rashid continued to sit silently.

"Very well, Hashir. It is understandable that you are confused right now. So was Humayun when we first met years ago. But as you can see, he is now quite enlightened."

Rashid could not resist and spat across the table at Humayun, yelling, "*Khayin!*" "Traitor!"

The guard grabbed Rashid's shoulders to keep him seated, but Rashid never attempted to stand. Harris waved the guard off.

"I'll assume that was not a compliment to Humayun," offered Harris with a grin. Humayun smiled, slightly nodding his head as he took a sip of water while using a napkin to wipe off the table.

Harris continued. "As you can see, you are not restrained. Your room, while admittedly a cell, is quite comfortable. And you'll find the food is excellent and compliant with your religious beliefs. Later, the guards will show you where you can do your daily prayers and eventually meet others who we have as our guests."

"What are you doing with my two brothers in the cells near me?" demanded Rashid. "Why would they not look up at me or say a word when I passed?" Rashid decided he needed to know what might lie ahead for him.

"I assumed you'd want to know. You are free to try to speak to all of our guests, Rashid. However, just as they will not respond to you, they ignore us. So for now, we keep them in their cells, hoping they will come around and accept our hospitality as it is intended. We do not mean to hurt them. But we do mean to educate them."

He realized then that the two silent inmates were intentionally placed near Rashid's cell as a subtle hint of what he would become if he failed to cooperate.

"Educate them? Why would you need to educate them?" asked Rashid.

Humayun interjected, "Because like you, Hashir, they lost their way as Muslims. We need to teach them the true ways of Allah. We need to teach them the peace of Allah and rid them of the lies of vengeance and violence you and I heard for years."

Rashid responded, "*Telhas bukshee.*"

That resulted in an immediate response from Humayun. "*Inti tel-ahsi lahalek!*"

The two stared at one another but remained seated.

"Interesting, and while I don't understand your language, my guess us the two of you weren't expressing your undying love for one another!" quipped Harris. Humayun mouthed "Lick my ass," to Harris, who grinned. "And your response?"

"I told him to go lick it himself," Humayun replied.

"Hardly endearments," Harris nodded. "OK, let's move on. Hashir, you'll be spending a few months here attending classes and having opportunities to speak to other guests who are in the program. Depending upon the speed of your progress, you will next visit one of our centers elsewhere in the world, where you will continue your education. Eventually, we'll talk about where you go when you're done."

I will fool you both. And wait for the chance to avenge Allah.

"And if you're thinking you can outsmart us into thinking you have been saved so you can then return to your terrorist jihad, that will not succeed. We're a lot better at knowing who is lying than liars are at fooling us."

We'll see. "I don't need to be re-educated. There is nothing you can teach me.

"That's what they all say, Hashir. That is what they all say," calmly responded Harris.

"I'll die in the name of Allah before I betray my brothers." Rashid's expression was defiant.

"Indeed, they all say that, too, Hashir," continued Harris. "And some get their wish. I hope you're not among them."

FIVE

ST. PETERSBURG, RUSSIA

"GOOD MORNING, MR. COOPER," SAID THE OPERATOR IN A VOICE TOO CHEERFUL FOR SUCH AN EARLY hour. "This is your 7:30 wakeup call. Would you like us to call again at 7:45?"

"No, thank you. I'm up." Even though the voice was a recording, Cooper felt obliged to respond. Electronic voice recognition as a substitute for human interaction was now the norm for most routine requests at hotels.

St. Petersburg's Lotto Hotel on Antonenko Lane was one of the newer hotels in Russia. Owned by a Korean hotel conglomerate, Lotte hotels are among the most luxurious in the world and fit well into the lifestyle of Francis "Frank" Cooper, a lawyer who knew how to help his international clientele launder money. Cooper did not care why they needed to wash their ill-gotten cash. As long as his very healthy fees were paid, he turned a blind eye to their business.

A nondescript man at five-foot-eight with light brown hair and dark eyes, Cooper was at least 30 pounds overweight and drank far too much. While he eschewed the drugs many of his clients offered, he loved the party life and the women that came with it. The fact that most women found him physically repulsive and boorish made no difference to him. His clients or his money always made sure he got what he wanted. That was his perk for loyalty and tight lips among the criminals he represented.

Following a post–law school stint with a small firm in New York City that specialized in criminal defense, Cooper was approached by an emissary of Constantine Petrenko, one of the firm's clients. Cooper had never met

Petrenko, as was the case with nearly everyone at the firm. Cooper had just finished a successful defense of one of Petrenko's executives, who had been accused of embezzlement. While the executive was clearly guilty of stealing millions from a cancer clinic in New York, Cooper got him off with a hung jury. No retrial occurred. Cooper did not bother to ask why two jurors, despite overwhelming evidence, refused to convict. Nor did Cooper care. As far as he was concerned, a win was a win, and he had a long string of them for Petrenko's business associates.

"Mr. Cooper," said Petrenko's messenger, "you are a very talented lawyer. But we think being in a firm holds you back. We have operations all over the world under constant attack by misguided and misinformed prosecutors. Someone who works only for us and defends our rights would be very well paid."

Yeah, thought Cooper, *you're crooks like most of my clients and want me to help you hide your money and cover your crimes. But so what? As long as the money is right, I'm OK with it.*

As Cooper's career progressed with Petrenko, the money became far better than Cooper had imagined. He never regretted that he wasted no time leaving the firm and accepting the proverbial "offer he couldn't refuse." For him, it was all about money and the high life. All about being out from under the constraints of a law firm that still believed in ethics. After all, as far as Cooper was concerned, he couldn't care less about the honesty of his clients, much less his own. His only condition was that he remain in private practice with a few other clients so he could insulate himself from being an alter ego for Petrenko. Doing so helped him avoid undesired scrutiny by government prosecutors. And when it came to protecting criminals from themselves, no one did it better than Cooper. So Petrenko agreed that Cooper could remain in private practice with other clients on the condition that Cooper made sure he was always ready for Petrenko. It was more of an order than a request. Cooper had a few other clients, but Petrenko represented most of his business.

The money was good. Very good. And it allowed Cooper to enjoy the lifestyle he loved. Wine, women, and all that came with it. Cooper lost all concern over legal ethics. He was as hardened a criminal and as corrupt as the clients he represented.

Cooper usually looked forward to seeing Petrenko, but today was not one of those times. Petrenko summoned him to St. Petersburg for a meeting that Cooper knew would be unpleasant. Cooper had failed to deliver on Petrenko's latest demand. Failing with Petrenko was not a healthy exercise, financial or otherwise.

As Cooper waited in the lobby for Petrenko's car to pick him up, he took another handful of Zantac, ignoring the label warning against taking more than two pills at a time. He was convinced he'd developed ulcers soon after he got Petrenko's call.

Scanning the newspaper, he noticed an article on the third page about an explosion at an oil refinery in Kazakhstan, killing a dozen workers. While the blaze was contained in relatively short order, the reporter wrote that the explosion was caused by a faulty electrical system, and no one suspected sabotage or an act of terrorism.

I bet, thought Cooper. *In the former Soviet Union, nothing happens that is not suspicious. If it was not terrorism, it was most definitely sabotage.*

Cooper wondered if Petrenko owned the refinery. But that was something no one, even Cooper, knew. Petrenko kept all of his Russian holdings in a complex labyrinth of companies under a series of fictitious names. Discovering the truthful owner was near impossible.

The car arrived, and Cooper began his day.

SIX

RESTAURANT CATHERINE THE GREAT, ST. PETERSBURG, RUSSIA

THE RESTAURANT RUN BY ST. PETERSBURG'S HERMITAGE MUSEUM IS A MECCA FOR RUSSIAN hospitality and cuisine. Constantine Petrenko was a regular guest and like most other Russian oligarchs, received special treatment. That morning's meeting with Cooper was no different. While the hotel's Restaurant Catherine the Great was open only for dinner, the manager made a concession for Petrenko and set up a breakfast table for two.

Unlike most other oligarchs, Petrenko never sought public accolades. As far as he was concerned, the fewer people who knew him, the better. He liked being unknown, and closely guarded his ability to go wherever he wanted without notice. To many he was an enigma, to the point that some didn't believe he even existed. They thought of him as an amalgamation of characters operating as a syndicate, reaping illegal profits at the expense of innocent victims.

But Petrenko was indeed real. Born in Moscow, he was educated in England at the finest schools and made his fortune from Internet ventures. Like his idol, Vladimir Putin, Petrenko was in excellent shape. Nearly six feet tall, clean-shaven, with bright blue eyes and auburn hair, he struck a menacing image. Many said he looked like Vladimir Putin's younger brother, only in better shape. And considering the physical shape Putin was in, that was a serious compliment.

Even Putin grudgingly admired Petrenko but remained concerned with the oligarch's rising power, as Putin was with anyone who might someday become a challenge. While Putin appreciated the contributions Petrenko and others like him made to Russia's growing prosperity, and the political advantage of staying in their favor, Putin also knew that he could not let them grow too powerful. Putin, essentially Russia's president for life, intended to outlast world leaders, particularly United States presidents, beyond the record held by Cuba's Fidel Castro. Castro outlasted ten United States presidents. So far, Putin ruled Russia through seven. He had no intention of letting anyone threaten that goal, including Petrenko.

A threat to Putin's power and the likely reaction was something Petrenko understood, always endeavoring to keep himself an enigma that remained well hidden from would-be detractors and, for the most part, from Putin and his band of protectors, never hesitant to eliminate anyone who posed a threat. Petrenko took notice every time some other political or business figure was poisoned or vanished. He was not about to find himself on that list. So he steered very wide of Putin and was careful not to take on investments or public positions contrary to Putin's plans.

Early in his career, Petrenko's ventures were legitimate as he rode the wave of capitalism following the disintegration of the Soviet Union. But dissatisfaction with modest success eventually brought him into Russia's criminal underworld, where he quickly established his turf with money and blood.

Petrenko's first business was Images, a social media site that allowed those who subscribed to post pictures of themselves, friends, events, and the like. Anything that made them feel important. Essentially, it was the Russian version of Instagram.

Little did those who posted trivial photos and thoughts know that Petrenko accumulated detailed records on the millions of loyal subscribers and marveled at how easy it was to get them to reveal the most intimate of details about their lives and finances and, in particular, the lives and finances of others. Images, a seemingly innocent social media site, was anything but that. A repository of data, including bank accounts and personal information, it grew to be unlike anything else on the Internet. While sites like Facebook, Google, and Instagram compiled similar information, regulations and business ethics prevented full monetization of their data beyond aggregate demographics intended to address audiences of interest to marketers. That was not an obstacle for Petrenko. For popular sites, selling ad space and data feeds is the Holy Grail. For Petrenko, such information was just the tip of the iceberg. Petrenko was amazed at how people blindly click the "accept" button without any idea of what they're agreeing to. It didn't take long to convert Images from an innocent social media site to a vacuum for personal information that could be sold at a premium, particularly to criminals dedicated to siphoning money from the accounts of the naïve.

As Images grew, Petrenko learned to use the information as a pillar for his capitalist Utopia. Before long he controlled the destiny of not just individuals but of countries and multinational corporations as well.

Petrenko's second Internet venture, Peephole, was as controversial as it was popular. Subscribers could track the whereabouts of anyone they chose. Many of those who signed up had legitimate motives. Parents wanted to know what their children were doing. Employers wanted to track their employees outside the office while they were on business. Private investigators used it to track unfaithful spouses and deadbeat dads. Law enforcement used it to locate suspects. It all seemed so simple. For Petrenko and his clients, Peephole was a surrogate that spied on unwitting individuals, politicians, publishers, celebrities, and radicals at all points along the political and economic spectrum. They were all Petrenko's unwitting dupes, with no knowledge that they were revealing their deepest secrets and doing his bidding.

Petrenko amassed his fortune in three ways. First, he made money selling the data from Images and Peephole to whoever had enough money to afford individualized data unburdened by regulatory regimes. The more they paid, the better the data. Petrenko could deliver data far more granular than even that of the National Security Agency. That was not surprising, since he long ago hacked into the NSA without the agency ever being aware of the breach. The hacking continues, undiscovered.

Second, Petrenko made millions through trafficking robots throughout the Internet ecosystem. These "bots," man-made digital programs that imitate real people, systematically infect every computer on the Web, planting cookies and siphoning off advertising revenue pennies at a time. By having hundreds of thousands of bogus websites and an army of bots working 24/7, those pennies can grow to millions a day with virtually no effort by the programmers who control them. Just set them loose and the algorithms that power them take over.

Advertisers, obsessed with reaching Internet users, ignored the reality that vast numbers of supposed consumers viewing their ads were in fact non-human bots. The reason is simple. Media buying companies promise their clients incredible reach into Internet users. They promise millions upon millions of "eyeballs" measured through clicks or visits. So long as there is some sort of way to count, it doesn't matter what measurement is used. Petrenko's programmers, all of whom were better than any counterpart at Microsoft or Google, rigged statistics and delivered whatever a media buying agency's heart desired or whatever false information it wanted to sell to its clients. It all lined Petrenko's pockets with millions. Whenever white-hat hackers discovered a fraudulent scheme, the black-hat programmers employed by Petrenko made modifications that rendered the cleanup efforts worthless. It was not a game the good guys could win. They could only mount a good defense that reacted when possible. Fighting it was an around-the-clock effort that cost more than most companies could afford. So they just ignored the fraud. The advantage went to Petrenko and others like him, who routinely misappropriated billions off the Internet's money flow.

Last, Petrenko reaped in a fortune through ransomware. He high-jacked corporate databases, encrypted them, and then demanded a ransom to release the data. It is one of the most common of the digital crimes that Interpol and the FBI have been unable to stop. The key for a successful highjacker is a ransom that is affordable but not greedy. The vast majority of corporations that are faced with a ransom demand readily pay it to retrieve their data and continue uninterrupted operations, all while keeping the breach confidential. Victims of ransomware were loath to cooperate with regulatory authorities, particularly where they needed their data to compete.

—

Cooper was escorted to Petrenko's table, his chair pulled out for him by an attentive waiter.

"Good morning, Constantine. It's good to see you again." Cooper knew his greeting was purely perfunctory and that Petrenko never looked forward to seeing any of his operatives.

"Yes, of course," Petrenko offered as he stood and firmly shook Cooper's hand. Cooper always thought the strength of Petrenko's handshake was meant to send a message far beyond "hello." His handshake was always accompanied by a cold stare that could freeze anyone's soul. There was nothing kind in Petrenko's eyes.

Cooper was used to such meetings in otherwise public places that were emptied of all other people. It was all part of Petrenko's mystique, one way of showing those who he gave the honor of meeting him that he was always in complete control. This morning was no different. Cooper knew where he stood with Petrenko.

The two sat silently until the waiter brought them their first course of porridge, followed by rye bread and sliced sausage. Petrenko dove into the porridge, as he always did. His table manners were atrocious as he slathered his rye bread with butter topped with the sausage. While Cooper dutifully sampled it all, he never enjoyed traditional Russian meals, particularly breakfast. The only redeeming feature was the coffee. Nor was he about to tell Petrenko that he had already eaten at the Lotto, knowing he would have to deal with Petrenko's preferred breakfast at his meeting. Instead, he tried his best to control his disgust at the way Petrenko ate.

Petrenko finally broke the silence, "I pay you a lot of money, Mr. Cooper. No?"

Cooper wondered why foreigners always used "no" as if it were its own question mark.

"Of course, Constantine. You pay me well. And I appreciate it."

"So tell me, Mr. Cooper, why I pay you so well."

Cooper knew he was being baited.

"I like to think it's because I do a good job for you."

"Ah, yes," responded Petrenko with an icy stare. "I pay you because you do a good job for me. So what should I pay you when you don't do a good job for me? Or better yet, what should I do to you when you don't do a good job for me?"

Cooper was sobered by Petrenko's game, and also nervous. Alone with Petrenko, there was no telling what might happen. Cooper could easily be disposed of in Russia without a trace.

Cooper responded as calmly as he could, "Constantine, I know you are disappointed because I have not found someone to replace Raymond Steele. It takes time to find someone willing to play by your rules." Cooper knew that any replacement had to play by the rules of a pure criminal.

Raymond Steele was a commodities broker who did whatever Petrenko told him to do, knowing full well that the details he was given were all insider information and a precursor to how Petrenko would manipulate markets and arbitrage illegal gains. Always careful not to be greedy and to move trades through a labyrinth of companies that seemed to have no connection with one another, Steele was handsomely rewarded for his obedience.

However, Steele had grown less responsive than Petrenko wanted. Petrenko believed Steele's financial success, at Petrenko's expense, was making him lazy. Now in his seventies, Steele was losing his edge, and

Cooper suggested to Petrenko that he find someone to replace Steele. To Cooper's chagrin, Petrenko assigned that task to him.

It did not go without notice to Cooper that within a week after he told Steele he was being replaced, Steele was found dead in his home, hanging from a rafter in his den. It was ruled a suicide. It could have been, thought Cooper, but he had his doubts, all of which fueled his fear of Petrenko.

"Well, Mr. Cooper, if you know why I'm unhappy, why are you doing nothing about it?"

"Constantine, I am trying as best I can. It's not as simple as you may think it is." While it was never easy to be firm with Petrenko, Cooper knew that showing weakness was not an option.

"Not simple? You think it isn't simple to find some dimwit broker who will follow orders much like you do, Mr. Cooper?"

Cooper was used to Petrenko's insulting nature and not about to take the bait. Instead, he chose to use his own form of manipulation, which he had learned all criminals fall for—flattery.

"You are too important to leave any decision to the dimwitted, Constantine. Surely, you would not surround yourself with fools. So I am meticulous in my search to be certain that whoever I find will be up for the challenge and loyalty you require. The loyalty you demand," Cooper added with an ominous tone.

Petrenko took another gulp of coffee and a large bite of rye bread with sausage, pieces dropping from the corners of his mouth as he spoke. "Yes. Loyalty." Cooper knew pandering to Petrenko's ego was his best defense.

"Well, Mr. Cooper, perhaps I can help." Petrenko pushed an unaddressed white business envelope across the table to Cooper.

Cooper didn't touch it and asked, "Constantine, what is in the envelope? We've spoken about not exchanging anything in writing. Why don't you simply tell me what this is about?"

Cooper's preference for keeping communications oral was as much to protect Petrenko as it was to keep himself off the radar of authorities as well. He may have hated Petrenko, but Cooper knew where his bread was buttered. He always wanted to preserve Petrenko's right to deny whatever suited him. Written communications could be used to reveal the truth neither he nor Petrenko wanted anyone to know.

Petrenko nodded and pulled the envelope back to him.

"The envelope contains nothing, of course," lied Petrenko. "But if it did have something in it, it might have the name Darren White, a commodities broker in Chicago."

Cooper held back a smile at how Petrenko loved to play the spy game with vague references. He played along.

"I see," responded Cooper. "Perhaps I will look up that name. Perhaps I will talk to others to be sure I have his name correct." Cooper knew he could find out a lot from one of Petrenko's hackers, who undoubtedly used Petrenko's databases from Images and Peephole to find Mr. Darren White, the next unwitting dupe in Petrenko's criminal enterprise.

"Yes, that would be a good idea. I'll make arrangements."

Petrenko stood. It was the signal that breakfast was over and Cooper was dismissed. Nothing could have pleased Cooper more.

SEVEN

RITZ CARLTON, GRAND CAYMAN ISLANDS

SITTING POOLSIDE IN A PRIVATE CABANA AT THE RITZ CARLTON, DARREN WHITE FOUND THE humidity-free 98 degrees easy to handle. He liked the sun but hated the heat. He had been asked to meet a big investor at the hotel who was willing to pay all his expenses for five days. He immediately agreed, regretting only that he hadn't brought one of his girlfriends.

He arrived on a Saturday. The meeting was not scheduled until 2:00 on Wednesday, the last day he was expected to be there. The person who arranged the trip told him to go early and enjoy himself, so he did. He stayed on the grounds of the Ritz and charged everything to his room, assuming that the benefactor who brought him there would not mind. He included a few girls along the way. After all, he was told all expenses were paid.

By 2:30, White wondered if the mysterious executive was going to arrive. He ordered another Tanqueray gin and Schweppes Indian tonic with a twist, rather than a wedge, of lime. It was his pretentious way of ordering even when having a drink as mundane as a gin and tonic. He was now on his third and feeling fine.

"Hello, Mr. White," said a man who approached with hand extended. White rose and took the hand.

"And hello to you. I'm Darren White."

"Yes, Mr. White. I just called you by your name," responded Cooper.

Cooper wondered, *Geez, has this guy been drinking all morning?*

"My name is Frank Cooper. I appreciate your seeing me, and I hope you've enjoyed your stay so far." White thought Cooper seemed sincere.

"Yes, I have. And thank you for your generosity."

"Of course. But I'm not the one you should thank. The person who paid for all of this, and willingly so, is a man I've worked with for more than ten years. He is the benefactor for all of this." Cooper sat in the chair to White's left and told the waitress he'd have whatever Mr. White was drinking. And that Mr. White would have another one, too. Cooper figured he might as well learn something about the fool he was about to dupe into a deeper life of crime and the drunker White was, the better.

Seriously, thought Cooper. *Why did Petrenko steer me to such a pretentious putz?*

Cooper was tempted to ask White if the girls he had ordered to his room were as good looking as the waitress, but decided to hold that information for another day.

"In this weather, Mr. White, only a gin and tonic will do."

"I'm way ahead of you. And please call me Darren. May I call you Frank?" White was feeling comfortable.

"Sure, Darren. But I prefer Mr. Cooper." Cooper always wanted to keep a distance. Formality when being addressed suited him.

"And what is the name of the man who arranged for all of this?" White asked.

"Someone you've never heard of, Darren. And never will. He prefers to remain anonymous. With his wealth and power, it is better that few people know him. Instead, he works through lawyers like me. And pays us extremely well for the privilege of representing him." Cooper wanted to gag on the privilege part.

"I see," responded White, thinking this was more mysterious than he thought it would be but after three drinks and the lure of money, he was more than willing to listen.

When the drinks arrived, Cooper told the waitress to be sure to bring another pair as soon as it looked as if they were done with the ones she just brought.

"Of course, Mr. Cooper," she responded as she walked away. White took note that she knew him.

"So tell me, Darren, how old are you? I suspect you're about ten years younger than me. I'm forty-seven."

"Close. I'm thirty-nine. So only eight years apart."

"So tell me a little about yourself, Darren. What was your childhood and schooling like?"

The gin and tonics emboldened White.

"Frank. Sorry. I meant Mr. Cooper. Something tells me you already know the answer to those questions and frankly, my childhood is irrelevant. But I'm happy to play along. So why don't you tell me what you know, and I'll let you know if your researchers got it right."

Cooper smiled, "OK, Darren. Let me tell you what we know."

As Cooper took another sip of his gin and tonic, the waitress appeared with a fresh one in hand. Her smile toward White was more an invitation than a polite gesture. She'd been serving White at the pool for days and wished there were a way to get to know him better. At 5'10", 180 pounds, White was in excellent shape and his brown hair and brown eyes, together with a 5 o'clock shadow, was a fashionable look that caught many a woman's eye. This didn't go without notice to White, and he made a mental note to get to know her better later.

"As a young man, Darren, you were an underachiever through most of your childhood. You always wanted the good life and became motivated by money at a very early age. Your parents divorced when you were ten and you never saw your father again. A lot of people called you a mama's boy and often bullied you. You fought a lot in high school and never really had any close friends. In college, however, you changed and found friends. You also found drugs and alcohol. And women. You partied through Lafayette College and managed to graduate with a GPA of only a 2.7. That got you no job offers, so you took the LSATs and did well. But not well enough to get into a decent law school. Your GPA prevented that. So you enrolled in Brooklyn Law School, where you finally applied yourself and did well. Pretty good, so far, don't you think?"

"Yes. Who told you all of this?"

"You did, Darren. It's right there in the endless posting you and your friends make on social media. It wasn't very hard to learn just about everything we need to know about you."

"And why did you need to know so much? What do you want?"

"I'm on a roll, Darren. We'll get to that. But first, let me continue."

The waitress brought White a refill.

"In the summer between your second and final year of law school, you landed a summer internship at Skadden Arps. But you hated it and realized that even with a job at one of the world's top law firms, it would take you years of crushing hours before you'd earn what you considered serious money. Or as you often posted in texts to your friends, 'fuck you' money. So you turned down an offer from Skadden, dropped out of law school, and took an entry-level job at Merrill Lynch as a broker. You thought it was the brokers who made the most money in the shortest time."

"And I was right. I've proven that," White proudly boasted.

"Indeed you have. In no time, you became a superstar, receiving increasing bonuses and accolades year after year. However, as you succeeded, your personality became a liability. You were a loner who had no sense of team. You became abusive to fellow workers. Yet because your performance excelled above just about everyone, Merrill Lynch tolerated you."

"Yeah, you got that right. Most of the other brokers were assholes who didn't know a damn thing about making money."

"Making money for whom, Darren? Merrill or its clients?"

"Clients didn't make money unless Merrill made money," replied White.

"A convenient answer, Darren. Let me continue."

"I'm not sure I want you to. I'd rather you got to the point."

"And I will, Darren, but only at the pace my benefactor requires. You're free to leave if you're no longer interested."

"OK," responded White, "but now I'll add some to the story. By my sixth year at Merrill, I was working closely with the lead broker on a portfolio worth more than $500 million. I became his biggest producer and was paid more than $1 million a year in salary and bonus. They weren't paying me to be a nice guy to other workers."

"Don't get me wrong, Darren. I like the idea you don't give a damn about your colleagues and that you're in this all for yourself. I share that view. So does the man I work for."

"Fine, but I really am approaching the end of my patience. Please get to the point."

"Very well. You are very adept in trading commodities, bonds, and stocks. The full portfolio. You are particularly astute at predicting markets. That gives you an edge."

"Right, and that's why I left Merrill and went on my own."

"You did, but only after you were denied the bonus you thought you earned after you got a poor review on interpersonal skills. You were told that while your financial performance was outstanding, your behavior caused problems, particularly among women employees. They were increasingly complaining that your language was infused with sexual innuendos and insults. Some even accused you of improper touching."

"No one can take a joke any more."

"I agree."

Now past his fifth drink, White was obviously feeling no pain.

"What do you want? I'm tired of waiting and have better things to do than listen to my personal history."

"Ahh, Darren, you need to trust me that this is not a waste of your time."

"Fine, but please get to the point."

"Good, because this is where it gets interesting. Unbeknownst to Merrill, a client you originated was a fake corporation you set up right here in the Cayman Islands. And while you're here, no doubt you'll even visit the local agent who set it all up for you and move some of your ill-gotten gains to the secret accounts you have elsewhere. While Merrill should have discovered it, as long as you kept making them money, it was ignored. You funneled the fake company's monies to the Cayman Islands through a labyrinth of accounts to hide and launder the funds. Funds that you embezzled, at a small amount each time, from Merrill clients through fake trades. It didn't take you long to amass quite a fortune. An illegal fortune."

White's expression showed his concern that Cooper knew he owned a Cayman account. White never reported or posted anything on social media about it. No one knew. Except Cooper.

Cooper then outlined White's laundering process.

"Once a deposit goes into your Cayman account, it is immediately transferred to a second Cayman account. You like to call them Cayman I and Cayman II."

White could feel the fear as his stomach began to turn.

"Once in Cayman II, you wire the money to an account in Costa Rica where there was no extradition treaty with the United States. While the Cayman Islands also has no treaty with the United States, moving the money to Costa Rica is an insurance policy. From Costa Rica, you send the money to an account in the Isle of Man, a jurisdiction with virtually no reporting obligations. From there, the funds find their way back to the Cayman Islands into Cayman III, readily available to you. This all happens in a matter of seconds. As far as you know, the money is untraceable. But, as you can see, you're wrong," concluded Cooper with a stare that dared White to disagree.

"I don't know what you're talking about and I think it's best I leave."

"Oh, please don't. I need to continue with the best part of all. You have a checking account in a Bermuda bank under the name of Fredric Ansis.

What makes that interesting is that Fredric Ansis, at least the one owning the account, does not exist. And why did you do that, Darren?"

"I can't wait for you to tell me," responded White.

"Because you carry around a set of credit cards and IDs for Fredric Ansis and charge to your heart's content. Your Cayman bank makes sure all the bills are paid. Brilliant, Darren. Brilliant. But also very easy to find and it took us no time to figure out who the real Fredric Ansis was."

White was looking more and more petrified. "I'm sorry, Mr. Cooper. I am afraid I will have to take you up on your offer to leave if I am not interested. So that is what I'm going to do." White stood up.

"Sit down, Darren," Cooper ordered. White took notice that two men who White assumed were henchmen for Cooper started toward the table.

"I said, sit down," Cooper ordered. "Don't make me ask again."

White sat, took a sip of his drink, and nervously waited for what would come next.

Cooper waved his hand and his henchmen backed off.

"Mr. White, I'll make this simple. You're going nowhere. I never had an offer to make to you. Only an ultimatum. With your condo in Manhattan and a beachfront mansion in the Hamptons, did you really think people would never notice? Add your real estate holdings in Miami and here in Grand Cayman. Putting you up in the hotel was a ruse, Darren. You may be a fool, but you're a lucky one, since we found you first." Cooper's tone was growing ominous.

"What do you want?"

"Good, Darren. As you wish, we can now get to the point."

"*Thank God for that*," responded White, seeing that Cooper did not like his impertinence.

Cooper continued, "My benefactor has a network of hedge funds and stock trading concerns throughout the world. While he controls all of them, a complex labyrinth of ownership structures prevents anyone from knowing who he is or that he makes all the calls."

White could feel his stomach turn.

"And this is your big day, Darren. You are now going to oversee the entire operation and coordinate each hedge fund's and each broker's investments and operations. You will be dealing with billions. Exciting, huh?"

"That depends," responded White, who began feeling more sober with each image of the consequences a few days in the Caymans were about to cost him. "With all the risk I'll be taking, I expect an adequate reward." As nervous as he was, White believed that at this point, he had nothing to lose by being blunt.

"But of course, Darren. You are taking considerable risk. If the structure goes south, you will probably spend your remaining years in prison. That assumes, of course, you are alive to serve a sentence."

Alive to serve a sentence! What White wanted most was to leave, but he was resigned to the blackmail Cooper had in his pocket. He had no doubt Cooper would use it. So White knew he had no choice.

"So, Darren, what is your price?"

White was surprised by the question. It was not the kind of negotiation he expected. But at this point, he saw no reason to negotiate against himself.

"Mr. Cooper, you may have me over a barrel, but that doesn't make me a fool."

No, just an idiot, thought Cooper.

Cooper sat silently, offering no response.

After what seemed to White as an eternity, he realized Cooper did not intend to make an offer. So it was now or never for White.

"OK, Mr. Cooper, have it your way. For what I suspect you'll be asking me to do, I want $5 million a year guaranteed against 1 percent as a management fee and 5 percent of the profits."

No reaction from Cooper.

Emboldened, White continued, "And I want the first year upfront divided among accounts I'll give to you. Accounts from which I'll immediately move the funds to deposits you'll never be able to find."

Cooper took out a cigar and pondered White's demands as he clipped it and rolled it between his fingers. Cooper favored a Padron 1964 Anniversary No. 4 in a natural wrapper. At $40 a stick, it was an expensive habit. After a few minutes, Cooper slowly lit the cigar and took a long drag. He leaned into White.

"Really, Mr. White?"

White had no intention of backing down.

"And, of course, I want all my expenses paid. In advance or from an account I control."

More silence as Cooper took another puff, blowing the smoke toward White. As soon as he began to take the puff, the waitress was at the table with an ashtray. It was not the first time Cooper had a cigar at the Ritz.

Just as White was about to demand a response, Cooper spoke.

"We have a deal. Imagine that. Over a few drinks, you've become a multimillionaire!"

Fuck, thought White to himself, *I should have asked for more?*

"And if you do well," continued Cooper, "I have no doubt my benefactor will be even more generous."

Shit, thought White, *who the hell is this guy? But if he's going to make me that rich, should I care?*

"Tomorrow I'll provide you with all the contact information you'll need," Cooper said. "All the companies already know to expect instructions from you."

White's stomach was in knots, wondering how Cooper could be so confident about the deal that he'd already told others White would be making the calls.

"When do I start?" White asked, dejection and defeat obvious in his voice.

"Come on, Darren, cheer up. For now, let us agree that in a week, you will provide me with a plan to move $1 billion in assets. It shouldn't take a man as smart as you are to figure out what to do with that kind of money.

If we like your plan, then we'll transfer your compensation to the accounts you provide to us and you'll get started."

Cooper's two henchmen approached the table.

Cooper rose. "Have a nice day, Darren. I'll call you in a week and arrange to see your recommendations. In the meantime, I'd recommend that you lay off a bit on room service girls."

Once Cooper strolled away with his cigar in hand and henchmen in tow, White could not have wanted to leave the Cayman Islands more. The reality that he no longer had control of his own life was sinking in.

EIGHT

ABU MUSE AL ZARQAWI CAMP, IRAQ'S NINEWA PROVINCE

ABU AL-BADRI WAS A STEREOTYPICAL TERRORIST WHOLLY IMMERSED IN THE IDEOLOGICAL quagmire of radical Islam, in which violence is the primary weapon. He, like most other terrorists, believed that eradicating the world of infidels was a mandate from Allah and the clerics who called for jihads against anyone who disagreed. Dying for the cause was the highest honor one could be given. Such a sacrifice was worth the rewards in heaven bestowed upon those loyal to Allah.

Al-Badri was recruited and trained by ISIS operators in Syria and Saudi Arabia. Included in his class was Hashir Rashid, an equally impressionable young Muslim prepared to die for the glory only a few were offered.

As comrades in arms, all the recruits—twenty-five strong in al-Badri and Rashid's class—became friends. Their training was hard, and no sacrifice was considered off limits. Those who knew what ISIS recruits were put through often compared it to the most rigorous parts of training received by U.S. Navy Seals.

The two often talked about death.

"Do you think you and I will be asked to sacrifice our lives for Allah and the greater good?" Rashid asked him.

"Hashir, I pray every day that I am so blessed," al-Badri lied. He was always curious why the likes of Rashid were so prepared to die. Al-Badri preferred a future of ordering others to die.

"Praise to Allah," responded to Rashid.

"Praise to Allah," repeated al-Badri.

As training ensued, the ISIS leadership recognized al-Badri as someone who would be better not sacrificed to Allah. He was smarter than any of his classmates. Like the others, he had been educated in London and was versed in Western ways. And he showed great potential as someone prepared to make tough decisions. Rashid and all of the trainees looked up to him. He became their natural leader. Leaders in ISIS were not sacrificed. Only those who are clearly expendable were given that honor.

When his training was complete, Rashid was sent off to bomb school to learn how to die and al-Badri went with the elders to Damascus where he assumed a leadership role in planning the ISIS Caliphate.

On his last day with Rashid, al-Badri feigned sincerity in his goodbye. "Hashir, I envy you. You will enter heaven with Allah's blessing. I can only hope I will one day meet you there."

Rashid seemed to believe him. "I will pray to Allah that your wish may be fulfilled," he responded. And so they parted ways, never expecting to see one another again in their life on earth.

Even with all the secretive communications measures taken by ISIS and their ilk, the addiction they all have to social media made discovering who they are and where they operate easy game for the likes of Petrenko and his hackers. Al-Badri and his addiction to reading and posting online did not go unnoticed by Petrenko. But unlike the beliefs al-Badri had in himself, Petrenko saw him and all his brethren as fools who could be used as tools in building his fortune.

"Mr. Cooper," Petrenko would often say, "with vision, we can convert the violence that men like al-Badri yearn for into profits. Knowing when he plans to attack nonbelievers opens up opportunities to manipulate markets."

With that vision, Petrenko once again dispatched Frank Cooper.

It was apparent to Petrenko that what terrorists lacked the most was money, weapons, and a clear long-term strategy. The kinds of things astute investors like Petrenko understood. And while ISIS was rumored to have significant funds, they had no idea how to manage them. Much was wasted. Petrenko decided he could bring something that ISIS and other terrorist groups needed—financial expertise and strategic planning. In return, he wanted to quietly oversee some of their terrorist attacks so he could manipulate markets. Both Petrenko and the radical terrorists would win in that game. He'd make money and the terrorists would fill their desire to kill infidels, innocent or otherwise. Petrenko really didn't care who or how many died as long as he was making money.

With Darren White, Petrenko had the first leg in the three-legged stool he required. Now he needed al-Badri, a radical terrorist, for the second leg. Arms dealer Philippe Lamont would soon fill in the third leg—weapons.

A radical terrorist willing to send innocent followers to die for a religious cause, a commodities broker who could be blackmailed to abide by whatever was needed, and someone willing to sell weapons regardless of the purpose the buyer intended were a perfect trio for Petrenko's plan.

NINE

FOUR SEASONS HOTEL, BEIRUT, LEBANON

IT WAS FAR EASIER FOR FRANK COOPER TO CONTACT AL-BADRI THAN HE HAD THOUGHT it would be when he had been given the terrorist's name. Petrenko's digital spiders combing the Internet could find anyone, anywhere; even elusive terrorists.

For al-Badri, the invitation from Cooper to talk about financial support for his cause was intriguing. He had to admit that the last person he ever expected to offer assistance would be an infidel. Always suspicious of a trap, al-Badri insisted on receiving Cooper's credentials and photograph together with assurances that he would be alone. They were all provided. While al-Badri was not yet on any most-wanted lists, he was still very cautious, as he had been taught to be.

For Cooper, it was unsettling to provide a known terrorist so much about himself before a meeting. He preferred it the other way around, as he did with Darren White. But Cooper also knew he had no choice. Orders from Petrenko were to be obeyed, and Cooper never wanted to find out what happened to those who failed to do so.

They agreed to meet at the Four Seasons in Beirut. Cooper found it ironic that he was meeting a murderer and religious zealot who eschewed Western ways in such a posh environment. When Cooper told him of the location, Petrenko laughed and observed that greed knows no religion.

Cooper sat on the balcony of his corner suite overlooking the marina, with a view of the Mediterranean Sea. The suite included a large living room and dining area, making it perfect to host meetings, confidential or otherwise.

It was now the third day Cooper had been waiting. Each day, he got a call that al-Badri would be delayed, telling him it was the Will of Allah. He had been warned to expect such behavior. A common negotiating tactic in the Arab world is to make the other party wait and grow frustrated. It also gave al-Badri's operatives the ability to observe Cooper and assure themselves that he was indeed alone.

As Cooper sat that afternoon on his balcony, bored and daydreaming amidst the beautiful view, a knock on the door startled him back to attention.

Finally, I can get his meeting started and leave Beirut in one piece.

On answering the door, he was greeted by three men, all dressed in traditional white Arab robes.

"Good afternoon," said Cooper. "Which one of you is Abu al-Badri?" he asked.

The tall one answered, "None of us. We've been told by Mr. al-Badri to meet with you first and discuss your needs."

Cooper was not pleased with this. Petrenko instructed him that al-Badri was to be the one he spoke to. No one else. Cooper knew better than to stray from the plan regardless of how frustrated he was in waiting for a meeting with al-Badri.

"Then I must disappoint the three of you," responded Cooper. "I have strict instructions that I cannot alter. I will only speak to Mr. al-Badri. And I must speak to him alone. No one else may be present. That's what we agreed to."

Cooper stared at the tall one and waited for a reaction. It seemed like an eternity, even though it was only a few seconds.

"I see," the tall one responded. "We will let Mr. al-Badri know what you've said."

The three turned and walked back to the elevator, pressing the down button.

Cooper saw no reason to watch further and shut the door, disappointed that he'd been wasting his time and shuddering at the thought of yet another report to Petrenko that he'd failed to solve a problem, this time in making contact with al-Badri.

A knock came again.

On answering the door, Cooper found that a man who appeared to be in his thirties, lightly shaven, stood before him. Unlike the past visitors, this man was dressed in a Western business suit and looked as if he'd be very comfortable on Wall Street.

"Good afternoon, Mr. Cooper. I am Abu al-Badri."

TEN

SOFITEL PARIS LE FAUBOURG, FRANCE

ALTHOUGH HE WAS A MUSLIM, ALGERIAN PHILIPPE LAMONT HAD NO ALLEGIANCE TO ANY cause. The only thing Lamont cared about was selling arms to the highest bidder. Although he had heard of Petrenko as someone who was never afraid to skirt the law to make a financial gain, as was the case with virtually every Russian oligarch, no one ever associated Petrenko with weapons deals. Nor did it matter to Lamont if that was true or not. He never saw reason to question any clandestine labyrinth his clients put him through to operate. Money, not knowing whom he was dealing with, made all the difference. Lamont was happy to deliver any weapon he could get his hands on to anyone with enough cash to pay for it.

Lamont had arms sources and caches throughout the world. His inventory included everything from small arms to rockets and vehicles of every nature, including tanks and mobile launchers. More important, he was amassing weapons with the technology necessary to deliver destruction wherever his clients wanted it.

While law enforcement authorities throughout the world knew of him, Lamont was a master at anonymity and evasion. He never stayed in one place long enough to be caught and kept his bank accounts in countries that protected his secrecy, continually moving money from one account to another. Even when his money was occasionally seized, it meant little to him. He learned to tolerate occasional losses. If Lamont suspected that someone within his organization might be cooperating with authorities, that person quickly vanished without a trace, often along with the authorities with whom they met and the entire families of both. There were never witnesses alive to testify against him.

In Lamont's world, communications were often a series of messages that seemed to have no connection to each other. Not code as spies understood such things in modern military parlance, but instead an occasional tweet, social media post, random encounter in a coffee shop, or a discreet call to meet somewhere safe and generally in the open. While organizations like the United States' NSA and the United Kingdom's GCHQ (Government Communications Headquarters) listened in 24/7 to all the chatter, it was virtually impossible in an encrypted world to put all the fragments together. In truth, Lamont knew that human intelligence, not algorithms or other technology scrubbers, were the most reliable sources to fight the terrorists. On more occasions than anyone wanted to admit, luck and a careless Jihadist brought about the most successful victories.

Lamont liked the Sofitel le Faubourg in Paris. While it was a very comfortable hotel on the Rue Boissy d'Anglas, it was not considered the kind of hotel a multimillionaire arms dealer would frequent, particularly in Paris, where options like Hôtel Barrière Le Fouquet's or the Plaza Athénée were more suited to what might be the stereotype outsiders expected. But Lamont avoided flamboyance. He reserved that for his wine and sexual dalliances.

The hotel was only a block from the United States Embassy, something Lamont liked. He took pleasure in doing deals so close to his biggest adversary. He thought of it as rubbing their noses in their own feces.

When Lamont entered the le Faubourg bar at 2:00, the appointed time, Cooper was already there. As usual, no one else was in the bar. It was small, and most hotel guests preferred to go to the larger, more stylish bars just feet away, like the lounge at the Hôtel de Crillon or the Buddha Bar across the street.

"Mr. Cooper, I presume." Lamont extended his hand as Cooper rose.

"Yes, and it is a pleasure to meet you, Mr. Lamont. With your permission, please call me Frank and if I may, I'll call you Philippe." Cooper was willing to dispense with formalities with someone like Lamont. Unlike Darren White, Lamont was a brilliant and accomplished criminal, every bit the match for anyone Cooper knew. That earned him respect from Cooper.

"But of course, Frank. By your accent, my guess is you're American. So call me Phil. Most folks from the States find it simpler to remember." Lamont actually preferred that no one refer to him by his actual name, first or last.

"Then Phil it is. Please sit. May I order you a cocktail?"

"Yes. What are you having?"

"A martini, straight up," responded Cooper as the waiter dutifully arrived.

"Aha. I'll have a Lillet."

These Americans are so uncivilized, thought Lamont, restraining a sneer at the drink. *Martinis are never appropriate in the afternoon. Particularly on a weekday. Lillet is the proper aperitif for this hour.*

Lamont could not care less about sizing up anyone he spoke to as long as the size of their bank account could match the cost of his services. Cooper was no exception. "This is such a beautiful city," commented Cooper. "And this hotel is very quaint. Not what I expected. It's certainly not what Sofitels typically look like."

"Yes, it's one of the few jewels in their collection. The building is historic and every room is different. So no matter how many times you stay here, it's always a new experience."

"Well, this is where I'll stay next time I'm here. The Ritz Carlton is too much for my taste," responded Cooper.

"Yes, indeed. I try to stay away from the pretentious spots of Paris as well. And that is not particularly easy!" joked Lamont.

They ordered a light lunch of quiche Lorraine and onion soup. Lamont had his with a dry sauvignon blanc Sancerre while, much to Lamont's disgust, Cooper ordered another martini.

Over espressos, the conversation got to the point of the meeting.

"Phil, it will come as no surprise to you that I have a patron who is interested in purchasing merchandise from you. A lot of it."

"Nothing would please me more. Do you have a better idea of what he or she is looking for, when they want it, and where they want it delivered?"

"It's a long list, so I've written down an inventory of my patron's needs." Cooper handed Lamont an envelope containing a list of two pages of items. When Lamont opened it and took out the papers, Cooper retrieved the envelope. It was the only piece of paper with his fingerprints on it. The list was clean.

As Lamont read, Cooper could see in his eyes that he was impressed with the magnitude of the order. This shipment would mean millions to Lamont.

"Frank, this is a very sizable order. And while I am sure I can fulfill it, I will need some time."

"Time you can have, Phil. Just give us a date."

"And I'll need a good faith deposit."

"That's fine, but why only a deposit? My patron is willing to pay all of it up front. He knows you as a man who can be trusted." The tone in Cooper's voice left no doubt that if Lamont did not deliver he would never live another day to see any further deliveries for anyone. The comment sent a shiver up Lamont's back, something he rarely felt. For the first time, he wanted to know the man who was behind all of this.

"And with an order of this size, I'll need to know the person at the top. I have to be careful in my business."

"Sorry, Phil, you can never know the patron for whom I work. That is entirely out of the question. I am serious when I say our lives depend upon it. So as my patron would say, the question to you is quite simple: how much do I have to pay you to make you a criminal? And since we both know you're already a criminal, the only issue is whether you're being offered enough for what we want. So give me your best price and never again ask me for a name. If you're not willing to do so, our business here is concluded."

As Cooper rose from his chair, Lamont motioned for him to sit down. The two spent the next hour going over the order and ended with Lamont's promise to get back to Cooper in a week with the price and delivery terms.

ELEVEN

THE GREENBRIER, WHITE SULPHUR SPRINGS, WEST VIRGINIA

CIA OPERATIVE RICHARD HARRIS WAS MEETING FBI AGENT CHANDLER THOMPSON AND Homeland Security's Oliver Grant at the Greenbrier Country Club.

As Harris sat in his suite waiting for Thompson and Grant, he opened the brochure describing the Greenbrier as "America's Resort."

Sitting on over 11,000 acres, the Greenbrier caters to the rich and connected, particularly wealthy lobbyists and politicians. But that's not what most fascinated Harris.

The Greenbrier is also home of the infamous underground bunker built to secretly shelter the United States Congress in the event of nuclear war. The bunker, an integral part of the Cold War apparatus, includes dormitories that can hold over a thousand people, a hospital, and a broadcast center. Shut down in 1992 after the *Washington Post* exposed the secret site, it is now a tourist attraction. But it still includes some secure rooms reserved for get-togethers no one needs to know about—a perfect place for a meeting between CIA, FBI, and Homeland Security operatives.

Answering the knock on the door, both Thompson and Grant arrived.

"Dick, I'm disappointed," observed Thompson. "I was kind of hoping we'd meet in a secret room in the bunker. Don't you CIA guys do that all the time?"

"Funny, Chandler," responded Harris. "As hard as it is for you to believe, even we can't make those reservations. So I'm afraid you'll have to settle for this twelve-hundred-dollar-a-day suite."

"It will do," Thompson replied.

"I'll say," added Grant. "You guys in the CIA sure have nice budgets. I'd never get away with this at Homeland."

"Ollie, what makes you think Dick has any budget at all?"

"All right, that's enough. Let's sit down and go over the objectives," inserted Harris, as he motioned his two colleagues to chairs.

Thompson spoke first. "Dick, a lot depends on your confidential informant. And I have to be honest that I remain skeptical about how much of a threat your source and his…or her…or their claims represent."

Harris knew that Chandler Thompson was a career agent. Educated at Princeton and Harvard Law, he began his career in law enforcement as a Manhattan Assistant District Attorney, where he worked with the FBI on joint domestic terrorism investigations. In a move some thought was a step down, he transferred into the FBI as a rookie agent. Thompson made it clear that he wanted to be in the field on the front line of domestic terrorism and believed that the greatest threat to America was homegrown extremist groups like the neo-Nazis, alt-right, and the Ku Klux Klan. Diverting attention from them to illegal aliens or foreign terrorist cells was to Thompson a waste of time and a shirking of the responsibilities of the elected government.

"Chandler, while I understand your skepticism and penchant that America's worries are limited to terrorists in our backyard, I can assure you my confidential informant is reliable. You need to remain open about the greater threat the global apparatus of terrorists represents."

"So what is your CI's name, Dick?" asked Thompson.

"Seriously, Chandler, you know better than to ask." There was simply no way Harris would reveal Rashid, at least not at this stage of the investigation.

"Can you at least confirm that you're not relying on one CI? If so, we're taking a pretty big risk on a single person's word, Dick," observed Thompson.

Harris responded truthfully that there was more than one CI. What he did not say was that he did not consider all of them, including Humayun, as reliable sources. He regarded that as something Thompson didn't need to know. The identity of confidential informants was often covered out of fear for their physical safety. Operatives like Harris knew how to protect sources and use informants—identified and unidentified—in his efforts to get to the truth.

"Perhaps your friends are right, Dick," responded Thompson. "But we have limited resources and should be focusing our attention on what's happening here, not what we speculate might be afoot in other countries. Let them address their own threats. We can't police the world."

Oliver Grant joined the conversation. "Chandler, I think you fail to see the connections clearly. To protect our homeland, we need to pay attention beyond our borders. While I'd like to think we can depend on our allies and perhaps even our civilized enemies to help, they don't. They're rightly concerned about protecting their citizens, not ours. They don't care what operatives in their countries might be hatching internationally. Indeed, we're the only country with a global perspective on the problem. Not even Russia cares about the world's threats as we do."

Grant, a career bureaucrat, grew through the ranks of Homeland Security to become its director of operations for the Eastern seaboard. Overweight and a heavy drinker, he had no prospect of advancing further. Unlike Thompson, Grant saw international terrorism as more centralized and organized than believed by his superiors. He fervently felt that those in control were professional financiers and foreign governments, some of which he believed were allies, rather than the supposedly smart Islamic radicals who Grant believed were singularly focused on killing, not financing. For Grant, this dark conspiracy—the deep state—was an unholy alliance that needed to be revealed and stopped at all costs.

"Ollie, as deputy director of the bureau's Joint Terrorism Task Force, I've managed more than one hundred operations around the country and share intelligence with the CIA and Homeland," Thompson said. "I know the big picture. I also know we have more to worry about here than we do with what's happening in Europe or anywhere else. Nonetheless, I've agreed to be part of this effort and will remain open-minded. But I need to see results quickly to stay on board."

"Gentlemen," interjected Harris, "can we dispense with further debate on the wisdom of a plan we've all agreed to?" Harris wanted to prevent the discussion from eroding back into a debate he considered closed.

"OK," responded Thompson. "Let's go over it again."

For the next two hours, Harris outlined the step-by-step tactics of an operation to uncover what the CI had told Harris was a well-funded and well-armed Jihadist group somewhere in the Middle East with connections throughout the world. Harris believed attacks were imminent, but they needed to know more. And quickly. By putting his sources into the field, he hoped to gather intel and maybe get a lucky break. But he also knew that there was risk involved, and the price could be lives.

"So we sacrifice a few to save millions?" asked Grant.

"I'd prefer not to use that cliché, Ollie," responded Thompson.

"I'm just calling it as I see it, Chandler. And I'm fine with that, cliché or not." Due process was never something that Grant let get in his way any more than Harris did.

TWELVE

ESPITA MEZCALERIA, WASHINGTON, DC

AS SHE SAT AT THE BAR IN ESPITA MEZCALERIA WAITING FOR A SOURCE NAMED LORI Torchia to arrive, Rebecca Taft ordered her usual cocktail, a Palo Alto, a drink described on the menu as a martini with a hint of tobacco leaf. While that would not sound appealing to most, its mix of tequila, alpine liqueur, and blanc vermouth, laced with blueberry and alpine amaro, gave it a smooth but spicy taste Taft enjoyed. It was a hot, muggy July day in Washington and the Palo Alto was just what she needed as she sat in air-conditioned comfort.

Taft particularly liked the bar at Espita Mezcaleria. The pours were generous, and the Mexican-inspired food more than satisfying. Simple in its décor with stools at the bar, she felt comfortable there. Better yet, no one bothered her except the occasional guy who tried to pick her up. But that was common for her in any bar she went to. Her attractive looks did her well, and she knew how to use them. With natural blond hair and blue eyes, she never lacked for suitors. When she walked into a room, everyone took notice.

Taft always wanted to be a journalist. She was a graduate of Columbia's School of Journalism, and had aspired to be a reporter for a top internation-al newspaper. It didn't do her ego any good when applications to the *New York Times* and *International Tribune* failed to even result in interviews. She settled on taking a research desk at the *Congressional Quarterly* and hated it from day one.

After two years at her dead-end job with the *CQ*, she thought about quitting entirely, maybe finding a wealthy tech-world thirty-something to marry and then spending her time in the Virginia suburbs raising babies and tending her garden. Then she got a call from a headhunter for *Axios*, a news and information website launched in 2017 by a group from *Politico*. The site's name means "worthy" in Greek. The job was to become a beat reporter on the Washington scene with the assignment to look into the private lives of senators and congressmen on both sides of the aisle. At her first interview Taft employed her charms, and the editors believed her when she insisted that she never would let anything get in the way of the truth. At least what she saw as the truth. They offered her a job, and she accepted.

As she warded off come-ons from barflies, Taft recalled the phone call from the day before that now had her waiting for Lori Torchia.

"Hello, Ms. Taft, my name is Lori Torchia. You don't know me. But I'd like to meet with you to talk about something that would be of interest to you and your readers." Torchia spoke almost perfect English, but Taft detected the Romanian accent.

"You're right, I don't know you. How did you get my cell number?" Taft was always suspicious of people who emailed her, let alone anyone who called, since she never gave out her cell phone number. She preferred to develop her own sources, and random emails or calls to the paper were usually from people looking for their fifteen minutes of fame at the expense of a naïve reporter. Taft was not naïve.

Torchia ignored Taft's question and responded, "I work in cyber. The dark side."

That intrigued Taft enough to continue the call.

"I see. And why do you want to talk to me?"

"Not on the phone. Can we meet? You can pick the place, as long as it's in public."

"Mysterious, huh?"

"Call it what you like, but I've been involved with a matter that has significant interest and could affect a lot of people."

"Affect them in what way?"

"In a bad way."

"And what is your involvement?"

"I won't talk about it on the phone. If you're not interested, that's fine. I'll find someone else."

"And how many reporters have you called who have turned you down?" Taft remained suspicious.

"You're the first I've called."

"Right. And why am I the one so honored?"

"I like some of the stuff you write for *Axios*."

Taft checked her calendar. "It's all a bit mysterious, but I can see you tomorrow. How about five o'clock at Espita Mezcaleria? It's at 1250 9th Street."

"OK. You won't be disappointed." Torchia hung up.

Now sitting and waiting, Taft ordered a second Palo Alto and Googled Torchia on her phone and found nothing. She tried Facebook, Instagram, and LinkedIn. She even went to foreign-based sites like Peephole, Images, and WeChat. She saw nothing that matched what little Taft knew. While there were more than a few posts by someone named Lori Torchia, none of them fit the profile of a techie, and no one was from the DC area. Taft could usually find a lot about someone from social media. Like any good reporter, she used social media as a screening device for sources. She always found something. Not this time. She wondered who Lori Torchia was.

Briefly distracted as she took another sip of her drink, Taft was caught off guard when Torchia sat on the stool next to her. She was wearing white linen gloves, as if she were going to church.

Taft observed that Torchia was a bit overweight, but not too much. Her brown hair was pulled back and she dressed in fashionable jeans with a blouse, highlighting her figure's best features. She was attractive but not in an approachable way. That set her apart from Taft.

"I'm Lori Torchia."

"OK, I'm Rebecca Taft. Now that introductions are out of the way, would you like a drink?"

"Sure. I'll have some iced tea. I don't drink alcohol."

Too bad, thought Taft. She preferred to ply her sources with alcohol. It made them more cooperative. The bartender took the order and quickly returned with the iced tea.

"So what do you want to tell me?" asked Taft.

"First, I want your assurance that you will not use my name or identify me in any way I could be discovered."

"Sure. Everything will be off the record. For now. When I'd like you to go on the record, I'll ask."

"I won't go on the record," responded Torchia.

"Have it your way." Taft was used to skittish sources. She knew she could maneuver Torchia to go on the record at the appropriate time. Every source wanted something and if that something was worth enough to them, they'd sell their souls to get it.

Torchia took a sip of her tea and remained silent.

"OK. So back to my question. What do you want to tell me?"

"I'm a hacker and work for people who trade on the dark web. I've been doing it for three years."

"Who do you work for?" asked Taft.

"I really don't know for sure. I am paid a lot of money to hack into sites and trade information. The usual. Social security numbers, driver's licenses, credit cards, and bank accounts. I used to hack into government sites, but the commercial side is more lucrative. So that's what I do."

"Right. You and about a million other hackers. Why should that interest me?"

"Because now I'm afraid I'm working for people who are supporting bad things. I believe they use the information I give them to hurt people. A lot of people. And I didn't get into this business for that kind of thing."

"Oh, so you've developed a conscience?" Taft asked sarcastically.

"I suppose." Torchia did not seem offended by Taft's tone.

"And what evidence do you have that you're helping terrorists murder people?" Taft noticed that Torchia did not flinch at the murder allegation or the reference to terrorists, neither of which Torchia had mentioned. It was no secret that some bogus sites were funding terrorists.

Torchia reached into her purse and gave Taft a thin, blank, letter-size envelope.

Now I see what's with the gloves. No fingerprints.

"Don't open it here. Look at it somewhere where no one is watching you. As it is, if my giving you this is recorded on some camera somewhere in this bar it could put my life in jeopardy."

Jesus, thought Taft. *She's not only odd, but paranoid too.*

"There are no cameras here," observed Taft. "That's why I like this place."

"Really? Just how naïve are you?"

Taft ignored the insult. She was interested in hearing more.

"Believe what you'd like," responded Taft. "So tell me what's in this envelope."

"It's a list. That's all I'll say. Goodbye."

Torchia abruptly got up and walked out of the bar. Taft asked for the check and when the bartender did not immediately respond, she threw a couple of twenties on the bar and went for the door, hoping to see if she could either catch up with Torchia or know whether she was alone. But Taft was too late. Torchia was nowhere to be found. She went back to her office, confident that no closed-circuit cameras were there.

THIRTEEN

AXIOS MEDIA

IN HER TAXI TO *AXIOS*, TAFT HAD A FEELING THAT SHE WAS GETTING INTO SOMETHING THAT was way over her head. She should probably throw the envelope in the nearest trashcan. Terrorism was not her beat and she knew almost nothing about the dark web. So why did Torchia pick her?

Back at her desk she nervously opened the envelope, feeling it must contain an omen of some sort. On the sheet of paper she pulled out was a typed list of ten random dates.

That's it? thought Taft. *What the hell am I to make of a list of dates? How does this relate to terrorists?*

She looked at the envelope and turned the paper over a few times, hoping for a clue. Nothing. She decided to put it in her drawer. She wanted get back to the article she was writing about developments in Congress on the president's latest efforts to expand the Patriots Act in ways her editors believed would further deny Americans their constitutional freedoms.

Taft often laughed at all the hysteria over privacy. Her generation had long since decided that their personal data was free game in exchange for posting meaningless tripe about themselves on social media. Whenever she needed a good quote on protecting our most sensitive information, she always went to the most senior congressman she could corner. The older they were, the more important they thought it was. The Patriots Act drove some of them wild. They could not figure out what was more important: protecting privacy or routing out terrorists.

She typed a few paragraphs, but couldn't get Torchia out of her mind. Torchia seemed genuinely concerned, including for her own safety. Taft took the list out and looked at it again. She entered each date on Google, searching for some terrorist connection to Torchia's paranoia about supporting terrorists. After a half hour, she matched something to all of the dates, some of which had matches she knew that didn't require any research:

- February 26
  o New York's first World Center Bombing in 1993.
- November 5
  o 2009 Ft. Hood, Texas, shooting that left 13 dead and more than 30 injured.
  o 2010 bombing at the Durra Adam Khel mosque in Darra Adam Khel, Khyber Pakhtunkhwa, Pakistan, killing at least 66 and injuring 80 others.
  o 2014 Hamas vehicular attack in Jerusalem that left three dead and several others wounded.
- January 7
  o 2010, Nag Hammadi massacre of Coptic Christians in Nag Hammadi Egypt. Seven Coptics killed and 1 Muslim bystander dead.
  o In 2015, first day in a series of attacks over three days in Paris killing 17 and injuring 22.
  o Zliten, Libya truck bombing at a police training camp in 2016 killing more than 50 and injuring more than 100.
  o 2016 attack on Paris police station. Terrorist shot dead. No other injuries.
  o 2016 car bombing in the Libyan oil port of Ras Lanuf, leaving 7 killed and 11 wounded.
- November 13
  o 2004 Indonesia bus-bombing killing 6 and injuring 3.

- o 2015 coordinated attacks in Paris that killed 137 and injured 368.
- o 2015 suicide bombing in Baghdad at Shia funeral. At least 21 dead.
- March 22
  - o 2016 bombings in Brussels airport that left 35 dead and more than 300 wounded.
  - o 2017 vehicular attack on London's Westminster Bridge that killed 4 and injured more than 45.
- June 12
  - o 49 people dead and 53 injured in 2016 attack at an Orlando, Florida, nightclub.
- July 14
  - o 2016 Bastille day attack in Nice, France, that left 87 people dead.
  - o February 18
  - o 2018 Attack in an Orthodox church in Russia's southern province of Dagestan, killing five women and injuring others.
- August 14
  - o 2007 coordinated suicide bombings in Qahtaniyah and Jazeera, Iraq, killing at least 500 and wounding more than 1,500 people.
- September 11
  - o 2001 attacks on the World Trade Center, Pentagon, and United flight 93, killing nearly 3,000 people.
  - o 2012 attack on American diplomatic compound in Benghazi, Libya. U.S. Ambassador Christopher Stevens dead.

Where is the pattern here? There didn't seem to be anything Taft could infer from the list other than it was a collection of terrorist attacks in the last thirty years.

What are you trying to tell me, Lori Torchia?

Stumped, she decided to share it with her editor, Michael Isselin. Isselin was an old hand at Washington politics and the intrigue that swirled around the proverbial—or as Taft liked to say, primordial—swamp. Isselin also played Sudoku as if it were his religion. Puzzles were something he could figure out. Taft found such games boring.

Taft knocked on his door, a bit fearful of the response she might get. Isselin was usually ornery and rude to all of his reporters. "Michael, do you have a minute?" she asked as she gently pushed open the door.

"If it's important, yes. If not, send me an email." He was in his usual mood.

"Well, I'm not sure it's important…" Taft started.

"Then send me a fucking email. Did you miss that idea when I first suggested it?"

"I would, but this may be time-critical and involves what seems like a puzzle or perhaps a code. No one can break a code better than you." She hoped the compliment and appeal to Isselin's puzzle obsession would work. It did.

"Really? Show me."

Over the next two hours, Taft and Isselin went over the meeting with Torchia and the list Taft compiled. Isselin was getting frustrated.

"Where did you get the events that match the list?" Surprisingly, he had not asked that at the start.

"Google and Wikipedia."

Isselin leaned back in his chair, stared at the ceiling and shook his head. That made Taft nervous.

"Of course. Another great source for a good reporter. Google and Wikipedia. In case no one told you, Wikipedia is as close to fake news as any Russian-backed propaganda campaign. So you really think you'll find a pattern based on Wikipedia? Why not just ask them and not bother me?"

Taft got up from her chair. "Sorry I bothered you, Michael. She's probably just some hacker trying to play with us. I'll drop it."

"Wait." Isselin was looking intently at the list. "There is one oddity in the list."

Taft felt the back of her neck tingle. She knew Isselin was about to reveal something ominous. She could feel it.

"Is this in the same order as the list she gave you?" asked Isselin.

"Yes."

He stared at the list, making notes and crossing things out. After a few minutes, he looked up with a clear sense of satisfaction—and victory—on his face.

"That's it. All the dates up until the last two can be placed in chronological order if you eliminate some of the events. Here, look at this order." Isselin handed Taft his handwritten list:

—

February 26, 1993—World Center Bombing

November 5, 2009—Ft. Hood shooting

January 7, 2010—Nag Hammadi massacre

November 13, 2015—Attacks in Paris

March 22, 2016—Brussels airport bombing

June 12, 2016—Orlando nightclub

July 14, 2016—Attack in Nice

February 18, 2018—Attack in a Russian church

—

"All of your references to August 14 and September 11 don't work in the chronology. They're out of order." His satisfied smile said, *There you go, I solved another mystery!*

"But what does that mean?" asked Taft.

"You don't see it? Think, Taft. It's right in front of your eyes."

She stared at August 14 and September 11, the last two dates on Torchia's list. They had nothing beside them.

Then it hit her, "The dates are in the future. She's telling us that there will be terrorist attacks on August 14 and September 11!" Taft felt sick to her stomach. Isselin didn't seem terribly bothered.

"Perhaps, Taft. I suggest you follow up. You can also assume that there must be some connection between all of the citations corresponding to the dates. Start digging. It's only six weeks away to what might be the next attack. And get your source—this Lori girl—over here ASAP. I want to talk to her."

"I don't know how to contact her. She left me no phone number or address. The number she called from the other day is blocked or from a burner phone. We don't know. So I have no way of finding her." Taft felt lost.

Isselin again leaned back in his chair but did not look up at the ceiling. He was thinking.

"OK. Torchia said she liked what you wrote in *Axios*. Do a simple, gossipy column on the bar where you met her. Write about how you met someone and wished you'd gotten her name and number so you could talk to her again. If she reads it, she'll reach out to you. Give it a try."

"Should I also contact the authorities and alert them?"

"What? Purely on a hunch from an unknown source after we might or might not have solved a puzzle? All they'd do is laugh at you. We'll keep the story in-house for now. And next time, do a better job in identifying your source." Isselin could not resist ending the meeting with criticism.

FOURTEEN

BUCHAREST, ROMANIA

ISSELIN'S IDEA OF A GOSSIP COLUMN WORKED.

As soon as Taft saw the call from a blocked number, she knew it was Torchia.

"Lori?"

"Yes."

"I believe we've figured out your list."

"Not on the phone."

"Then can we meet again at Espita Mezcaleria? Today? Same time?"

"No, I'm back in Romania."

"Romania? What were you doing in the United States when I saw you?"

"Vacation."

"With anyone?" Taft was searching for clues on the mystery surrounding Torchia.

"If you want to see me, you'll have to come to Bucharest."

"That's awfully far to go for answers to some simple questions. And expensive, too."

"Then don't come. You have what you need."

"But I don't know that I do, Lori. Since you won't talk on the phone, I'm not sure how to get to the bottom of this mystery. I need some help here."

"Then come to Bucharest. I will call you in two days at this time to tell you where we can meet." Torchia hung up. Taft's mind was racing. This was

Tuesday. She'd have to be in Bucharest by Thursday if she expected to talk to Torchia any further.

Taft was surprised Isselin authorized the trip. Coach, of course. She had never been to Eastern Europe so it was exciting, particularly with the intrigue that surrounded the trip.

"Don't come back without a story, Taft. I don't like spending this kind of money on a wild goose chase. And keep the hotel under a hundred a night. I hear stuff's cheap in Romania." Isselin was as cheap as he was rude.

The next day, Taft boarded United flight 52, departing Washington's Dulles airport at 5:55 p.m. for the eight-hour flight to Zurich. After a four-hour layover, Taft connected to United 9782 for the two-plus-hour flight to Otopeni airport in Bucharest, arriving at 3:10 local time on Thursday afternoon. With the layover in Zurich, door-to-door was more than fourteen hours.

Taft was exhausted but on the ride from the airport to the Hilton Garden Inn in the Old Town section of Bucharest, she understood why travelers used to call Bucharest the Paris of the East. With its wide boulevards and gothic-style buildings, it was easy to imagine how in the good times one might think they were on the Champs Elysées with its boutiques and cafes. But these were no longer the good times in Romania. Still reeling from a weak economy and corruption at virtually every level of government, many of the once magnificent buildings were sorely in need of repair. While there was an occasional fancy shop, most of the businesses on the street were nondescript. Nonetheless, Taft could feel her energy returning as the taxi driver gave her a grand tour of what she was seeing.

At $89 a night, the Hilton fit Isselin's budget. Taft was jet-lagged and desperate to get some sleep. She was warned, however, that the worst thing she could do was go to sleep upon arrival. Unless she held tough and fought through that first day, her body would never acclimate to the time change.

Besides, she was scheduled to return on Saturday, so she had no time to sleep. After unpacking, she decided to take a short nap.

She woke up at 2:00 a.m., lying on the bed, still in her clothes. So much for following the advice she'd been given. She spent the next six hours watching CNN International, checking social media on her phone, and fading in and out of sleep.

On a lark, at 8:00 a.m. she checked her Starbucks app and to her utter delight discovered that even Bucharest had a Starbucks. Located on Strada Franceză, it was just a six-minute walk from her hotel according to Google Maps. She finished unpacking, showered, and got ready to begin the adventure that lay ahead.

It can't get better than to have my morning six-shot skim Grande cappuccino. It's just what I need.

A strong cappuccino was the way Taft jolted herself awake every morning in Washington. As she walked, she hoped she could use her Gold Starbucks card and earn some stars too.

Never hurts to get a free coffee.

At the counter, she ordered and gave the barista her Starbucks card. The blank stare returned by the barista gave Taft the impression that Romania had not yet joined the Starbucks reward program! Undaunted, Taft opened her Starbucks app with its autopay feature, which also tracked stars. To her surprise, the barista nodded and scanned the barcode on the phone. Success. Taft earned more stars. Technology delivered the rewards.

As she sat to enjoy her coffee, the phone rang at 10:30 a.m. with the now usual indication that it was from a blocked number. The call was earlier than Taft expected, but she was sufficiently confused with the time zone changes to not be sure when the call was supposed to come.

"Hello, Lori. I'm in Bucharest," Taft answered.

"I know. I saw your booking on Trip Advisor."

"How did you see my booking?" asked Taft, now feeling as if she was being manipulated.

"Really, Ms. Taft?" Torchia responded, a raspy tone in her voice. "What do you think I do for a living? I know everywhere you've been in the past year. You don't exactly hide very well."

The response shocked Taft. She wondered if it would be best to cancel the meeting and let this story be told by someone else. Taft always thought she was careful on the web, changing her passwords every two months and never turning on geolocation unless she was using Google Maps for directions or Open Table for a local restaurant.

Taft responded, "It makes me very uncomfortable that you know so much about me. You sound like you have a cold."

"I'm fine. Just stuffy from my allergies. Pollen counts in Bucharest are off the charts. And don't worry that I know so much about you. Lots of people do. I'll show you how to be invisible on the web and why you couldn't find me despite all your efforts."

"Thanks. I guess," responded Taft, now looking around the Starbucks, convinced it was filled with spies and wondering why her allergies had not been a problem if the pollen count was so high.

"Meet me at one o'clock at Restaurant Daryus," instructed Torchia. "It's at 62 Boulevard Dacia, only a fifteen-minute taxi ride from your hotel. Don't be late. I only have an hour off. It has a nice bar downstairs. I'll meet you there. And, Ms. Taft, you really should consider cutting back on your coffee. Six shots of espresso? Really?" Torchia laughed. Taft didn't see the humor at being so exposed.

"How do you know where I am?" Taft asked but after a silent pause, added, "Never mind. We'll talk about it when I see you."

"Yes. You have to stop them."

"Stop who?"

"The Russian and the Syrian. I'll explain later. I don't like talking on the phone and I've probably said too much already. And be careful; don't talk to anyone unless you have to."

Taft, now getting nervous, tried to relax as she finished her coffee and enjoyed a buttery croissant. The croissant wasn't as good as the ones in Washington, but it fit the bill.

She needed to walk. At 11:30, she set out for Restaurant Daryus, a 30-minute walk from the Starbucks according to Google Maps. Taft decided to take her time and look in some of the shops along the way. The directions took her through the old town, so she knew it would be an enjoyable and leisurely stroll with lots to discover around Strata Lipscani. Trip Advisor listed the street as the place where Taft would find the best shopping in Bucharest. She was in no rush. It was a sunny day and the warm air felt good.

Lipscani, once a thriving shopping district, had become overcrowded with bars and nightclubs, often spilling into the streets late into the night. But it was the hot spot for thirty-somethings, and Taft was comfortable walking its neighborhood.

After window shopping and buying nothing, Taft arrived at the restaurant a half-hour early. At that point she needed a cocktail and was happy to be at a bar.

Torchia was right. The restaurant was inviting, with red painted floors surrounded by brick walls and archways. Walking down the curved stairway, she felt as though she were entering a grotto in Spain.

The bar was roomy with a dozen leather-topped, but comfortable, stools. It had tables that could seat another twenty-five or so patrons. Taft immediately liked it.

She asked the waiter for his best brandy. He spoke English.

"I'll bring you pălincă, from Transylvania. Even Dracula likes it," he said with a grin.

"No doubt," Taft responded, noticing that he was quite attractive. "If it's good enough for vampires, I'm sure I'll like it."

"Where are you from?" he asked.

"Washington."

"And where are you staying while in Bucharest?"

Taft remained silent, declining to answer. She remembered Torchia's warning and decided that the fewer people in Bucharest who knew about her, the better. He got the message.

"Would you like something to eat? We have some of the best Iranian food in Bucharest."

"Not yet. I'm waiting for someone."

"OK. What is his name? I should let them know upstairs."

"Lori." Taft decided to stick with the first name only, mindful of Torchia's admonition to speak to no one.

The bartender smiled. "And here I thought someone as beautiful as you would be waiting for a man. Such a pity."

Taft knew he was waiting for a response that would spur him on, but she'd had enough of his awkward advances. So she just smiled and with that, settled in to enjoy the brandy. The bartender walked into the back room behind the bar.

Taft began worrying at 1:30. Torchia insisted she be on time. When it was half past four the bar began filling up as local workers gathered to talk about their day. Taft gave up and resolved to return to her hotel. Her flight was in two days, so she had some time to wait and see if Torchia reached out to her again. If she didn't, then Taft had no time left in Bucharest to figure out the mystery. Isselin's budget would not permit a longer stay.

Back at the hotel, she went online and again tried to find what she could about Lori Torchia. But just as Torchia told her, she was invisible. So Taft rechecked her flight information and checked in online. That was easy. And something the entire world now knew she did.

Taft's flight back was as uneventful as the day before, when she wasted her time hoping for a call from Torchia that never came.

PHASE TWO

CULTIVATING THE GARDEN

FIFTEEN

AXIOS, WASHINGTON, DC

ISSELIN WAS VERY UNHAPPY WITH TAFT'S REPORT.

"What do you mean she never showed up?"

"I don't understand it," responded Taft. "We spoke just hours before and she was insistent I be on time. Then she never showed up and never called me again."

"Did you feel that anyone in the bar was suspicious? Was anyone watching you that might have scared her away?"

"No. The only other person in the bar was the bartender. No one else came in until after Torchia was supposed to be there. And other than the bartender, none of them seemed suspicious or the least bit interested in me."

"But you were suspicious of the bartender?" asked Isselin.

"No. He wasn't suspicious in that way. I thought he was coming on to me. That's all," replied Taft.

"OK. So that was an expensive dead end. You didn't even get laid by the bartender. Maybe there is no story after all."

Taft chose to ignore the insult. "But Torchia said we had to stop some unknown Russian and Syrian. That's a hint. And we have the dates, too."

"And what are you going to do with dead ends like that, Taft? It's a big world out there with lots of Russians, Syrians, and dates. You honestly think you can connect those dots?" growled Isselin.

"Maybe. Why don't I use the trick you taught me?"

"The trick I taught you?" responded Isselin. "What trick?"

"Gossip. I'll put some feelers out there about a Russian and Syrian up to no good and see if I get a bite. I have to believe that if there is a grand conspiracy like Torchia fears, then there will be people here who are involved. Or at least know something. If I don't get a bite, then the story ends. But if I do, then we might be on to something."

"OK, Taft. Play your gossip card. Just be careful and keep me informed. If you go anywhere to follow up on any lead, I do not want you going alone. So keep me in the loop and I'll assign someone to be with you. Understood?"

"Understood."

Taft returned to her desk and began typing.

> *Barroom Boasts from Russians and Syrians*
>
> *You never know who you might meet in a bar. The other night around 11, while pub-crawling in Georgetown, my girlfriend Lori and I stumbled into Clyde's on M Street. We had been to about four bars by then and after finishing my Cosmo, I was ready to text to Uber and call it a night. But Lori had other ideas and started playing up to a couple of guys at the bar. I was tired and not particularly interested but could see Lori was enjoying it and when the Russian ordered the two of us another round, who was I to say no and prematurely spoil Lori's night? After all, the two were quite mysterious. So I joined in the fun and asked what they did. The Syrian said they were spies. "In Washington, everyone is a spy," quipped Lori. "Who are you spying on?" I asked. "No one in particular but you'll find out soon enough." "Soon enough?" asked Lori. "That won't do." Leaning flirtatiously toward the Syrian, Lori insisted, "And we need to know what and when right now!" Lori was drunk at this point and slurring. While I wasn't slurring, we'd both clearly had enough to drink. So had the Russian and Syrian. But the Syrian, caught up in his macho persona, took the bait. Sort of. "You'll know on August 14." Lori responded, "Know what?" The Russian grabbed the Syrian's arm and clearly wanted him to shut up.*

"It's time to go. We've all had enough to drink." Lori was crestfallen. It was not like her to let any man wander off into the night without at least having them make an advance at her that she could either entice or reject. Lori wanted to set the rules. Now the Russian took that choice away from her. The night ended and Lori was not happy. So here's an invite to our mysterious duo from the other night: On Friday night, meet Lori and me at Clyde's. 10:00. And bring the answer to Lori's questions.

Rebecca Taft, Reporter

She put the article in the outbox to make that night's online release. Then she dropped an email to Isselin with a copy of the article and a request that he assign Carol Bernstein, another woman from the office, to accompany Taft to the bar. She said she needed someone to play Lori.

"Taft, I'll do that but I'm also sending Gordon. There's no way I'm trusting two women in a bar who could be in harm's way."

Jason Gordon was a reporter on the crime beat. He had been with *Axios* about a year. After five years with the *Chicago Tribune*, he decided to join *Axios* to pursue criminals higher up in Washington instead of the inept Cook County politicians he'd become bored chasing. As far as Gordon was concerned, if he was ever going to win a Pulitzer, he needed to be in the center of the action.

Taft was not very fond of Gordon. She thought Gordon was overly self-assured and generally obnoxious. He loved to tell anyone willing to listen how great a reporter he was and how he uncovered major scandals. Trouble was, most people had no idea of any of the scandals he claimed to uncover. But that never stopped his bravado.

Gordon also thought himself quite a man's man and kept himself in excellent shape. He particularly liked boxing and often bragged how he could knock any man twice his weight to the ground with one punch. The humor most found in his boast was that soaking wet, Gordon might have weighed 150 pounds. He stood five foot five, and his pugilistic prowess was missed by most.

In the afternoon of the appointed night, Isselin summoned all three to his office.

"Let me just say that I think this is a very stupid idea. If Taft is right that the Russian and Syrian might be terrorists, then the three of you could be walking into a serious trap."

"Come on," protested Gordon. "Rebecca and Carol will be in a public place, and I'll be watching from a safe distance. If anything looks suspicious, our plan is that I come over and act like the long-lost boyfriend and break up the rendezvous. Simple. No one is going to do anything in a public place like Clyde's."

"Unless they're willing to die, too," responded Isselin, leaving the consequences of such a suicide mission hanging awkwardly in the air.

Bernstein broke the tension. "Don't worry, Michael, I have no doubt Jason can put rain on any parade. Even one led by the Unabomber. After all, wasn't that one of the scoops Jason unearthed?" Bernstein loved to poke fun at Gordon. He had nothing to do with the discovery of the Unabomber, of course.

"Yeah, Carol, tell me that after I save your ass from some nut case," Gordon added, apparently insulted by the ribbing. Gordon had a very thin skin.

"That's enough!" Isselin did not see the humor, and he was not someone who allowed others to waste his time.

"Just be careful and don't take any risks," Isselin continued, now turning to Taft and Bernstein. "Under no circumstances are the two of you to leave with anyone, man or woman. You are to find out what you can and then leave together. I've arranged for a car to be out front. It will be a blue Chevy. Nick Breen from legal will be driving. Do not vary from this plan. Is that clear?"

"Yes," both Taft and Bernstein said in unison.

"And Gordon, you stay and watch from a distance what the mysterious duo do, assuming anyone actually shows up. Do not engage with them.

Just watch and report to me. You can take a taxi or Uber home when it's all over. Just make sure you are not followed. Got it?"

"Got it."

The three left Isselin's office, feeling an excitement that made the assignment even more intriguing.

As they walked down the hallway, Bernstein asked, "Do you think Lori Torchia might show up?"

The question made Taft stop in her tracks.

"I hadn't thought of that," responded Taft. "If she does, it could get pretty awkward. I have to assume she's read the post. But given her desire to be hidden in the shadows, I doubt she'll show. Besides, it's not that easy for her to fly from Bucharest on such short notice. But if she does, I'm sure she'll only be watching out of sight and not interested in spending time with the two people she says we have to stop." With that observation, it finally sank in to Taft that there might be something dangerous about the night. She felt a chill.

"OK," responded Bernstein, seemingly oblivious to the dangers that might lie ahead. "If you do spot her, let me know somehow. I would like to meet her. She sounds so mysterious."

"Or maybe she's dead. Did you ever think of that, Rebecca?" suggested Gordon. "After all, she did fail to show just a few hours before she said she needed to meet you."

"Stop it, Jason," responded Taft. "You're being silly. I'm sure there's an explanation and if she wants to come to the surface again, she will."

"Unless she's six feet under," added Bernstein with a laugh.

"Both of you need to stop. This is not funny. If what Torchia tried to warn me about is true, it's serious. I would appreciate it if both of you would have the right attitude. This is not a night on the town."

"If Isselin is paying for the drinks, it's a night on the town for me," concluded Bernstein. Gordon smiled. Taft gave up trying to make either of them understand.

SIXTEEN

CLYDE'S OF GEORGETOWN

TAFT DRESSED FOR THE ROLE. IN A LOW-CUT DRESS WITH A SLIT UP ONE SIDE THAT TOYED at being higher than appropriate, she looked the part she wanted to convey. The mesh stockings and spike heels completed the ensemble. She looked very much like a woman willing to attract a man and engage in what could be a fantasy worth pursuing. She told Bernstein to dress suggestively as well. While she knew that might draw a lot of come-ons at the bar, she wanted the two of them to be noticed. After all, she thought, if you want to catch a big fish, you need bait that will attract them.

When Gordon arrived, he was dressed as he always did when he was hunting at bars, something he did just about every weekend. Free from any relationships, he was continually looking for one-night stands and took great pride in his occasional success. Wearing a Brooks Brothers white-collared shirt with the buttons opened two down from the top, a gray sport coat, and blue slacks, he looked too confident and someone any self-respecting woman would want to avoid. Of course, Gordon never looked for self-respecting women. His appearance was fine with Taft. She wanted Gordon to be paying attention to them, not some possible dalliance.

Bernstein had followed Taft's instructions, perhaps a little too enthusiastically. She arrived dressed in a business suit, but it could not have been tighter and showed off her ample breasts as though they were invitations to linger.

Maybe we're overplaying this, thought Taft. As her colleagues joined her in the bar, Taft feared that she and Bernstein looked more like sluts than potentially available women. But it was too late to worry.

Clyde's of Georgetown, on the ground floor of a three-story brick building, was a popular spot. The mahogany bar in the brick-walled lounge was always the main attraction for the Friday-night crowds. With dozens of model airplanes hanging from the ceiling and paintings of aircraft strewn on the walls, it was among Washington's favorite watering holes. The clientele were ready to drink and mingle. The ten-foot-tall nutcracker out front was Clyde's trademark, and a centerpiece for selfies to be posted on Facebook and Instagram. The back bar had every libation a patron could ask for. Its reputation as one of the best singles bars in the District was well established. It attracted those interested in exciting nights that might also lead to breakfast in bed.

The threesome arrived early, before the usual crowd. Taft wanted to be sure she and Bernstein got a seat at the bar. She positioned herself on a corner with Bernstein to her right. Gordon lingered at a distance with his Maker's Mark Manhattan in hand.

Taft told the bartender to give her a cranberry and soda in a martini glass, making sure it was slightly pink and included a wedge of lime on the rim. Taft instructed him to make sure that was all she was served. He understood that Taft wanted what looked like a Cosmo but without the vodka. He was used to such instructions, as many women kept their wits about them in singles bars by only appearing to drink alcohol. Taft suggested that Bernstein do the same, but Bernstein would have no part of that. She ordered her usual Don Julio tequila on the rocks accompanied by three wedges of lime, which she carefully squeezed into her glass.

"Carol, please keep your senses about you. I don't need you getting drunk tonight."

"Stop worrying, Rebecca. I can handle it."

Right. That's certainly not your reputation. Maybe I should have asked for someone else, thought Taft.

Taft ordered some freshly shucked oysters, a specialty of the house. She thought that would help with the scene. And besides, she was hungry and loved oysters.

By six-thirty, the bar was beginning to fill up. Taft felt nervous. As she looked at the men arriving, she realized she could not spot who among them might be Russian. And there were more than enough who looked like Middle Easterners. Any among more than a half dozen in the bar could have been Syrian.

By eight o'clock, Bernstein was three deep in tequilas and Taft had no doubt Gordon was keeping pace with his Manhattans. What concerned her most was that Gordon was apparently on his own agenda, approaching women at the other end of the bar with abandon, rejected by one after another.

So much for staying at a distance, lamented Taft to herself. *Didn't he hear what Isselin told him?*

Believing the night was a bust, Taft broke down and told the bartender to forget her previous instructions and to give her a Cosmo with Grey Goose vodka. He obliged. Bernstein ordered her fourth tequila.

At nine o'clock, after Taft and Bernstein had rejected a half-dozen advances from men who couldn't have been further from the prey they sought, a man in a business suit approached them from behind, positioning himself between them, and ordered a Macallan fifteen-year-old, straight up. Prepared to reject him if he made any effort to engage them, Taft was taken aback by what he asked.

"You're Rebecca Taft, right?"

Taft felt her blood pressure rise. She forced her words.

"You know me?"

"No. But I know your reputation."

"And what do you think that reputation is?" responded Taft.

"I guess I'd have to say you're a good reporter but one who can get in over her head."

Bernstein, now well oiled with four tequilas under her belt, interjected, "And what does that make you? Some barfly without a head?" She thought it was funny. Taft did not. No one did. It made no sense. But Bernstein was drunk and any attempt to be articulate was futile.

The man didn't take Bernstein's bait and calmly replied, "Not really. My name is Chandler Thompson. I work for the FBI. I read your post the other night and I think we should talk."

"About what?" asked Taft.

"About why you're looking for Lori Torchia, a Russian, and a Syrian."

Taft felt her stomach churn. She hadn't used Lori's last name in the article.

"I don't know what you're talking about," responded Taft, noticing that Bernstein appeared to be in shock and tongue-tied, something not typical for her.

"Look, Ms. Taft. I'm not here to make your life difficult. But we need to talk. And not here. Whoever you thought might show up tonight, it's not likely to happen. People like the men you hope to meet don't work that way. If they want to meet you, they will do it where and when they decide. They don't fall prey to amateur invitations like the foolish one you posted two days ago."

Gordon, watching from the opposite end of the bar, had just been rejected yet again and decided it was time for him execute on Isselin's plan and intervene. From a distance, it looked to him that Taft and Bernstein were in a jam. He was right.

As Gordon approached, he shouted out, "Hey Rebecca, funny seeing you here." Taft could smell the Manhattan on his breath.

"Mr. Gordon, no need to interrupt," said Thompson, holding up his hand to stop Gordon. "No one is in trouble here. At least not yet. I'm

Chandler Thompson." Thompson extended his hand to Gordon. "I'm with the FBI."

Gordon froze in his steps as he took Thompson's hand, immediately feeling the very firm handshake that conveyed a clear message to stand down.

Two more men approached the bar, immediately behind Thompson. They were obviously fellow agents.

"May I suggest we find a quieter place to talk? Our car is waiting outside."

"I'm not going anywhere," barked Bernstein, now obviously scared.

"That isn't a problem. I didn't invite you. You are free to go wherever you would like. That's your decision. But I'm afraid your Mr. Breen is not waiting to give you a ride. He has been convinced it is best that he tend to something else. So we're the only ride Ms. Taft has, and the two of you are on your own."

"And if I refuse to go with you?" asked Taft.

"Then you're making a mistake. Frankly, we are not particularly interested if Mr. Gordon or Ms. Bernstein join us or not, but if it makes you feel better, they can join us too. But you, Ms. Taft, are well advised to comply with my request," answered Thompson, in a tone that was more of an order than an observation.

"Am I being arrested?" asked Taft.

"Of course not," replied Thompson. "What could possibly be a reason to arrest you?"

One of the agents leaned forward and said, "Don't worry about the check. We'll take care of it."

Deciding she had no choice, Taft complied and over the objections of Gordon and Bernstein, followed Thompson outside to the waiting car, leaving her two companions behind with instructions that they get word to Isselin that she was with the FBI.

Observing all of this from a booth in Clyde's, Frank Cooper enjoyed his dinner and called for the check when Taft left with her newly found escorts. He made a call.

SEVENTEEN

FBI, WASHINGTON, DC

THE RIDE TO FBI HEADQUARTERS SEEMED LIKE AN ETERNITY. TAFT SAT IN THE BACK SEAT between the two agents who accompanied Thompson. He sat in the front passenger seat.

"Where are you taking me?" asked Taft.

"You'll know soon enough," Thompson replied, without turning to look at Taft. His words chilled the air. Taft could see Thompson was grinning, pleased with his little inside game.

"Do I need a lawyer?"

"Only if you've done something wrong. Like withholding evidence that might be a risk to national security. Or if you've published false reports of encounters with foreign agents. Stuff like that. But since you'd never done any such things, I don't think you need a lawyer." Thompson could barely hide his smug look.

"I haven't done anything wrong, but I still think I want a lawyer before we go any further."

"Well, Rebecca," responded Thompson, "since we haven't charged you with anything and do not believe you are a person of interest regarding any commission of a crime that we are actively investigating, you're not yet entitled to a lawyer. After a few questions, you are free to go and hire all the lawyers you'd like. But first things first."

Taft suspected Thompson was lying. It was her understanding that anyone questioned by the FBI is entitled to a lawyer, even if they are not accused of anything. But for the time being, she decided to wait and see.

After the car pulled into the garage under the FBI offices, Taft was escorted to a small interrogation room. It was the first time she'd been in one. It looked like a scene right out of the movies.

Fluorescent lighting recessed into the ceiling lit a small metal table with a chair on one side and two others on the opposite side. The mirror on the wall was clearly two-way. Nothing more was in the room. Taft was shown the single chair.

The agent escorting her asked if she would like a cup of coffee or something to drink. Taft declined.

A few minutes later, Thompson entered, carrying two cups from Starbucks.

"A six-shot skim cappuccino if I'm correct," said Thompson as he set the cup in front of Taft.

How does everyone seem to know so much about me?

"I prefer something a lot less lethal," continued Thompson. "Mine is just a blond roast, black." As he sat down, he put the folder he was carrying on the table, placing it between them as if to entice Taft to look inside, which was precisely what he wanted her to do.

"First, Ms. Taft, please let me apologize for the cloak and dagger. I meant it when I said you didn't need a lawyer, but you are entitled to one if you really insist. I was just having a little fun with you. I got a kick out of your Nancy Drew move to ferret out the mysterious Russian and Syrian. It might have worked if they were idiots. But of the little we know about them, they're anything but idiots." Thompson gently pushed the folder toward Taft.

"Go ahead," he suggested. "Take a look."

Taft slowly opened it to find a stack of eight-by-ten photos, some black and white, some color. The one on top showed Lori Torchia coming through U.S. customs at Washington's Dulles airport. Pushing that one aside, Taft saw that the next three showed her with Torchia sitting at Espita Mezcaleria bar. The bar where Taft was convinced there were no cameras. The fifth photo showed Torchia, outside the bar, getting into a car. Now Taft understood why she had vanished so quickly. The sixth photo was someone Taft did not recognize.

"Who is he?" asked Taft, putting her finger on the man in the photo.

"His name is Frank Cooper. More on him later. Interestingly, he was at Clyde's tonight. Keep looking."

Next was a picture of Cooper with Darren White apparently having breakfast at some nondescript restaurant.

"And him?"

"Darren White, a particularly stupid and very greedy broker. We have reason to believe he works for Cooper. Problem is, we don't know who Cooper works for."

"Could he be the Russian or Syrian Lori told me about?"

"Perhaps. We don't know for sure."

"What do White and Cooper do for their mystery boss?"

"We assume whatever they're told to do. Our guess is you don't refuse an order regardless of what it is."

Thompson reached forward and gently pushed the photo aside to reveal the next one of a man walking down the steps of a hotel.

"We believe this is a picture of Abu al-Badri leaving the Four Seasons Hotel in Beirut. In what we don't regard as coincidence, Frank Cooper was registered there on the same day."

"So you think the two of them met?"

"Outstanding, Nancy Drew. You're getting better." Thompson smiled, but this time in a pleasant way. Taft was beginning to think he might not be the asshole she first thought he was.

"Is he…"

"Syrian? Yes," said Thompson, completing Taft's sentence. "We think he's former ISIS, assuming anyone can formerly be with ISIS."

"So Cooper, White, and al-Badri may all be working for the Russian Lori feared," observed Taft.

"We don't know. In fact, we can't be sure that Torchia's description of the mystery man as a Russian is even right. More often than not, lower-level players like her have little accurate knowledge of who sits on the top of the food chain," responded Thompson. "Nor can we be sure the others Torchia referred to are Cooper, White, or al-Badri. We've never seen her with any of them. And after all, she never physically described anyone to you. Is that correct, Rebecca?"

"Yes. She only referred to a Russian and Syrian and insisted we have to stop them."

As Taft put her finger on the photo of al-Badri to move it aside to the next one, Thompson placed his hand on her finger.

"You're not going to like the next one," he warned as he gently guided her hand to reveal it.

It was Lori Torchia, dead on a slab in the Bucharest morgue. Taft felt sick to her stomach. It was the first time she'd seen a picture of a corpse, let alone of one she knew in life.

"Her real name was Florentina Dumitrescu. She was a Romanian who started off on the legal side of computer programming before succumbing to the lure of the money she could earn as a hacker. When we read your post, we put one and one together and confirmed that you were in Bucharest the day she died."

"I knew she was a hacker. She told me she worked in the dark web." Taft's eyes were affixed to the photo as tears welled up with the fear she had something to do with Torchia's death. "How did she die?"

"Poisoned. A pretty standard way spies dispatch people they don't like. We assume the mysterious Russian was behind it and she died in a taxi on the way to see you. We believe that about two blocks from the restaurant, she passed out in the back seat and died within minutes. She was buried in the Jewish cemetery just minutes away from the bar and then forgotten to the world."

"Why did she have to die that way?" asked Taft, now in tears.

"Because we asked the Romanian government to do so until we determine how she was involved. Her reference to you of a Russian and Syrian puts you in the middle of the mystery. We've been following Frank Cooper for some time, believing that whoever he works for is manipulating financial markets throughout the world. So we look into anyone who meets Cooper. As we pieced the puzzle together, we realized we were looking at something far more dangerous than financial schemes."

"Terrorism?"

"Most likely. The scary part is that when someone with unlimited funds appears to see radical Islam as a tool to advance his interests, it's a new game. As dedicated as the radicals are, they usually lack financial resources.

"And even when they have money, they spend it foolishly. But ISIS changed that with its own financing through oil. Even then, they still lacked the contacts they needed for the kinds of weapons they craved and operations they wanted to undertake."

"Nuclear?"

"Exactly. We know that nuclear weapons are on the market. They have been for years. But sales have been few, and we've been able to intercede so far. If you only knew what that takes, you'd realize how scary this could get if those weapons became more available. That is now the new normal. It has every right-thinking person, even some Russians and Chinese, concerned. The united alliance against this is decidedly an odd family."

"But what do you think I can tell you? I never got anything important from Lori. All she told me was that we needed to stop the Russian and Syrian and she gave me a list of dates."

"List of dates? What list of dates?" Taft realized that Thompson didn't know.

"She gave me a list of dates that chronologically corresponded to terrorist attacks. But two didn't fit into the chronology."

"Which two?"

"August 14 and September 11."

"September 11? How can you say that didn't correspond to a terrorist attack?"

"Of course, it did. But not in the chronological order she gave us."

"Please explain."

Taft told Thompson the story of how she and Isselin pieced it all together. That her bait to meet with the Russian and the Syrian was an effort to find out why and what was coming next.

"If you're right, then something is going to happen in a few weeks. Did Lori tell you anything more?"

"No. That's all I know." Taft felt a pit in her stomach. This had all become too real for her. Sitting in a small room with an FBI agent who didn't have the answers only made it worse.

The door opened, and another man walked in holding a folder. Taft could see the label: "TOP SECRET."

"Rebecca, this is Richard Harris. CIA. He and I have been working together for the past year. Homeland Security is also involved."

Harris sat down next to Thompson.

"Ms. Taft, you're going to help us," Harris concluded, ignoring any effort to make a polite introduction.

Help you? I'm just a reporter after a story. A story I wish I never pursued. You're the ones who are supposed to help, not me.

"I don't know what I can do to help you. I know so little," responded Taft.

"True," replied Harris, "But we believe those who are looking at you think differently. They know that you and Dumitrescu—Lori Torchia to you—met. We also know she worked on dark web operations used to disrupt markets with fake news. She takes her orders from somewhere in Eastern Europe, but we don't know from where. Not yet. And we don't know who Dumitrescu worked for. But whoever it is, they may think you know or were told, since you spoke to her and were going to meet with her. So we have to assume you pose a threat to them."

"You're scaring me," Taft replied

"We understand," responded Harris. "You have reason to be scared. But we can provide you with some protection. To be honest, we're surprised you're still alive."

Still alive! I want out. Now.

"I'm not comfortable with all of this and I'd like to leave."

"No doubt you would, Rebecca," interjected Thompson. "But I'm sorry to say, that's not really an option anymore. This is a matter of national security and whatever rights you think you have serve no purpose here."

Harris placed his folder on the table in front of Taft and opened it to the first picture.

"Ms. Taft, this is a photograph of Cooper meeting with Philippe Lamont, one of the biggest arms dealers in the world. He has access to just about anything. And while we don't think that includes nuclear weapons, we can't be sure." It was the only photo in the folder.

Can't be sure? What kind of bullshit is this?

"I don't understand. If you don't know what to do, what makes you think I can help? What could I possibly do?"

Harris and Thompson looked at one another. Thompson nodded to Harris. Harris spoke.

"All we want you to do is keep writing stories. We believe you can help us connect the dots and get to the truth about what's going on. And because August 14 seems to be a flashpoint, there isn't much time." Taft realized Harris must have been listening from the other side of the mirror.

The door opened again, and another agent entered, handing a briefcase to Harris. Once Harris took it, the man left without a word.

Harris opened the case and took out a phone and a necklace, pushing both across the table to Taft. She stared at them but didn't want to pick them up.

"What kind of phone do you have, Rebecca?"

"An iPhone," she replied, still staring at the phone and necklace in front of her, feeling in her gut that she wanted nothing to do with either of them.

"Good. Then you're familiar with the phone. Please pick it up. It won't bite you." Harris pushed to phone toward her.

"I have a phone. Why do I need another one?"

"Because this phone is encrypted. But unlike your other phone, we don't want you to use this phone for calls. Use it only for texts." Harris pressed the button on the phone and brought the screen to life. It had only one icon on it—a text bubble like Messenger but blue with the bubble surrounded by a dotted line. Taft stared at it but didn't pick it up.

"In fact, we don't want you calling us any more from any phone." Harris pushed the phone closer to Taft. "See this blue icon?" Harris pointed to it on the phone's screen. "It's an app called Signal. As long as both sides of a conversation are using it, it's encrypted and untraceable. Impossible to hack into."

Thompson continued, "Signal is the most popular app of terrorists, particularly coupled with an iPhone. Between the password protection of the iPhone itself and Signal's enhanced encryption, it is virtually impossible to break into a conversation and gather intelligence in a time frame that makes an investigation possible. Unlike Android phones, the iPhone shuts down for five minutes whenever the wrong password is entered six consecutive times."

"And that's why we've sued Apple for a solution but keep losing in court. Unfortunately," interjected Harris, "our courts are more concerned with protecting terrorists than Americans."

Thompson placed his hand on Harris's forearm to keep him from going on a political tirade that he knew would offend Taft.

"So using automated password-cracking software is exponentially slower with an iPhone. With an Android, cracking software will eventually generate the right password within weeks because it does not have the same protection. With an iPhone, it can take years, far longer than any law enforcement investigation can afford."

Harris continued, "But we've learned to play the same game and take advantage of the same security. So we use iPhones with Signal."

"That's great," said Taft. "So neither of you know what one another are doing. I imagine that's a great way to stop terrorists," she added sarcastically.

Harris ignored the remark and continued, pressing the icon for the Signal app. "When you open it, you see a picture of the American flag. That means you are connected to us. As soon as you open the app, we'll know you're online. You begin by pressing the icon. Do not press the compose button in the corner for a directory. We're the only contact in the directory, so pressing the compose button is an unnecessary step. Simply press the American flag." Harris pressed it and the new message box appeared. "Then type your text and press send. It's simple. Just like any other texting software. We'll respond immediately. Do you understand?"

"Yes."

"You are to keep the phone with you at all times. And don't forget to charge it. The charger is included with the phone."

"I'm not an idiot. I know how to charge a cell phone," replied Taft, obviously losing her patience with Harris.

"I apologize, Rebecca. I'm used to dealing with people far less intelligent than you. So please forgive me if I seem to be disrespectful. That is not my intent."

"Well, you should start working on your social skills," responded Taft as she continued to stare at the phone, not touching it. Harris then put his hand on the necklace, pushing it toward Taft.

"The necklace is a transponder. The phone is too, but we like backup just in case. Wear it at all times. It will tell us where you are, anywhere in the world. Take them," Harris ordered.

Taft picked up the phone, her hand shaking. Thompson rose, picked up the necklace and walked behind her.

"Please allow me." Thompson placed the necklace around Taft's neck, clasping it from behind. Taft thought it more of a noose than jewelry. Thompson sat back down.

As she fumbled with the phone, Taft observed, "My editor won't let me write whatever I—or you—want. So I still don't understand how—"

"You needn't worry about Mr. Isselin. We'll take care of him."

"Just like you're taking care of me?" angrily responded Taft. "By putting me one bullet away from some fucking terrorist with my only protection being secret texts and a cheap necklace? I can't wait to hear how you're going to protect Isselin! Or does taking care of him mean something other than protection?"

Neither Harris nor Thompson responded.

EIGHTEEN

M STREET NW, WASHINGTON DC

JASON GORDON PUNCHED INTO HIS LYFT APP FOR A PICKUP OUTSIDE CLYDE'S. AFTER CALLING Isselin and reporting what happened, he and Bernstein were told to meet Isselin at the office. Immediately.

By now, M Street was crowded with Friday-night revelers and bar hoppers.

A Toyota Corolla with a trademark pink Lyft logo taped to the passenger window pulled up, and the two got inside. Gordon preferred Lyft over Uber, ignoring Isselin's instructions to take either Uber or a taxi.

"You Jason?" the dark-skinned driver asked.

"Yes."

He pulled from the curve and drove off down Michigan toward Route 29.

"What just happened?" asked Bernstein.

"I don't know, Carol. All I can think is we're deeper into this than we thought. The fucking FBI for Christ's sake! *They* even scare me."

"Where are they taking Rebecca? How did they know we were there?"

"I don't know any more than you do, Carol. All we can do now is tell Isselin what happened."

"You were supposed to protect Rebecca, Jason. You let her get into a car with three men who claimed they were from the FBI. Did you see any IDs from them? Why didn't you ask?"

"Fuck you, Carol. You could have asked, too."

Five minutes into the ride along Route 29, the driver failed to make a left onto North Highland Drive, the right direction to *Axios*.

"Hey, driver, you missed the turn," Gordon ordered. "Turn ahead onto North Kirkwood and take that road."

"Sorry, my GPS is taking me this way," the driver said apologetically.

Turning to Bernstein, Gordon complained, "These fucking Lyft drivers and their damn GPS. They never know where they're going." Gordon then noticed the car had no GPS.

Not following Gordon's order, when the driver got to Highland, he turned right onto the North Spout Parkway.

"Hey, what the fuck are you doing? You just missed Highland. You should have taken a left, not a right, you idiot. What the hell is going on?"

"Relax, Mon."

"Jason, I'm scared. Where are we going?" asked Bernstein.

"Stop this car," ordered Gordon. "Stop this fucking car!"

The driver responded, "OK, OK. You don't have to get so angry. I'm just trying to do my job."

"Pull the fuck over, damnit," shouted Gordon.

The driver pulled into the Fort Strong Apartments parking lot, stopping next to a black Range Rover Evoque that was backed into a spot. He parked too close for Bernstein to open her door.

Putting the Toyota in park, the driver jumped out and slammed his door behind him. Gordon tried his door, but it was locked. The driver had turned on the childproof option. The rear doors would not open.

"Oh my God, Jason. What's going on?"

Gordon was about to climb into the front seat when the driver's door opened again, and a man threw a small canister in. He slammed the door and got into the Range Rover, not pulling forward out of its spot beside the Toyota.

As the gas filled the car, Gordon and Bernstein began chocking in seconds, desperately trying to pull on the door handles but to no avail. They mercilessly died in less than thirty seconds. As designed, the gas that suffocated them dissipated into the air, leaving evidence that they had died of carbon monoxide poisoning.

The driver donned a gas mask, returned to the car, opened the door, turned off the childproof locks, and removed the canister. He closed the front door and opened the door next to where Bernstein's body now lay. He reached back and tore open Bernstein's blouse and lifted her bra, exposing her breasts. He reached in further and unzipped Gordon's pants, exposing his penis. After he rejoined his comrade, the Range Rover sped away.

On receiving the report once the assignment was completed, Petrenko could not help but marvel how stupid people were about getting into a car with a logo on the side without ever questioning who they were trusting with their lives. It was so simple to hack into the system and monitor any Uber, Lyft, Via, or other ride-sharing apps. Petrenko's driver had all the logo'd cards he needed. He simply had to place the one Gordon called on the window. It was lucky for Petrenko that Gordon and Bernstein didn't just take a DC taxi for the eleven-minute ride to *Axios*. As one of his team once told him, "The only thing you can't hack is a hack in a taxi."

"What about the other two, Taft and Isselin?" asked Petrenko's head of security.

"Don't worry about them. I want to see what they do. Just keep an eye on them. They're small fish. Now that the FBI seems to be involved, I want to know who is behind this. We need to get to the top. That is the head of the snake we need to cut off. We'll let them hang by a thread for now. This will be a sobering message for them."

After investigating, the police reported the tragedy as a death of two lovers on a tryst in the rear seat of a car, succumbing to carbon monoxide poisoning. The police reported that the Toyota was registered in Gordon's name, a simple ruse for Petrenko to arrange. The report noted that the two had been seen frequenting a District bar, leaving quite inebriated. The fact that Bernstein was partially clothed when found added to the narrative that they appeared in the throes of ecstasy when they were overcome by the carbon monoxide. Equally simple for

Petrenko to arrange. It only took a couple of days for the social media chatter, questioning the deaths and suggesting there was more to the story, to fade away. That was also easy for Petrenko's programmers to accomplish. Facebook posts weren't immune from the superior talent Petrenko employed in Eastern Europe.

NINETEEN

PODGORICA, REPUBLIC OF MONTENEGRO

TAD DORDA WAS SCROLLING THROUGH THE MORNING'S REPORTS. OVERSEEING A TEAM OF over one hundred programmers strewn throughout Eastern Europe, he was responsible for the most talented of Petrenko's hackers.

As punctual as ever, Paula Janković, his top hacker, walked into Dorda's office with the obligatory cup of black coffee as her offering to him. It had become a tradition of sorts she never forgot. A leftover from the Communist regime, Dorda expected special treatment from his subordinates regardless of how important they might be.

It helped that Janković was stunning by any man's standards. At five foot seven, auburn hair, and a flawless body and complexion, it was impossible for any red-blooded man not to fantasize about her. Dorda was no exception, but he also knew that his position made Janković off limits. That didn't stop Janković from obviously enjoying the game.

"Good morning, Tad. I hope your evening was a pleasant one and you're finding today's reports informative. Once again, I spent an evening alone wondering where the men are in Podgorica."

"There are plenty of men in Podgorica, Paula."

"Yes, Tad. But not like you," replied Janković with a sultry tone.

"That's enough, Janković. You know better. Now what do you have for me this morning?"

Satisfied that she'd made Dorda uncomfortable, Janković continued, "We were able to find quite a bit about our new friends in the United States."

Janković handed Dorda a file that he took a few minutes to absorb as Janković sipped her coffee.

"So I see," Dorda finally said. "Your work is as outstanding as ever, Paula. Are you sure these people have no way of knowing we're tracking them?"

"Absolutely. Our spiders and bots are unmatched. Their signatures last one nanosecond and then morph into new ones, passing on their knowledge to the next one. Coupled with the algorithms and encryption codes embedded in each of them, no one can hack into them. It is machine learning at its best."

"So it acts like a virus?" asked Dorda.

"No, Tad, more like cancer," responded Janković. "A virus shuts systems down. They can then be rebooted. My algorithms kill them."

"And we keep the codes secure?" Dorda knew that answer but liked to ask Janković every day. Another part of their morning ritual.

"Yes, more secure than the formula for Coca-Cola. And we change them every hour."

"So tell me more about how you're collecting today's catch."

Janković knew that compiling personal dossiers is far easier than many people thought. Her hackers running Petrenko's social media websites, Images and Peephole, used complex algorithms proprietary to Petrenko to locate and track anyone who used the Internet. Hacking into Google, Facebook, YouTube, Instagram, and Twitter was child's play for Janković and her team. It didn't matter if people on social media used a computer or other mobile device. She could track it all and she was growing tired of telling Dorda time and time again how she did it. But she also knew she had to indulge his repetitive questions as though she was always being tested.

"Tad, we simply connect the dots between searches, purchases, reservations, postings, photos, and anything else someone puts on the Internet, by putting cookies and digital robots—called bots—on individual computers throughout the world. No one knows we're doing it and no one is immune. The owners of every device have no idea the cookies, bots, and our other malware are operating behind the scenes whenever the device is on," explained Janković for what seemed to her like the hundredth time.

Dorda continued the narrative as if he actually knew what he was talking about as opposed to repeating what Janković had told him countless times in the past, "Our bots gather information from emails, calls, and posts that contain data. It is all streamed back to Petrenko's servers placed throughout the world, mostly in countries that have lax laws on privacy and laws of extradition."

"Tad, why do you find it so interesting to repeat what I've told you? You're certainly not impressing me."

"Because, Paula, I like to remind myself of what we're doing and how we do it. Sometimes, Paula, I'm not certain you're telling me everything, so repeating it gives me some comfort that you are. You are telling me everything, right, Paula?" Dorda's tone was menacing.

"Yes, Tad, I'm telling you everything you need to know," responded Janković.

"That's the problem. You're telling what you think I need to know. So indulge me, and tell me again how it works. Perhaps someday I'll see you've left something out."

"Don't you trust me, Tad?" asked Janković sarcastically.

Dorda's stare made it clear he didn't think he had to respond.

Indulging Dorda as she always did, Janković continued, "Even in countries with strict laws and significant regulatory surveillance, it doesn't really matter. All of Petrenko's data is backed up in multiple places; all of it encrypted at a level impossible to penetrate within any reasonable period of time. Even supposedly passive devices like Amazon's Echo or Internet-based home security systems are not immune from our bots. Such hardware is never off. It's always listening and watching. All that information is captured and stored. The claim that Alexis or Google Home only listen for a few seconds, while literally true, fails to disclose that whatever it's listening to is transmitted and preserved in a database. It is only erased on the device, not the server. Something as seemingly harmless as a Ring doorbell is receiving video feeds and sending them not just to a user's cell phone but also to the server that makes the entire system work. And if you're carrying your phone or wearing an iWatch, your location and speech can be tracked 24/7. All with your permission. People freely consent to enjoy all the marvels they crave. And it can all be hacked."

Known as "big data," the trillions of bits of information can be mined and categorized in unlimited ways to create something as simple as personal and financial dossiers or something far more nefarious that give hackers like Janković complex psychographic profiles. Profiles that can predict how someone might act with the right stimulus.

When Janković first embarked on compiling big data for Petrenko, he used it in legitimate ways to track financial trends that could be used to make trades on exchanges throughout the world using algorithms capable of taking advantage of price movements that occurred in milliseconds. Petrenko would then arbitrage the stock using those trends and make a small profit with each trade. Since he could make millions of trades through his algorithms, profits mounted quickly.

Petrenko was not alone in using algorithms to replace human judgment. For years, sophisticated traders at large mutual funds and portfolio managers used the same system. Stock markets no longer needed anyone on the so-called floor to execute trades. It was all done with algorithms that over time were capable of actual learning. While not artificial intelligence per se, machine learning through processing millions of bits of data faster than humanly possible was about as close as one could get to artificial intelligence. The fact was that a machine could learn and store unlimited amounts of data and translate it into trends that could more accurately predict a price move than any human analyst could. While that occasionally caused extreme movement in markets in which indexes like the Dow Jones could jump or fall by hundreds of points in an hour, most markets had some controls to prevent a complete meltdown while programmers feverishly adjusted their computations to bring back some stability. The reality was, however, that markets were completely mechanical, proving that the proverb about the rich getting richer was true by making money in both bull and bear markets. Those who were particularly sophisticated could manipulate the markets to respond with significant movement up and down to ensure that those profits were unending.

"So we now know who Rebecca Taft has met with and her entire network of confidants?" asked Dorda.

"Down to a person, Tad. And we've now eliminated three of them: Lori Torchia, Jason Gordon, and Carol Bernstein. We can take care of the rest whenever we get the order. We're learning more every day as Taft turns on her computer, makes a call, charges a purchase, walks by a CCTV camera, or posts a pretty picture. We know more about her than she knows herself."

"So who are her friends at the FBI?"

"Special FBI agent Chandler Thompson is her primary contact. But he's not solo. He's part of a trio—the Three Stooges as I like to call them—who have been entertaining her. In addition to Thompson, there's a guy named Richard Harris. I think he's most likely CIA. The third stooge is Oliver Grant with Homeland Security. Taft hasn't met him yet."

"How did you identify all these people? Most law enforcement in the United States stays off of social media," observed Dorda.

"Many do stay off, but many don't. Even when they stay off, others post about them. Family, friends, general observers. No one is immune from being on social media. And besides, they're all in the Homeland Security TSA database."

"You hacked into Homeland Security? Isn't it encrypted and hackproof?"

"Tad, as I've told you countless times, no database is hackproof. Devices can be, but not databases. There is always a door in. And I find them. As for the Three Stooges, it was easy. We identified Grant and Harris from posts and confirmed Thompson though facial recognition on the CCTV cameras that picked him up when he whisked Taft off to a meeting from the bar where Cooper surveilled them. Like I said, it was easy."

"So what do we know about Thompson?" asked Dorda.

"He's a career agent. Decorated. A real Boy Scout."

"Anyone else involved from the FBI?"

"Mostly other lackeys at the Bureau," Janković replied. "But Thompson's acquaintances outside the Bureau are more intriguing to us."

"Harris and Grant?" asked Dorda.

"Perhaps," responded Janković. "I'm wondering if my Three Stooges might be just the tip of the iceberg. This kind of shit attracts all sorts of flies."

Janković loved to toy with Dorda. She always made sure his morning reports left out some juicy details. It was her way to make sure an algorithm would never replace her. While it annoyed Dorda, he was resigned to let Janković play her game. As long as she always brought him a cup of coffee for their morning briefing.

Dorda pushed on. "And who would those acquaintances be, Paula?"

"More agents from the CIA and Homeland Security. Perhaps from Congress or even the White House. I don't know yet," lied Janković. She had no reason to believe or suspect that there were others. She just wanted to keep Dorda on the hook. Petrenko, too.

Janković continued, "Thompson recently checked into a posh resort in West Virginia, foolishly using his own name and credit card. The hotel's CCTV camera picked up the other two Stooges going to his room."

Dorda was growing tired of the cat and mouse game.

"Paula, enough with your fun. You know who they are. Now, what are they planning?"

"They are all mid-level operatives except for Harris. He appears to be more important and has a budget to back him. As far as we can tell, Thompson and Grant are not key players in any of their organizations. If I had to guess, they've gone rogue and are planning something that is not sanctioned."

"Why do you say that?"

"Right now, it's just a hunch. We're not finding much interaction between the three that links them to enough other people to create a profile of a larger operation. But we're still digging."

"Petrenko will not like that answer, Paula."

"Then let him come here and tell the programmers how to do their job." Janković was very protective of her team and any challenge to their ability to do their jobs elicited an insubordinate comment.

"Right," responded Dorda, "I'll be sure to tell him that. You're dismissed. Come back when you have the answers I need."

Janković rose.

"Wait, Paula."

She stood silently.

"How are you doing with our other project?"

Janković sat back down.

TWENTY

THE SELFISH LEDGER

"WE'RE NOT THERE YET," JANKOVIĆ ANSWERED. "PETRENKO'S THEORY MAY BE SOUND, BUT the idea of using subconscious digital manipulation to force an action otherwise against one's self-interests is something else. It's like the notion that you never die in your dreams because you have no motivation to die when you're awake."

"So you can't make someone do something that will hurt them against their will, right?" Dorda asked.

"That's the theory. And while we've often seen people sacrifice themselves for causes they believe in—foolish or otherwise—our challenge is to get them to act against their self-interests without needing a cause to do so. We want to compel them against their will without them knowing they're doing our bidding."

"And knowing you, Paula, you have a plan to do just that," replied Dorda with a tinge of sarcasm in his voice. He was tiring of the game.

Janković shifted in her seat. "Have you ever heard of the *The Selfish Ledger*?"

Dorda frowned. "Some. I know it concerns the theory of something called the Selfish Gene. But I imagine you're about to enlighten me."

"Exactly. It's a concept Google suggested in an internal video titled *The Selfish Ledger*, which was leaked in 2016. Apparently, it caught Petrenko's eye, and now it's his dream to use the concept for his benefit.

"It all starts with a nineteenth-century evolutionist named Jean-Baptiste Pierre Antoine de Monet, chevalier de Lamarck. Quite the name, huh, Tad? Sure beats something as mundane as Thadeus Dorda, doesn't it?" quipped Janković.

"Very funny, Paula. So what did this Frenchman have to say?"

Janković clicked on the link and began *The Selfish Ledger*. Dorda frantically scribbled notes, knowing he might have to sound intelligent about it to Petrenko. And sounding stupid to Petrenko was not something Dorda was willing to risk.

The narrator described de Monet as an evolutionist who in 1809 theorized that every living thing has a code at the cellular level that is passed on through generations to define the physical characteristics each generation inherits. As this code is passed on, it adapts to the changing environment.

"Those early thoughts are really nothing more than a theory of evolution," Janković interjected. "But it's the seed that underpins *The Selfish Ledger*."

The video then explained how William Hamilton, a twentieth-century evolutionary theorist, advanced de Monet's idea with his theory that an individual's genes, not their brain, determined how one acted and reacted to stimulus. Hamilton postulated that the way a person behaves is not based upon what is necessarily in their best interests but what is best for the gene and its evolution.

"In other words," Dorda commented, "the gene ensures that a particular behavior is what is best for itself and its continued propagation. It's the rush to survival of the fittest."

Janković nodded and paused the video.

"Now it gets interesting, Tad," Janković prodded. "Pay attention to the theories of Richard Dawkins."

Dawkins, a 1970s evolutionary biologist, coined "selfish gene" to describe a gene over which individuals have no control. Dawkins believed that individuals are merely vessels for their ever-evolving genes.

Janković paused the video.

"In other words, Tad, if Dawkins is right, individuals have no control over what they do unless their genes—their internal code—believe it will benefit evolution."

"So in theory, Dawkins would have believed you can die in your dreams," suggested Dorda.

"Now you're thinking!" Janković replied. "The idea advanced by Google suggests that if one can accumulate all the data on a person in today's digital world, that data can be harvested and manipulated to produce the equivalent of de Monet's code. In turn, this digital DNA can be used to predict an individual's actions, decisions, preferences, movements, and relationships. As individuals react online, these attributes develop and form into a digital DNA. Google describes the science as an epigenome, a multitude of chemical compounds, which in this case are points of data that tell a genome what to do."

"This all sounds nice, Paula, but Petrenko won't care if you can't deliver."

"Tad, try to follow along here. It's not that difficult," Janković snapped.

"If data is regarded as the equivalent of Dawkins's selfish gene and supports the theories of de Monet and Hamilton, computers can accumulate and manipulate user data and not only predict, but actually control how an individual behaves. The more that individuals share data about themselves and others, including what others share about them, the more behavior can be directed, robbing individuals of choice. You understand?"

While she had no intention of giving Dorda any more information than he needed, Janković knew that data companies like Google, Facebook, Peephole, and Images would become the custodians of this data and in theory steward it for the good of humanity. Indeed, the more an individual operates in the digital world, the more he or she can be served up options based on goals presumed by that behavior. Over time, as this data is harvested, sorted, analyzed, and manipulated, the popular end game is to deliver products and services that assure achievement of an individual's goals.

"It all sounds like a fantastic story and obviously what marketers do every day with those annoying ads popping up on the screen," Dorda observed. "But how is that useful to Petrenko?"

Janković never ceased to be amazed at how thick Dorda could be with what she thought was simple logic.

She responded, "Tad, what I'm suggesting goes way beyond selling products and services. At some point, this data can be gathered over generations and used to develop a deep understanding of all sorts of behaviors and issues, such as depression, health, and poverty. If we're right, and I believe we are, the data genome can not only predict behavior but can also modify it to cause a desired result. Now all I need to do is prove it to Petrenko."

"And you don't have much time, Paula," concluded Dorda.

—

Petrenko, unbeknownst to Janković and Dorda, was watching IBM in addition to Google.

IBM was using its supercomputing program, Watson, to detect moods as users surfed websites. The innocent goal was to deliver an offer to purchase a product that was irresistible because Watson knows your mood. Watson knows what you want and when it's best to offer it to you. Petrenko speculated that if Watson knows what you want and when you want it, why can't Watson also know what you will do—and perhaps then do more than simply entice you to act, but rather compel you to act?

For Petrenko, it all came together when he saw a TED talk by Zeynep Tufekci, a Turkish-born professor and "techno-sociologist." She was particularly critical of Google, Facebook, and other online data collectors for manipulating individuals through algorithms mining big data. One example Tufekci gave struck Petrenko and gave him his inspiration.

What if a system, Tufekci suggested, harvested data knowing that it's easier to sell sojourns to Las Vegas to people who are bipolar and about to enter a manic phase, because medical science knows that manic-depressive people tend to become overspenders and potentially compulsive gamblers? So what might appear as an innocent offer to have some fun in Vegas was in reality an invitation to self-destruct.

In its purest form, Petrenko saw the reality of this effect through the success of Peephole and Images and their advertising targeted to consumers based on their searches. If you can identify a person's desires, reasoned Petrenko, then you can also exploit their weaknesses, both physical and mental, through algorithms that serve up alternatives as subliminal tools for behavioral manipulation.

Petrenko saw *The Selfish Ledger*, IBM's Watson, and the theories of Tufekci as much more than speculation. He believed that when taken to their logical ends, they could be used to subconsciously direct consumer behavior and ultimately remove choice. In other words, to make his targets do precisely what he wanted them to do, violent or otherwise.

He could program killers.

—

"But as I said, Tad, we're not yet certain we can predict or manipulate someone's behavior subconsciously or against their will," Janković continued.

"But you're not saying it's impossible."

"Not at all," Janković replied. "I'm just saying we're not there *yet*. We've seen countless times how willingly zealots will die for a cause, believing that is what they must do. But in their cases, doing so is not against their will. They believe in a greater cause. Our challenge is to find the triggers that turn a sensible person into a zealot who believes that what they're doing is right. Or better yet, what they're doing is what *we* believe is right. And we want to do that without creating any connections back to us or, for that matter, to anyone authorities can discover. Therein lies the wonderful chaos a Selfish Ledger can create."

Tad could see that Janković was more than academically interested in proving her theories. She was physically excited, almost as if succeeding bordered on sexual pleasure.

"At this point, I can do it on a small scale. But we want to do it on a large scale. We'll get there eventually."

"And when is 'eventually,' Paula?"

"I don't know," Janković said, her eyes shifting back to the computer screen in a dismissive gesture to Dorda. "We'll get there when we get there. That's all you can pass on to Petrenko for now."

"Paula, that's not enough. I need more."

"OK, then you can also tell him we're about to conduct some experiments to see if our ideas have any merit."

"What kind of experiments?"

"It's a bit complicated, Tad. Petrenko has two dupes he finances: Darren White, his boy toy in the commodities trading world, and Abu al-Badri, his friendly ISIS terrorist. We've been tracking and accumulating data on White for more than a year and have what just about everyone else on earth has said about him. We've watched him make thousands of trades that help fill Petrenko's pockets. We know how he thinks. At the same time, we've been watching al-Badri and identified and tracked a dozen wannabe terrorists who follow him but lack the infrastructure to take action. Or perhaps lack the nerve to join Allah and al-Badri's jihadist cause. So we're developing some digital interfaces that target them to see if we can subconsciously direct them to take a particular action."

"That sounds impossibly complicated, Paula. Can you put it into simple words?" asked Dorda.

"Because to prove it works," Janković replied, speaking slowly, as if to a simpleton, "we have to cause someone to take action that is against what is personally best for them. In effect, to prove it to Petrenko, we have to make our dupes do something that will piss him off. Then he'll know we've succeeded."

"Something against their better good, Paula. But pissing off Petrenko is another thing. Why do you need to do that?"

"If we're to convince him, Tad, we have to give Petrenko a clear message. The more shocking, the better," responded Janković.

"Paula, that's very dangerous. Why can't you prove your theory to Petrenko without pissing him off, particularly with people he relies on? You need a different plan."

"OK, Tad. Calm down. Maybe I'll come up with something else. But whoever it is we set down a path we control, he or she has to be someone close to Petrenko. Otherwise, he'll think it's a setup or just a parlor game."

Dorda knew he needed to be careful and keep Janković from going off script and doing something foolish that could put them both at risk. Or dead.

"Thank you, Paula. You know my concern is with your success, and pissing off Petrenko is not the way to go. Let's come up with someone else who he knows but does not rely upon. That's as far as I'm willing to go."

"I understand," replied Janković. She knew that Dorda was right, as much as she didn't like it. She yearned to teach Petrenko a lesson. "But he needs to feel it or our efforts are nothing better than a suggestion that he can either adopt or reject. And knowing him, he'll simply reject it. If we are to prove our theories, choice must be removed from someone he knows and trusts. Our messaging must force that person to follow our will, not his."

"You want to make someone he knows a Manchurian Candidate?" responded Dorda. "That's interesting as long as the target is someone Petrenko believes is expendable. Keep moving forward and keep me posted."

"Will do," responded Janković, knowing full well that she'd only tell Dorda what she wanted him to know and nothing more.

TWENTY-ONE

PENINSULA HOTEL, HONG KONG

THE CONCEPT OF TRUE ARTIFICIAL INTELLIGENCE WAS PETRENKO'S OBSESSION.

He had read extensively about the Summit Supercomputer, housed at the Department of Energy's National Laboratory in Oak Ridge, Tennessee, and in China's Sunway TaihuLight computer, located at the National Supercomputing Center in Wuxi, Jiangsu province, China. Both are exascale supercomputers that can process data at petascale speeds. Petrenko knew that there was a positive side to the supercomputer's abilities. After all, it could process massive amounts of data and perform simulations of environmental and biological systems that might discover answers to questions about climate change, drought, and the spread of disease, or predict geological disasters and the likelihood of terrorist threats becoming a reality.

Exascale computers process trillions of bits of data, connecting one to the other in nanoseconds. The more data available, the more accurate an analysis or prediction will be. And because these computers have the ability to digest data at unlimited scales, there are no restraints on how such data could be used if it were to fall into the wrong hands.

And in those wrong hands, the darkest theories of *The Selfish Ledger* could become a frightening reality. In Petrenko's mind, such computers could control anyone who lives in the digital world. A population that will eventually include everyone. As the race for ever-increasing computer speed continues throughout the world, including the unprecedented speed users experience with 5G smartphones, Petrenko's real fantasy and obsession was the possibility of true artificial intelligence—not just the machine learning being used for myriad practical applications.

How long, he mused, will it take for the world to dissolve into a cesspool of fear and chaos once true AI is achieved? How long before a superpower chooses not only to influence the behavior of its own population but to use that power to direct the politics of other countries that do not have benefits of exascale computers? The world will then enter a period of new colonialism controlled by a group of superpowers with supercomputers. And the cost of such powers will be a fraction of what those countries spend today in exporting their political, economic, or religious beliefs.

Petrenko prided himself on being a realist. While others kept making things faster, he saw the potential as really quite simple. The more powerful the computer, the more data it can digest and the more modeling it can perform. The more modeling it performs, the more reliable its prediction will be. It is clear that as capacity increases, such computers will process and evaluate data far faster than any human could ever imagine. In essence, a single exascale computer is better at solving complex problems than is any collection of the smartest people in the world. Or in history for that matter. In Petrenko's mind, the country—or individual—that has exascale computing capacity controls destiny. To Petrenko, the quest was not AI but what he liked to call AP—artificial persuasion. Coupling the principles of the Selfish Ledger with machine learning that retrieves and regurgitates what a person wants to hear again and again, he could possibly persuade that person to do his bidding, essentially robbing them of their free will.

But as a realist, he knew that to reach his goal would cost more money than even he had.

His only option was to hack into the most secure networks in the world at NSA and in China. Petrenko believed that those were the only two systems he needed. While Europe was impressive, its economy paled in comparison to the United States and China. It was also clear to Petrenko that the twenty-first century was about the competition between those two superpowers. The rest of the world, including Europe and Russia, were mere bystanders.

So while China and the United States invested billions in the technology revolution, Petrenko quietly hacked their networks, manipulated the data, influenced decisions, and extracted billions in profits in search of his ultimate goal—control of the world's Selfish Ledger.

Petrenko began his master plan within months of Google's release of *The Selfish Ledger*. His first target was China. Not because he believed that the Chinese had more valuable data, but because a failure to succeed in China was not as devastating as a failure to succeed in the real jewel, the United States. In China, Petrenko could afford early mistakes so long as his programmers eventually cracked the codes.

For this task, he ordered Cooper to enlist Pak Heir Zhang, a renowned Hong Kong computer scientist who turned dissident when China took back the Crown Colony of Hong Kong from Great Britain in 1997. Zhang was sent to a rehabilitation camp in 1998 after refusing to cooperate with the China Central Committee's plans for him to work on its supercomputer program. He accepted the hard labor and resisted the brainwashing efforts of his captors for three years before Petrenko saw him as presenting an opportunity.

As always, Petrenko resorted to his time-proven way to approach the otherwise non-corrupt and get what he wanted. He sent emissaries with briefcases full of money with the question he loved the most: "How much will it cost me to make you a criminal?" He felt safe with that question because the answer to how much money it would take was almost always less than he thought they'd want. If too high, Petrenko's emissary walked away, usually quickly followed by the disappearance of the person with the greedy answer. And if that didn't work, he'd find out what they wanted beyond money. That was usually something that Petrenko could use as blackmail to ensure compliance. His approach never failed.

By 2012, Zhang was back in the good graces of China's committees and, unbeknownst to them, also on Petrenko's payroll. The bribes Petrenko needed to pay were a drop in the bucket for the benefits he'd receive. Working inside China's Ministry of Industry and Information Technology, Zhang slowly rose in stature as he developed China's supercomputing power.

Petrenko left Zhang alone until 2017, when Zhang was promoted to head up China's supercomputer program. Petrenko's plan worked perfectly. As he would often remind his overly aggressive partners, patience pays. Particularly in China.

Not trusting anyone with his master plan, Petrenko sent Cooper to meet with Zhang on a regular basis, always in different locations within China and usually corresponding with trips by Zhang to inspect sites and operations throughout the country. Keeping a low profile was not that difficult, and Petrenko had sufficient dupes in China's immigration ministry to keep Cooper's travels off the radar of authorities and away from watching eyes.

As Petrenko learned, money alone was not necessarily the only way to control—and eventually own—an individual. Petrenko always looked for other weaknesses in people that he could satisfy and further compromise them or risk their freedom. For Zhang, it was young boys. So Petrenko made sure Zhang had an ample supply wherever he traveled. It repulsed Petrenko that Zhang engaged in such debauchery, but it was behavior Petrenko was willing to tolerate to achieve his ultimate goal. Morality was not something Petrenko let get in his way. Besides, reasoned Petrenko, when he no longer needed Zhang, he would make sure Zhang endured appropriate pain when he died for all his sins. In the interim, it provided additional leverage should Zhang suddenly find a conscience.

—

"Mr. Cooper, thank you for your hospitality on my visit to Hong Kong. It's a pleasure to return." Zhang was always very formal when he addressed Cooper.

No doubt, you enjoyed the little "gifts" we conveniently provide you for your sick pleasures on returning to Hong Kong.

"Hong Kong is one of my favorite cities," Cooper lied. "Its newly found combination of British history and Chinese philosophy makes it a truly fascinating place. I always enjoy coming here." Another lie.

And I certainly do not like spending any time with a pervert like you.

"And what would you have of me this trip, Mr. Cooper?" Zhang asked. "I imagine you have instructions for me."

"I do." Cooper slid a piece of paper across the table.

As Zhang put his fingers on it to pick it up, Cooper stopped him. Zhang seemed startled.

"Zhang, that piece of paper has a phone number on it. It is a number you will enter into the phone we gave you. Do you understand?"

Zhang read the number and entered it into his phone directory. He decided to label it "Báichī," Mandarin for "Idiot," knowing that Cooper would never understand the insult.

"Mr. Cooper, I'm more than capable of understanding instructions. Just what is it you want me to do?"

"You will give access to the Sunway computer to the person at the other end of that number. Using the Signal app we've been using all along, you will text instructions and provide answers if asked."

"And who is that person, Mr. Cooper?" asked Zhang.

"That is not for you to know or care about. Simply do as you're instructed, or all the favors and fun you enjoy on our little visits together will end. And end badly."

Dorda and his programmers had the access codes they needed the next day.

TWENTY-TWO

KEY WEST, FLORIDA

COOPER LOVED KEY WEST AS MUCH AS HE DESPISED HONG KONG. TO HIM, IT WAS A MANAGEable version of New Orleans, another of his favorite towns where conventional behavior was the exception rather than the rule. He was pleased that he'd left Zhang after a successful mission and was now back on his home turf. When he was in the United States, Cooper felt safe. He knew that was largely an illusion, but it served to calm his nerves.

Tonight, Cooper was enjoying music at his favorite bar—the Green Parrot on Whitehead. A neighborhood dive, the Green Parrot was a Key West landmark that was devoid of the hectic pace of Duval Street, where most tourists spent their dollars. Emblazoned with signs that professed "No Sniffling" and "Excess in Moderation," the Green Parrot epitomized the Key West philosophy. While not truly a place reserved to locals, most who spent time there were as local as an immigrant could be to the Conch Republic, the romanticized hopes of Key West citizens to secede from the United States to form their own laid-back version of San Francisco's Haight-Ashbury.

Sipping an IPA from Key West's Water Front Brewery, Cooper would have preferred to listen to the band and forget about Petrenko's agenda, but he was there on business. With Petrenko, business always came first.

As Cooper ordered his second pint, Scotty Weinreb arrived.

Weinreb was a nerd by every measure. At five foot nine with unkempt blond hair, he looked the way one would expect a computer geek to look.

Devoid of any social skills, Weinreb spent most of his childhood playing video games. He continued his obsession into his adulthood and eventually landed a job programming computers for the NSA. He fancied himself a rebel with no allegiance to any state. In his naïveté he believed that he was doing God's work in cooperating with Cooper and the promise that Cooper would lead Weinreb to a path of righteousness in a socialistic world, a world order where the common man controlled his own destiny.

Weinreb took a seat at the bar next to Cooper.

"What are you drinking?" Weinreb asked.

"An IPA I particularly like," responded Cooper, knowing that Weinreb had no appreciation of the subtleties of an excellent brew.

"I'll have what he's having," Weinreb told the bartender.

Cooper quietly pointed to an envelope on the bar. Weinreb quickly picked it up and put it into his pocket. Over the past year, Cooper passed similar envelops to Weinreb that contained far more money than Weinreb would ever earn with the NSA. And as always, Cooper never touched the envelope on the bar. It was always clean of fingerprints.

Like most people, Weinreb was willing to accept such bribes as payments for his idealism.

The band at the bar, a collection of misfits from any variety of hopeful, but professionally suffering musicians, launched into its cover of the Allman Brother's "Midnight Rider."

> *Well, I've got to run to keep from hiding*
> *And I'm bound to keep on riding*
> *And I've got one more silver dollar*
> *But I'm not gonna let them catch me, no*
> *Not gonna let 'em catch the midnight rider*

"Why haven't I gotten what I've been asking for?" asked Cooper.

Weinreb took a sip and responded, "It's not as easy as it sounds."

"Bullshit, Scotty. We pay you well for what we ask you to do. For what you agreed to do. We're losing patience with your progress."

Petrenko wanted results, not promises.

"Hacking into the NSA computer isn't easy," offered Weinreb.

"Are you telling me you can't deliver, Scotty?" asked Cooper.

"No. Not at all. I'm just saying it takes time." Weinreb didn't like the ominous tone of Cooper's voice. After all, they were comrades in fighting the callous bureaucracy that stifled their freedoms. Why would Cooper be so threatening?

> *And I don't own the clothes I'm wearing*
> *And the road goes on forever*
> *And I've got one more silver dollar*
> *But I'm not gonna let them catch me, no*
> *Not gonna let 'em catch the midnight rider*

Cooper sensed Weinreb's fear. "OK, Scotty, calm down. We're just anxious to get started. Together, we can change the world, but we need your help. Let me make this clear to you, Scotty. We pay you a lot of money. The people who expect results are growing inpatient. All they care about is you delivering the access they need. It's that simple."

"I know. I will get you what you want. It just takes time. I'm no use to you if the NSA catches me. I'm scared they're on to me. So I have to be careful."

Weinreb took another sip, his hand slightly trembling. He was legitimately afraid of and often wished he had never met Cooper.

> *And I've gone by the point of caring*
> *Some old bed I'll soon be sharing*
> *And I've got one more silver dollar*
> *But I'm not gonna let 'em catch me, no*
> *Not gonna let them catch the midnight rider*

Cooper ordered another IPA.

The two sat for a few minutes enjoying the music before Cooper spoke again.

"Fine, Scotty. Take the time you need. We don't want you to be caught. What you're doing is important. For a lot of people. For Humanity. You understand that, right?"

"I understand." Weinreb understood he was too deep into Cooper's game to respond in any other way.

No I'm not gonna let 'em catch me, no
Not gonna let them catch the midnight rider
No, I'm not gonna let 'em catch me, no
I'm not gonna let them catch the midnight rider
But I'm not gonna let 'em catch me, no
Not gonna let them catch the midnight rider

"Good. I'll expect progress in a week."

Cooper put fifty bucks on the bar.

"Enjoy your beer. And the music."

Cooper left.

Weinreb sat alone, remembering his journey to cooperation with Cooper.

A graduate of Carnegie Mellon University, Weinreb learned his craft with finesse. Programming came naturally to him. Regarded by many to be a computer genius with code, he quickly found a job with Intel in its computer science department, assigned to programming for its high-tech chip designs.

But as always seems the case with geniuses, Weinreb grew impatient. He felt underappreciated and, consequently, underpaid. As Weinreb kept working more and more hours, he resorted to cocaine as a way of pushing himself to keep at it. He was no different from just about every other programmer in Silicon Valley, where the crush of long working hours and drugs went hand in hand. The difference with Weinreb was that he also lacked a moral compass that kept him on the honest side of technology.

It didn't take Weinreb long to learn that freelancing was a way to make some extra bucks to support his growing cocaine habit. From there, it was a short step to black hat hacking.

That made Weinreb easy prey for Petrenko. The fool loved posting pictures on Petrenko's social media sites from parties he'd go to on weekends when he thought his addiction was nothing more than fun. Until it got expensive.

Weinreb was quickly identified by Petrenko's algorithms. It took no time to target him as a potential insider in Petrenko's game.

In the beginning, Cooper reached out to Weinreb for some freelance programming. Innocent stuff. Hacking into some sites of corporations that exploited consumers. The goal was to expose the hypocrisy. Out the companies that abused innocent consumers. Do what was right and bring justice to a corrupt world.

It didn't take long before Weinreb's drug addiction got the better of him. He needed his fix. Cooper was there to help him get it with the money he needed. One step—one hit—at a time.

When Weinreb was asked to hack the NSA, it was no longer a matter of choice. By then, he was a felon, and Cooper made it clear to Weinreb that refusing was not an option. Besides, Cooper assured Weinreb, they wanted the same thing. They both wanted to bring Big Brother to its knees. It all made it easier for Weinreb to justify his crimes.

How much will it cost me to make you a criminal?

For Weinreb, the price was very small, and giving Tad Dorda the encryption key into NSA was worth forfeiting his soul to the devil. Six weeks later, he delivered it to Dorda.

TWENTY-THREE

SKYPE

"WHILE WE CANNOT SAY WITH CERTAINTY THAT ASIANS REACT TO SUBLIMINAL SUGGES-tions the same way Americans might, with a sample size in the millions, I believe we can extrapolate some correlations that provide directional insight and satisfy norms and projections at a statistically significant level," Janković explained on Skype to Dorda.

By China's standards, Nanjing is a small city, with fewer than 12 million inhabitants in roughly 2,500 square miles. By comparison, New York City has 8.6 million people crammed into 303 square miles. Nanjing is dense, yes. But it is not as crowded as most people picture Chinese cities to be. That was important to Dorda. It made it easier to catalog and follow its population.

As hordes of China's working class toiled through their daily routines, oblivious of the games Dorda and Janković were playing, the conversation continued.

"Paula, I appreciate the egghead that you are, but would you mind speaking in terms we mere ignorant simpletons can understand?" asked Dorda.

Janković responded, "With a sample size this manageable, it's easier to predict that someone or some group in a new sample will do the same thing regardless of where they live. And that 'thing' we want them to do is whatever we tell them to do."

"And they won't know we planted the seed?" asked Dorda.

Again, the same questions. Will this idiot ever ask me something only once?

"They won't have a clue," responded Janković. "As far as they'll be concerned, everything they did was by their own free will for a cause they believe in. It won't matter whether they'd done what we bid voluntarily or otherwise. They'll just do it and never know why."

"And how do you do this?" asked Petrenko from his Skype connection to Dorda and Janković.

Janković felt the bile in her stomach surge to her throat. She knew that whenever she spoke directly to Petrenko—whenever *anyone* spoke directly to Petrenko—the words needed to be clear and unequivocal. Those who were vague with Petrenko did not live long lives.

"For two years now, we've been mining China's Sunway TaihuLight Supercomputer with Pak Heir Zhang's help and NSA's Summit computer through Cooper's boy, Weinreb. Our algorithms are now working their magic 24/7."

"And what does that mean, Ms. Janković? I do not have all day," snapped Petrenko.

"Mr. Petrenko," responded Janković, "it means we've been mapping the behavioral traits of millions of people applying the principles of *The Selfish Ledger* and believe we know what motivates them at the subconscious level."

"Go on, Ms. Janković," said Petrenko. "I find this all very fascinating."

Fascinating? You have no idea how this is a lot more than fascinating! thought Janković.

"Our real breakthrough has been our algorithms, which have taken machine learning into something as close to artificial intelligence as anyone can get. While it's not literally AI, it's all we need to essentially let the programs run themselves. All we need to do is make suggestions," explained Janković.

Petrenko continued, thinking of his idea of artificial persuasion as the true goal to control. "And doing so means…"

"…We can subconsciously control their behavior." In her excitement, Janković had not been able to restrain herself from completing Petrenko's sentence. "And best of all, they have no idea we're doing so, much less who we are."

Petrenko, ever mindful to keep boundaries intact but intrigued by Janković's commitment and energy, responded, "Ms. Janković, while I am not one who tolerates people putting words in my mouth, I'll make an exception here. Your news is very encouraging. When can you make it a reality? Only then will you have done the job I generously pay you to do."

Dorda understood a threat veiled in a compliment when he heard one. He expected it from Petrenko, together with a firm understanding of the gravity it engendered.

"We will do everything we can to achieve your goal, Constantine," interrupted Dorda, one of the few people in the world on a first-name basis with Petrenko.

"I know you will, Tad. You never disappoint me."

Petrenko moved his attention back to Janković.

"So when will you test your theories, Ms. Janković?" continued Petrenko.

"It's already started, sir. We hope to have results by this weekend but cannot make any guarantees." It was Wednesday.

"Then you have until Sunday," responded Petrenko.

Dorda had just enough of Petrenko's arrogance with Janković.

"Constantine, Paula will let you know when she can let you know. Such things cannot be rushed simply because you want your toys sooner than we can deliver them. You have to be patient. It's as simple as that."

The nonresponsive silence hung in the air like an eternity.

Finally, Petrenko responded, "Very well, Tad. It's your call…"

Right, you asshole.

"…And your responsibility," concluded Petrenko as he terminated the Skype connection.

TWENTY-FOUR

NANKING, CHINA

TWENTY-YEAR-OLD YU YAN CHIANG CONSIDERED HERSELF AMONG THE ENLIGHTENED Chinese. Her name meant "someone with beautiful smiles." She lived up to it. Always happy, she made people comfortable even in tense situations. As a somewhat rebellious teenager, in a society with newly found freedoms denied their parents and grandparents, Yu Yan had many opportunities to hone that skill. And while attractive with dark black hair, brown eyes, and a thin figure weighing less than 120 pounds, it was her personality that made her so many friends.

Yu Yan was the only child in a traditional Chinese family, and as such, she knew she was a disappointment to her father, who always wanted a son—as did all Chinese fathers burdened with the state mandate of one child per family.

Undaunted, Yu Yan excelled in her education, trying to justify her existence as a daughter who deserved and yearned for the love of both her mother and father.

Yu Yan regularly posted on China's version of Facebook, WeChat, expressing her thoughts, even when they might be considered controversial. As part of the new generation of Chinese, she felt social media gave her freedoms her parents had never known. She was willing to push issues even when she knew her posts might get her and her family into trouble. Part of her didn't care. Yu Yan wanted to say what she believed. And sometimes what one believed could be a crime in China.

She didn't consider herself a radical. Yu Yan just wanted her friends to know what she believed. She desired to be free of state restraints and rejected those who would have her toe the line of the Communist state. She recoiled from demands from those who would dictate her thoughts, desires, and dreams.

Janković and her algorithms combing the social media found the impressionable Yu Yan early in her newfound digital freedom and subtly began the examination and indoctrination that would build her Selfish Ledger.

"Yu Yan," her mother would tell her, "you need to stop saying such things."

Her father was less vocal. He worked twelve hours a day in a filthy factory that made components for cheap Chinese electronics. Most were exported to more prosperous economies where Yu Yan assumed toys were more important than ideals. To her, China was poisoning the world, and her father was a mere dupe in the game.

"Mama, don't worry," she would say, "and don't be so blind. Don't you see what's going on? Xi Jinping is no better than Hitler. A puppet for suppression."

The eighteenth Central Committee of the Communist Party elected Xi Jinping general secretary of the Communist Party and chairman of the CPC Central Military Commission, making him China's paramount leader. Self-appointed for life, Xi Jinping was following in the footsteps of the oppressive Mao Zedong, the master architect of China's communist boot heel on the country's freedom.

Of late, however, Yu Yan found herself posting increasingly subversive statements, even when she knew they might come to the attention of the Ministry of State Security, China's KGB. The Ministry had already punished her with a one-week suspension from using the Internet because of her posts. A short suspension was the first step the Chinese government used for outspoken social media users. The next infraction could bring a far more severe consequence.

China, more than any other nation, has an iron grip on the Internet together with the most sophisticated surveillance technology in the world. Unhampered by laws of privacy, due process, or individual rights, the Chinese government watches every social media post and processes them through complex algorithms churning away as ones and zeros in the Sunway TaihuLight Supercomputer and its nationwide network. With a huge capacity and lack of any laws to stop them, China has the most extensive array of CCTV cameras in the world coupled with the latest in facial recognition. No one can be anonymous very long in China.

Planning was also well under way to add voice recognition to the abilities of the Sunway network. While voice recognition is nothing new, finding a way to match it to a face and plot out who else was involved in the conversation remains the challenge. For China, finding a solution to accomplish the goal was not just a matter of time but a national security necessity.

Under Xi Jinping's master plan, the Chinese authorities wanted to know who you are, where you are, where you've been, what you've done, what you failed to do, what you've said, and more. Better yet, they wanted to know the same thing about every one of your friends, family, and colleagues; about every citizen and visitor. In that sense, they were not much different from Petrenko. China, however, wanted the information to control their population. Petrenko wanted it to build his fortune to unprecedented heights. Either way, both wanted the power that came with reaching those goals.

While China's clandestine activity intrigued Petrenko, there was another trend in China that particularly caught his attention.

China was years ahead of other countries in ridding itself of paper currency. Because there were more smartphones in use in China than anywhere else, cybercurrency, with government support, was fast replacing cash. Economic forecasters predicted that China will be an entirely cyber-economy by 2030 if not sooner. In 2016, WeChat's payment system reported over 600 million users processing more than $550 billion in transactions. In 2019, Alibaba's Alipay, the other leading payment app in China, predicted that there would soon be more than a trillion dollars in yearly processing through cybercurrency. That's the well Petrenko wanted to tap. The potential to skim funds from such a massive monetary system wholly dependent upon digital security made the profits Petrenko realized from Images, Peephole, and his ransomware look like petty change. And breaking digital security was something Petrenko found easier by the day.

For anyone who cherishes freedom, China's surveillance capacity and long-term plans are the worst of the nightmares envisioned in any dystopian novel. For Yu Yan and her friends, the fear of government suppression of not just actions and words but of thoughts themselves was their worst nightmare. This gave Yu Yan and others a cause to fight for. After the generations that had been imprisoned in China under the failure of Communism, the newest generation tasted a liberalization that was anathema to the hardliners now wanting to regain control.

"We need a digital Tiananmen Square," Yu Yan posted. "We need to say 'no' to the puppet masters pulling our strings. We are not marionettes."

That was the post that got Yu Yan suspended from the Internet for a week. Now she was on the watch list and fearful of the consequences if caught again. Little did she know that Janković and her programmers controlled her posts.

China's Internet police learned quickly that suspension from the Internet—the most important thing to the youth of China—was the best form of discipline. Very few would risk a second or third violation and the prospect of imprisonment, reindoctrination at a Chinese educational center, or a lifetime ban from online access. Instead, they'd stick with the old school of secret meetings and whispering in late-night bars and dark alleys.

For Paula Janković, Yu Yan's fear was just what she needed to test her theories. Yu Yan should not willingly put herself at risk again. If caught and disciplined, the consequences could be imprisonment, so she would logically never knowingly violate the rules. Janković wanted to break down that logic and get Yu Yan to unwittingly, yet willingly, trip on her fears.

With easy access to China's computer infrastructure thanks to the efforts of Pak Heir Zhang, Janković could load anything she wanted on to any computer in the country, including Yu Yan's. No firewall, spam filter. or virus blocker could stop Janković. Most important, the Chinese authorities could not stop Janković. They couldn't even find her. She was a ghost planting propaganda at her whim, most of which was anti-establishment and outlawed by the Chinese regulators. It was not as though they didn't see the posts. They were all out in plain sight. The authorities just didn't know how to trace them or do something about them. When Janković began her cat and mouse game, the Ministry of State Security put four full-time agents to work trying to break the code and stop Janković. But you can't stop something you can't find.

Instead, Chinese authorities claimed the posts were subversive attempts by Western powers, including the United States, to undermine their government. Of course foreign powers all denied any involvement. But it was the most convenient excuse China could use to keep its investigative incompetence under wraps.

All this was part of Janković's plans. She knew authorities would search for her, so she would often lead them on to dead ends and plant false positives linking posts to other governments, all frustrating China's efforts. It was child's play for Janković.

On occasion and for her personal entertainment, Janković would even push the envelope to see if she could be caught and stopped. She loved the risky game. Dorda often cautioned her not to be so foolish. But Janković looked on such cautions as fuel to take more risk to prove to Dorda—and the world—that they were wrong. Her firewalls were impenetrable.

In Janković's game, Yu Yan was a mere pawn in the complex scheme. Janković would sacrifice her without hesitation. Indeed, she fully intended to do just that and eliminate any leaks. The same was true of Zhang. Once he served his purpose, he needed to be removed before he became a liability. It was only about when, not if.

For two years, Janković monitored everything Yu Yan did, using her activities, posts, and photos to plot out her individual profile. Her Selfish Ledger. Millions of data points that made Yu Yan tick were analyzed to determine how one action triggered another. How those triggers interacted to provide the basis for the map of Yu Yan's mind—her mental DNA—that Janković needed to prove she could manipulate at the most subconscious of levels. If nothing else, Janković could be patient, even under pressure from Dorda and Petrenko. She knew it was better to be late than wrong, particularly with Petrenko.

"Yu Yan, you have to stop posting such stupid stuff," warned her best friend, Mochou Yuanzhang. "You've already been caught once."

"I know, Mochou, but sometimes I get caught up in the moment when I read posts that show what Xi Jinping is doing. We can't sit by idly and watch."

"What posts are you talking about, Yu Yan? You seem to be the only one who sees them. Show me."

"I've tried, Mochou. You know that. But every time I try to find them, they're gone. Maybe the authorities are trying to test me."

No one else would ever see the posts Janković uploaded specially for Yu Yan. Posts with triggers to see how she'd react.

In the beginning, there was no reaction at all. Janković could only guess at Yu Yan's feelings. This was all part of building Yu Yan's Selfish Ledger.

Janković also posted innocent, happy things to monitor reactions and found out quickly that Yu Yan loved her parents, wished she could prove to her father that she was worthy of his love, and adored Chinese traditions that preached inclusion and respect.

It didn't take long for Janković's algorithms to post and predict Yu Yan's reaction to the things she loved. And the things she hated. Using those motivations were keys to discovering Yu Yan's triggers. Not only what they were but also when they could be tripped, even down to the hour of the day and, for Yu Yan, the time of the month. Indeed, Yu Yan's reactions swung significantly during her menstrual cycle, when her emotional state affected her reasoned thought. That nuance often dictated Janković's posts. Such nuances could never be identified by human intelligence. They were too subtle. Only the computing power at Janković's disposal could undertake that task. All of this went into Yu Yan's Selfish Ledger, each piece of data connected one to the other.

TWENTY-FIVE

WASHINGTON, D.C.

THE CIA KNEW THAT IF YOU WANTED INFORMATION FROM SOMEONE, YOU COULD WATERBOARD them. You could torture them and use drugs that eventually destroyed their minds. But some in the CIA didn't care. Once the information was downloaded, the prisoner was expendable and either hidden in some dark cell or mysteriously missing.

But all the information and intelligence in the world was only useful, at best, in finding the next bad guy and either draining him of what he knew or killing him. It was a never-ending cycle that had no winning strategy. It was nothing more than kicking the can down the road.

Torture and drugs were also increasingly ineffective in breaking the spirit of zealots obsessed with a cause. Pain can break a body, but not a mind that has been wired to hate since birth.

To win in the war against radical Islam, you had to change the way a radical Islamic terrorist thought. Not to convert them, but to create an evangelist for peaceful Islamic causes—what they came to believe was the will and way of Allah. You needed to show them that faith in Allah was not death for all infidels. You needed to do that one person at a time, selecting the best among them, who could then preach the new Gospel of Allah that sought peace, not war. You needed to make them think like loving mothers, not vengeful fathers.

That was Richard Harris's plan. Create new recruits to the cause and deploy them like a virus within the radical Islamic community, where they could act as double agents who saw themselves not as tools for capitalism but disciples of a just Allah. Their cooperation with the infidels would be to further Islamic doctrine, not Christian or Jewish beliefs. Their goal needed to be to bring their beloved Muslim nations to peace and prosperity not through violence but through love and enlightenment. The fact that Harris now had two working operatives was encouraging. But now he had to sell it to his own boss, Michael Hellriegel, the director of the CIA. Hellriegel was definitely not getting it.

"Dick, I'm not sure your plan is novel at all. Reindoctrination and double agents are tactics as old as war itself. Why is this any different?" Hellriegel asked. "What is it about your plan that makes it more reliable than any other, justifying that we allocate assets to it?"

Harris was never comfortable sitting in Hellriegel's office. Harris was a field operative, and being surrounded by walls strewn with pictures of politicians and supposed patriots made him want to leave the moment he arrived. Harris was also not used to taking orders, particularly from a political appointee sitting in a comfortable chair behind an ornate desk while Harris sat in an uncomfortable chair.

"Director Hellriegel, the difference is that reindoctrination, as you call it, fails because it tries to convince a believer to reject what they've been taught since youth simply because you promise them a better way. The best example I can give you is the failures of Christianity."

"Failure of Christianity, Dick? That's what you want me to sell to the president?"

Who are you kidding, thought Harris, *history has one story after another where Christianity failed to bring peace.*

But Harris knew that being tactful was a smarter approach with Hellriegel.

"Of course not, sir. But hear me out."

"I can't wait," responded Hellriegel.

Harris began. "The Crusades ultimately failed because making everyone believe in Christ was a doomed plan from the outset. The idea of Christ as the Savior meant that what converts had previously been taught by their parents or elders was wrong. The only way to win them over was to convince them that Christianity would reward them better than their old ways did. Promises of a better life were central to convincing someone to change."

"But every religion promises a better life, Dick. What's your point?"

Undaunted, Harris continued, "OK, let me try another approach. The same thing is true with the missionaries who converted Native Americans to Christianity. They believed their mission was to bring right thinking to a race they considered heathens through conversion rather than education—indoctrination—to an enlightened life. While there were some early successes, over the long term, the targeted populations have all returned to their core beliefs. And those who did convert became outcasts from their own people. It created a form of segregation that represented the antithesis of the teachings of Christ. Worse, those who returned to the beliefs of their birth grew to have even greater animosity toward Christians. And that led to more, not less, bloodshed."

"I'll give it to you, that your ideas are novel. And while I'm not sure they'll work, I'll give you the benefit of the doubt. I sometimes wonder why we have these meetings at all, since I can't remember the last time I said no to you!" laughed Hellriegel. "So what do you need?"

"I need more funds to identify and stop whoever the Russian is behind the plans we now suspect will be a series of terrorist attacks in just a few weeks. At this point, we only know dates. But my operatives can be planted where we think leads can best be pursued. And I need this quickly. We're running out of time."

"So all you need is money? You already have a virtually unlimited budget. Why do you think you need more money?"

"I don't necessarily need more, but I don't want you to be blindsided when you see the bills. This isn't cheap. But I do need something else."

"Why am I not surprised? You always have one extra ask every time we meet," responded Hellriegel with a sly smile.

"I need the cooperation of the president."

Harris outlined the program to Hellriegel and produced a top-secret CIA report. A report that could never be leaked without exposing the plan and dooming it. So no one except Harris, Hellriegel, and the president could know of it.

—

Hellriegel brought up the idea as he sat in the Oval Office for his weekly briefing.

"Mike, do you think what Harris says has any merit?" asked President Samantha Harrison.

"I remember Harris well from his handling of past terrorist attacks," she continued. "While he certainly has my respect, I'm not sure you can get more out of your intelligence apparatus than you do from any double agent network you spooks have been building for decades. Why dedicate scarce assets to such a venture? Are you sure it's reliable? The idea of some unholy alliance between ISIS and some Russian seems an awful lot like fictional hopes. No other intelligence source you've provided supports it. And frankly, this plan risks substantial unrest with both our allies and enemies. You'd better be sure your intelligence is right if we're to take such risks."

"Madam President, I can't sit here and tell you that agent Harris's plan is that different from any other program used to create our network of spies. Infiltrating enemy leadership is as basic a doctrine as any espionage operation could have. But the threat is real. Harris has more than enough intel to give credence to his concerns. While risky, I think we need to give him what he needs."

Harrison had no patience for terrorists, and had led the nation through some of the most horrific terrorist attacks in history. When she appointed Hellriegel to the top spy post, she did so because she knew him to not only be strategic and tactical but to be heartless when he needed to be. The director of the Central Intelligence Agency of the United States needed to be heartless. And the president of the United States needed to be a politician.

"It doesn't sound like you're convinced either, Mike."

"Here's the thing, Madam President. Harris is one of the best agents we have. You know that. He's working with Chandler Thompson at the FBI and Oliver Grant at Homeland Security. I trust their judgment. Collectively, they may even be the best. Their intellect is unmatched, as is their capacity to absorb and evaluate complex data. It's like nothing I've ever seen. At times, it's as if Harris, in particular, is a human computer. I have no doubt he is convinced of the intelligence he's receiving. That alone gives all the reason I need to support it."

Harrison pressed a button on her desk and Joyce Marcus, assistant to the president, walked in.

"I'll have another Diet Coke, Joyce. Thank you. And Mr. Hellriegel will have—" Harrison looked toward Hellriegel.

"Nothing, thank you," he responded.

"As you will recall, Madam President," Hellriegel continued, "Harris originally estimated his success rate would be one out of three or four recruits. So I had low expectations of success. As a result, I kept the program small. But Harris was confident that if he could show his ideas worked, he'd get more funding."

"And you're satisfied that his ideas have worked?" asked Harrison.

"Yes. True to his estimate, the first two Harris tried to convert, one from Hamas and the other from Al-Qaeda, failed miserably and had to be placed in black op locations in Africa. Harris could not afford to put either of them in any general prisoner population for fear they'd reveal the program."

"And then he found Farid Humayun?" asked Harrison.

"Yes, Madam President. And now he also has Hashir Rashid."

"Then why do you need my approval to continue? Since when do I need to give the green light to the CIA for what sounds to me like an operation supported by the director? Isn't that what you're paid to decide, Mike?"

"Of course, Madam President. I'm just keeping you posted of our intelligence efforts and the plan Harris has proposed," responded Hellriegel, resigning himself to realities of politics and plausible denial. The president made it clear she can play Pontius Pilate if the plan failed. The failure would fall on him.

The next day, Hellriegel gave Harris enough men and money to recruit more operatives and to get his plan under way.

TWENTY-SIX

PARIS

IN 2015, FARID HUMAYUN WAS READY.

He was ready to kill infidels in the jihad and welcome his own death for the glory of Allah if that was his destiny. Humayun was completely committed to the narrative infused in him from his earliest childhood.

Humayun was part of a cell working in Paris plotting the 2015 attacks that killed hundreds. A master at explosives and weapons, he was as much a dedicated radical as one could be.

In the attack on the French satirical newspaper *Charlie Hebdo*, led by Saïd and Chérif Kouachi on January 7, 2015, twelve were murdered and eleven injured. Humayun was supposed to be among the triggermen. He knew it was probably a suicide mission but didn't care. Succeeding was Allah's command; death was his reward and key to Heaven. Humayun was ready.

But on January 5, he got sick. His temperature was over 104, and he couldn't stop vomiting.

"Farid, you can barely even hold a gun, let alone aim it," Chérif Kouachi told him the morning of January 7.

"I'll be fine, Chérif," Humayun insisted. "Just let me rest."

"You can rest in the car tonight, Farid," added Saïd Kouachi, "We'll take Omar with us and let you drive the car instead."

Omar Abazo was supposed to drive one of the getaway cars. His job was to get the Kouachi brothers and Humayun safely to a meeting point where they would be moved back to Syria under ISIS protection. To accomplish that task, he had to be at a specific place at a particular time, engine running.

"Omar? He doesn't have the training, Saïd," objected Humayun.

"No arguments, Farid. Omar will be fine. And you will be sure to get us home safely. We will die for Allah on another day."

While disappointed that he would not have the opportunity to kill—or perhaps even die—for his cause, Humayun followed orders. There was no other option. Each person served a purpose in Allah's plan, and a future opportunity to be in the center of an attack would someday come. Humayun had to be patient and do as he was told.

While Al-Qaeda's branch in Yemen took responsibility for the attack, that was an ISIS cover. In truth, ISIS was the architect of the slaughter at *Charlie Hebdo*. But not the part where the brothers improvised and took hostages at a signage company in Dammartin-en-Goele. That move became necessary when Humayun failed to show up at the extraction point, leaving the Kouachi brothers with no escape route.

Before he could position himself, Humayun's temperature of over 104 triggered a seizure and he lost control of the wheel, crashing into a telephone pole. He was unconscious when the ambulance arrived and took him to a hospital, where he was admitted on the edge of death. When the Kouachis were gunned down on January 9, it was because Humayun failed in his mission.

Humayun lay in the hospital for two weeks, at first just another John Doe who carried no identification but had injuries severe enough to be admitted even absent a name. Not that it really mattered. France had a health care system that was free and open. Whoever you were, you were welcome in France's hospitals. With a broken hip, broken femur, and fractured skull, Humayun was going nowhere.

As the events surrounding the *Charlie Hebdo* affair unfolded, pieces began to come together. Dots were connected. One of those dots was Humayun.

At first, the attendants assumed his incoherent rants were the aftermath of the trauma he suffered. Rants by patients with severe injuries and potential brain damage were common. But when Humayun started mentioning the Kouachis, the focus on what he said took a new direction.

The authorities decided to wait patiently until Humayun healed and was in a condition to talk. The decision was made not to rush him and to keep his capture and identity secret. Humayun was too valuable an asset to have his name appear in the French press. His tirades were vivid enough to give authorities reason to believe he would have very valuable information once he became lucid.

Interpol, pursuant to a long-standing routine of sharing information about terrorist activities, notified the CIA about Humayun. The reference was filed among the many reports the CIA received daily from around the world. It would have probably been lost among them all if Richard Harris had not taken a particular interest in the *Charlie Hebdo* attack. His instincts told him that the sophistication of the attacks in France represented an escalation beyond the typical suicide missions commonly used by terrorists.

Harris wanted first crack at Humayun.

"So you simply want me to release this terrorist to you without an explanation? Why should I do so?" asked Daniel Kadar, an agent with France's equivalent of the CIA, the Direction Générale de la Sécurité Extérieure, or DGSE.

Kadar and Harris had worked together on some joint operations, and each trusted the other.

"Yes, Daniel, that is precisely what I'm asking the DGSE to do. And to also destroy any records of your apprehension of him."

"Why, so you can take credit for it? It was not Americans who died, Richard."

"I know that, Daniel. I feel for your country's pain. But I need you to trust me that I have my reasons. If he turns out to be a dead end, I'll return him to you. If he is who I think he can be, he'll be part of a much bigger plan to fight terrorism. And this has nothing to do with taking credit for anything relating to the *Charlie Hebdo* attack. You can take all the credit you want. Just not for Humayun."

"I believe you, Richard, but what do you mean by Humayun becoming who you think he can be?"

"I can't tell you that. Not now. But when I can, I promise you'll be among the first to know. In the meantime, I'll owe you one, Daniel."

"Yes, you will."

Owing a fellow agent in their world of espionage was not a lightly taken promise.

In the dead of night on February 15, Farid Humayun was taken out the back of the hospital into a nondescript, windowless van. It was a short drive to the small, private airstrip where a Mooney Acclaim Type S, the fastest single-engine plane in the world, awaited them. Powered by a 301 horsepower Teledyne Continental TSIO-550 engine, the Acclaim was capable of speeds of 240 knots or more than 275 miles per hour and was one of Harris's many toys. Importantly, it could take off and land on short runways and was perfect for quick, clandestine CIA operations.

After landing outside Florence, Italy, a couple of hours later, Humayun was taken by boat to Gorgona, the entry point into Harris's program.

At first, Humayun responded like the others. Defiant. Dedicated to ISIS. Harris fully expected to fail again and see his program go up in smoke.

When Harris was ready to give up, he confided in one of Humayun's attending physicians what he was trying to do. At that point, Harris determined that his program was going to fail, so it made no difference that someone else knew about it.

"Mr. Harris, why do you think you can change Humayun's convictions simply because you believe the way he thinks is wrong?" asked Sylvia Benoit, the CIA psychiatrist Harris assigned to Humayun.

"Because no religion preaches murder as a way to heaven. Devoted believers in Islam know that the way radicals are twisting the Quran is an abomination. A right-thinking man cannot possibly defend the killing."

Harris was beginning to think it might be best to let Humayun rot in a cell on this God-forsaken island.

"Why not?" responded Benoit. "As you said yourself, Christians did the same in the Crusades under what they believed to be the sanctity of the church. And wasn't the Inquisition just another form of terrorism led by right-thinking men of their time?"

Harris failed to see the analogy, but enjoyed the conversation. He needed an intellectual challenge after weeks of trying to convert Humayan and making no progress.

Harris continued the interaction with Benoit. "Let's assume you are right, Dr. Benoit. Then all you have proven is that history can repeat itself. That does not make history right."

"No, it does not. But it does question your belief that good will win over evil once evil has been enlightened. Somehow, I doubt the Crusaders or Grand Inquisitors died repentant for all their wrongs even after they were judged."

"So what is your point, doctor? Certainly, a good Christian, or Jew for that matter, does not believe their God has ordered them to kill anyone who does not believe in Islam."

"Now you're being naïve, Mr. Harris. One of the Psalms in your Bible tells us, 'I have pursued mine enemies, and overtaken them: neither did I turn again till they were consumed.' That is hardly a forgiving sentiment. Nor is it anything new or isolated in the Christian religion."

"For a psychiatrist, Dr. Benoit, I'm surprised you seem to find justification in scripture and not in science."

"But it is science. The simplest science of psychology. In Dominion theology, Christians believe God has ordered them to subjugate people and establish dominion over all things. It's believed to be a holy prerequisite to the second coming of Christ, a hope that every true Christian longs to see as the ultimate redemption of their sins. So you can perhaps understand that killing in the name of a God is not unique to Islam. It's in every religion. You cannot expect to change a person's views by brainwashing them to believe that one man's violence is another man's salvation. That will not work with someone who is already devout in their own religion. You can convert weak thinkers, Mr. Harris. But you cannot convert the strong with conventional arguments about just or unjust religious dogma."

Harris was trying to absorb Benoit's argument.

"Do you believe in God, Mr. Harris?" asked Benoit.

Harris wondered if the conversation was bordering on a theory that meant little to his mission. Benoit was now asking what Harris considered canned questions out of Religion 101. But he resolved to continue.

"You want to know if I believe in God. OK, I'll play along. Yes, I believe in God. But not a God who teaches His flock to kill for no just reason no matter what Psalms or theology you recite. If killing is His message, then whatever I believe in, it is not in Him."

"Or Her, Mr. Harris?"

"Or Her, Doctor. But somehow I doubt Islam thinks its God is a woman. No offense, Doctor," Harris responded.

"No offense taken, but if you are a believer, then perhaps you, and most men, need to be more open to the concept that God's gender is irrelevant. Perhaps it is even inaccurate in the writings, like your Bible's reference to the Holy Trinity as God the Father, God the Son, and God the Holy Ghost."

"Why do you refer to the scriptures as 'my Bible,' doctor?" Harris responded. "Let me ask you. Do you believe in God, Dr. Benoit?"

"Mr. Harris, I believe in science and logic. So no, I do not believe in God. But that means nothing to the problem you're trying to solve. Humayun believes in God. He believes in Allah. He believes in Muhammad as Allah's messenger just as Christians believe that Christ is your God's messenger. So what I believe is irrelevant. You need to deal with the reality that the concept of God is the stumbling block you need to overcome with Humayun."

"Doctor, this is a wonderful debate, but so far you're not helping me at all."

"Please bear with me, Mr. Harris. By now you know that psychiatrists never get to their point quickly."

"Fine, go on, Doctor. Have your fun, but your humor is not amusing," Harris responded with an impatient tone.

"Mr. Harris, the gentler side of most people's lives lies with their mother. While the joke may be that all of your neuroses are the fault of your mother, the truth is that most of us learn compassion and love from our mothers. We learn aggression and a lot of antisocial behavior from our fathers. If there is any lesson we can learn from history, it's that."

"So I need to convince Humayun that his father was a failure and his mother knew of a better way? That he should learn from his mother and that he could help us bring his kindred brethren down the right path? That's quite a stretch, doctor. So how do you suggest I appeal to the feminine side of a dedicated terrorist?"

Benoit remained patient. "Try showing him how common thinking among all religions is the right way. Not how Christians found Christ to be the son of God and their savior any more than Muhammad was to Allah. But that both were flawed men no different from all the people in the Bible, the Quran, or the Torah."

Harris was beginning to warm up to Benoit's idea, but needed more.

"And that will somehow teach Humayun the right side of Allah? I'm not following you, doctor."

"OK. Try to understand how the mind works," responded Benoit. "Our brain is the most complex computer ever created. But unlike conventional computers, our minds also reason. No matter how much faster we make computers, they will never have the reasoning power of the human brain.

Computers can only get more and more logical. And the more logical they become, the more incapable they are of making humane decisions."

"Like Mr. Spock on *Star Trek?*" Harris interjected with a condescending tone.

"You can laugh, Mr. Harris, but you will only succeed if you find a balance between the logical and emotional side of Humayun and a way to let him reject the violence he was taught by his father, not his mother. You will never get him to embrace the principles of Christianity or any teachings you put under some holy cross. Teach him that religions built upon the violence of men in ignorance of the kindness of women have led us all down a path of destruction. Get him to believe in the flaws of your God, and he will come to see the flaws of Allah. You need to get him to embrace Her as his God."

In the weeks that followed, Harris dropped all reference to any single religion. He accepted Benoit's advice and accepted Her as his God. Humayun soon followed.

PHASE THREE

HARVESTING THE CROP

TWENTY-SEVEN

GUANTANAMO BAY

HASHIR RASHID WAS READY.

It had been over five years since his failed adventure in Florence. After weeks in Gorgona prison, he spent months with Farid Humayun and Richard Harris at dark sites in Africa and the Middle East, where he was treated well and given the time he needed to understand why Humayun told him that he had seen the error of his own ways once enlightened through education about the failings of all religion. It took time, but Rashid came to accept the wisdom of peace as the ideal to die for, not the killing of innocent people with beliefs contrary to yours.

Instead of attacking radical Islam, Humayun attacked the teaching of all organized religion—Christianity, Judaism, Buddhism, Islam—as based in the hypocrisy of selfish men seeking personal gain at the expense of others.

Humayun focused on nonviolent teachings of modern men like Mahatma Gandhi and Martin Luther King Jr., and women like Mother Theresa and A'isha, wife of Muhammad, to show Rashid how he himself had found enlightenment through peace, not murdering. How he came to embrace a path to righteousness that was paved in sunlight, not through dark alleys.

Truly God instructs me to be humble and lowly and not proud, and no one should oppress others (Islamic Hadith).

The process was slow. But those whom Rashid first saw as captors and later as comrades were patient. Harris and Humayun did not judge Rashid or say that what he believed was wrong. Instead, they told him what was right rather than telling him about the Quran, the Bible, or the Torah. Rashid listened to what was wrong with organized religion and violence.

We have appointed a law and a practice for every one of you. Had God willed, He would have made you a single community, but He wanted to test you regarding what has come to you. So compete with each other in doing good. Every one of you will return to God and He will inform you regarding the things about which you differed (Surat al-Ma'ida, 48).

Rashid saw what was right about peace and nonviolence. Over time, he came to realize that whatever his beliefs should be, they were not the teachings of radical Islam.

Spend in the Way of Allah and do not cast yourselves into destruction with your own hands; do good, for Allah loves those who do good (Quran 2:15).

Rashid came to accept that while dying for a cause was just, dying for an unjust cause was not. And violence in the name of condemning those who did not see God as he did was an unjust cause.

After a year at dark sites in Africa and two years on Guantanamo, Rashid finally heard the words he waited for and his chance to atone for his past transgressions against a God he wanted to believe in, but only one with an enlightened side.

"Hashir, you're being exchanged in a prisoner swap and will be sent to Kuwait. From there, Saudi operatives will take you to Syria, where others will pick you up. We want you to go back in, Hashir," said Humayun.

"And do what?" asked Rashid.

"Listen and watch," interjected Harris.

"What makes you think they'll let me in so easily? How will I explain my return? I've been gone for years with no explanation."

"Of course there's an explanation," Humayun replied. "Guantanamo. You've been together with your fellow unjustly imprisoned comrades, proving every day your allegiance to the greater cause of Allah and the jihad. No more an explanation than that will be needed. Hashir, you're trusted by the other inmates. You have eaten with them. Prayed with them. Convinced them you're still a believer."

"I am a believer, Farid. Just not a believer in the teachings of Abu al-Badri and his followers. I once was, but I no longer am."

Anyone who walks with a wrong doer in order to strengthen him knowing all the while that he is a wrong doer, has departed from Islam (Islamic Hadith).

"After all these years," Harris continued, "we've arranged for you and some other prisoners—good and bad—to be exchanged for four Americans held hostage by Middle East radicals from Hamas and Al-Qaeda. They specifically asked for you this time. We suspect your old ISIS friends are behind your being included in the lucky bunch. None of those exchanged know you are working for us. Any more than you know if any others among those exchanged are working for us as well."

Asshole, thought Rashid. *You want me to know you don't trust me. I'm being watched like all the others.*

Rashid liked Humayun but believed Harris was no more interested in peace than were Rashid's misguided radical brethren.

"Once back in Syria, we're pretty certain you'll eventually be reunited with Abu al-Badri, the man who asked you to die in Florence," added Harris.

"Al-Badri didn't ask me, Harris. I volunteered. Like a fool."

Rashid's mind was racing. He was finally getting out of Guantanamo.

"He certainly didn't try to stop you, did he?" interjected Harris.

"Hashir. Hashir!" Humayun's voice rose in tone. "Are you listening to us?"

Humayun's voice brought Rashid back to the moment.

"I'm sorry, Farid. I'm thinking about how this day is a glorious day."

"Yes, Hashir, it is," responded Humayan. "You've done well."

"I suppose," Rashid replied. "But sitting silently while al-Badri continues to kill innocent people in the name of Allah isn't what I'd call success."

"Hashir, al-Badri is a small fish," responded Humayun. "We want the head of the snake. To sacrifice a few is a small price to pay. Even the innocent sometimes die for a greater cause."

"I believe that Farid, but only when they do so of their own free will. That is not an option al-Badri gives them."

"And that may be true, Hashir," continued Humayun. "But now we have a chance to know who pulls al-Badri's strings. So you need to continue the charade until he plays his hand."

"The Will of Allah, Farid?"

"The Will of whatever God you choose to believe in, Hashir," interjected Harris. "Or the Will of no God at all. The Will of what's right."

TWENTY-EIGHT

CAESAR'S HOTEL, LAS VEGAS

"A CHOPIN MARTINI, STRAIGHT UP WITH THREE OLIVES," ORDERED COOPER.

He was sitting at the Montecristo cigar lounge on Nobu Way at Caesar's Palace, enjoying his Padron cigar, sipping his drink of choice, and waiting for Darren White, Petrenko's broker.

So far, White had done well. Within only a few months at the job, he understood the structure. He logged hundreds of thousands of miles in the air and his trades were shrewd. While the initial plan that White had given to Cooper a week after the two men had met in the Cayman Islands was relatively conservative, that's the way Petrenko wanted it. Until now.

The lounge was much to Cooper's liking. Comfortable with twelve LCD displays of baseball and soccer games. He was pleased to see the game between his Chicago Cubs and the hapless New York Mets was fast coming to a successful end in a Cub's rout. The Cubs led the division by five games with the Mets firmly ensconced in last place in their division. Could the Cubs win their second world championship? Only the Boston Red Sox stood in their way, with most analysts predicting that matchup in the World Series. Cooper loved the Cubs.

White finally showed up, late.

"Nice of you to join me, Darren. I don't like waiting."

White looked tired. For a good reason. After losing six thousand dollars playing craps, he decided to salve his wounds at Crazy Horse 3, a strip club on West Russell Road. He did not get back to the hotel until 5:30 that

morning, just in time to see a sunrise. He tried to sleep, but could not stop thinking about the stripper he met in the VIP Room. Two hours with her cost him $1,000 and three bottles of overpriced champagne. The "extras" cost him another $500. But at least he got something out of his investment, which felt a lot better than seeing $100 chips vanish at Caesar's tables.

"Sorry, Mr. Cooper. I had a long night." He sat across from Cooper and immediately felt nauseous from the cigar smoke. It didn't help that Cooper kept blowing it in White's direction. Purposely, as far as White was concerned.

The waitress arrived, and White ordered coffee. Black.

"I'd think that a man of your intelligence would have learned to pace himself, Darren," Cooper suggested with thick sarcasm.

What an asshole, thought White, his head throbbing from far too much cheap champagne.

"After all, marijuana is legal here in Vegas. It is a far better way to get high than the bottle, White. And cheaper. A brownie or two is all you need for an entire night."

It was something Cooper loved about Vegas and its scores of dispensaries filled with all sorts of cannabis edibles that gave you a buzz without the hangover. Two brownies cost about $40. While Cooper had historically eschewed drugs, he found Vegas brownies an acceptable alternative. He still felt relaxed from his "snack" the night before. It also helped that he had won a few hundred at blackjack. Unlike many gamblers in Vegas, Cooper had no desire to earn comps from casino pitmen by pissing away money at games like craps and roulette. Instead, he always found a twenty-five-dollar blackjack table with correct 3–2 odds and the right to surrender a hand if dealt bad cards. Even with a ten-deck shoe, Cooper could count cards well enough to bring the odds with the casino near even. But not well enough that the casinos ever noticed. With discipline, he rarely walked away down on chips. While Cooper never had a great night, his losses were always low.

He particularly enjoyed his reward of a good martini for brunch once he filled his pockets with a previous night's winning chips.

Cooper blew a few more puffs toward White, enjoying the response. Making White feel worse than he already was pleased Cooper.

"Mr. Cooper, I'd like to get some sleep," said White, waving the smoke away with his hand. "So why did you make me come to Vegas for this meeting?"

"I'll get to that in good time." Cooper loved the game of playing with dupes like White.

A few more puffs on his Padron. All in White's direction.

"Would you like a cigar, Darren? I'm smoking a Padron, a cigar from Nicaragua. I think it's the best cigar in the world. Even better than a Cohiba from Cuba."

"I'll pass. I don't smoke, and the smell of cigars makes my stomach turn."

"Oh. I'm sorry to hear that. I suppose I could put mine out, but that would be a waste of $40," Cooper responded with a smile. "I'm sure a financial guy like you can understand that."

Asshole. "Whatever, Mr. Cooper. Please get to the point before I puke."

"Very well, Darren. I will get to the point. After I order another Chopin. I always get them with three olives. You know why I want three olives, Darren?"

"Not that I care, Mr. Cooper. But I guess you're going to tell me."

Cooper waved to the waitress, pointing at his drink to let her know he wanted another one. His third for brunch.

"And get my friend another cup of coffee," Cooper added.

He finished the martini he had and ate the remaining two olives.

"You see, Darren, it's bad luck to have less than or more than three olives in a martini. That rule dates back to Prohibition days and the mob. The capos always felt three was a lucky number."

"Fascinating," responded White, with no interest in Cooper's story.

"Darren, the proper martini has three olives. You eat the first one when you get the drink. That cleanses your palate. And then you enjoy the last two as a finish. You really should try it sometime. It is very civilized. And from the way you look, you could use a lesson or two in being civilized."

The waitress brought Cooper his martini with three olives and White's fresh cup of black coffee.

White motioned to the waitress.

"I'll have what he's having," pointing to Cooper's martini. "But I'd only like one olive."

Two can play this game, White decided.

Cooper smiled. "Be careful of your choices, Darren. You need all the good luck you can muster. But with a good martini, now you can relax. Good. Because we have a lot to talk about."

The waitress delivered White's martini, one olive. White removed it and put it on the napkin the waitress placed under his glass.

"My, my, Darren, you do like to live a life of danger, don't you?"

"I live whatever life I choose, Mr. Cooper. Or at least I did until I met you," White responded as he took a healthy sip of his drink.

Cooper, unimpressed by White's bravado, continued. "So let's get to business. Have you taken care of Fredric Ansis as I asked you to do, Darren?"

"Yes," responded White. "I closed all of his accounts." Cooper did not want any of White's past following him further into Petrenko's world after the next set of instructions.

"Good, Darren. And you're exclusively using the credit cards and IDs I gave you for your travel and expenses?"

"Yes. I use different IDs and cards once I'm in a country than the passport I used to get in. Just as instructed." White was tired of all the rules but knew better than to challenge them.

Cooper took another sip of his martini and a drag on his cigar, taking his time and contemplating his words.

"I want you to know my benefactor is very pleased with your handling of his funds. You've made some good moves."

"Indeed." White wasn't about to give Cooper the satisfaction of acknowledging that many of the trades he did were from instructions he received from Cooper. White intended to take credit wherever he could.

"But now, Darren, we're about to get very serious."

White leaned back in his chair. "I'm not surprised. Whoever the benefactor of yours is, I can tell he's not in this for the long game. I think he prefers it short and sweet and is getting impatient. That's fine with me just so long as he appreciates that impatience leads to losses. It never leads to gains."

Cooper knew White was right.

"Perhaps. But soon you will begin making specific trades, spread throughout the world and closed at random times. We want the moves to be as under the radar as possible. Do you understand?"

"Perfectly. So what kinds of trades are you suggesting?"

"I'm suggesting nothing, Darren. I'm ordering. There is no suggestion here at all."

"Fine. What am I to do?" Between his hangover, the martini, and the rancid cigar smoke, White had a splitting headache. All he wanted to do was get away from Cooper. He would have sold him his mother if that's what was needed to end this meeting.

"Do what you do best, Darren. That is what we are paying you for. Run our hedge funds and, as the saying goes, invest wisely."

"And what would wisely be, Mr. Cooper? I thought you said I was being ordered."

"Since you ask, let's assume that one day you buy credit default swaps throughout the world because we believe there will be massive loan defaults due to an economic disaster that only we can predict. Wouldn't you think that's a good bet to make, Darren?"

"Mr. Cooper, that's the *Big Short* all over again. That game is over. Now there are simply too many regulations in place to make such a move profitable. The risks are too balanced today. So I'd respond, no, that's not a good bet."

As Cooper well knew, the *Big Short* was a 2015 movie based on the 2010 book *The Big Short: Inside the Doomsday Machine*, by Michael Lewis. The film was a dramatization of the 2008 financial collapse of sub-prime mortgage-backed securities and complex collateralized debt obligations triggered when the housing bubble burst. It brought down Lehman Brothers and nearly bankrupted the world's banking industry. Those few who predicted it made billions. But most didn't see it coming and lost billions more. Only through massive government intervention did the world avoid a depression. Instead, the global economy limped through a major recession. Legislation was passed to prevent a replay. At least that's what regulators believed. Petrenko knew the intervention was only temporary and that markets would eventually adjust and return to taking risks with the greatest rewards through a variety of financial instruments, including credit default swaps.

"Wait," continued Cooper. "Let's assume you can make that bet at an unprecedented scale, believing that a cataclysmic crash is just a month away. Might that change your perspective?"

"Mr. Cooper…"

Cooper held up his hand to stop White from finishing his sentence.

"And assume further, Darren, that you spread that risk across hundreds of transactions throughout the world, making any appreciable volume in any one of them unworthy of notice, with overall trades impossible to trace back to any one source."

Cooper could see thoughts beginning to spin in White's head. Cooper knew he had caught White's interest largely because Cooper was suggesting the biggest play in Wall Street history. There wasn't a broker in the world who didn't want to predict and win in the next Big Short. Cooper sat silently, letting it all sink into White's mind.

After a few minutes, White responded, "Mr. Cooper, that strategy presupposes a global economic meltdown that is one hundred percent predictable. Certainly, not even your mystery boss can predict, much less want, such chaos. Even if he could cause some cataclysmic calamity to happen, the risk is too great that governments will intervene to restore control and market stability."

Cooper could see White's energy returning. Nothing like dangling illegal gains before a corrupt broker. That pleased Cooper.

White continued, "Worse, very few markets have enough capital to handle the size you'll need. Brokers talk, Mr. Cooper. Eventually, even your friend might stick out like a sore thumb despite the global spread of the trades. I can only hide so much. How will we explain that he's suddenly the richest man in the world through such astute moves that no one else saw? Someone would figure out quickly that what he did could not have happened without knowing what was going to happen. Trading everywhere would be suspended. Markets would close. Billions would be lost, including his."

Cooper had no intention of letting go. "That may be true, Darren. But with the right knowledge ahead of time, total market chaos might not be all that bad. And you have a network of brokers to do your bidding. So you spread the risk in markets worldwide and among brokers strewn throughout globe. Make sure none of them knows one another. Just imagine buying on the way down and selling on the way up as no one has ever done before. It can't get any better than that, can it, Darren?"

"I still don't buy it," responded White, not convinced Cooper's plan made any sense. "But it's your money to waste and my orders to follow."

"I'm glad you understand. So you'll do it, Darren, with a combination of credit default swaps, collateralized debt obligations, and short sales."

A credit default swap—a CDS—is basically an insurance policy. If one party believes there might be a future default on investments others have made, and he wants to cash in when that default occurs, he finds someone who thinks the investment is sound and who is willing to pay him any losses he incurs if a default occurs in exchange for a monthly premium. Another variation is the collateralized debt obligation, or CDO. With a CDO, investors are promised periodic payments in exchange for the investments they've made. It's akin to a loan that comes fully due by default, by liquidation or transfer of the collateral given to secure the obligation.

Sounds simple enough, but when the hedge funds get in the game, the scale changes and billions are at risk. By moving in and out of CDS and CDO markets, the manipulation, if correctly timed, can earn fortunes every day. When algorithms are added to the trading mix, the potential becomes geometric.

The problem is that over time, if no default occurs, the premiums paid on a CDS can exceed any hoped-for gains. The risk taker remains obligated to pay the monthly premium. But if the gamble is right, the investor can make a fortune, just as Michael Burry did in 2008 when he predicted the collapse of the mortgage-backed securities market that was the basis for the *Big Short*. No one believed Burry until it was too late for those who sold him credit default swaps. When the world's markets went into a chaotic fall, Burry made a killing. If he had been wrong—as many people believed he would be—he and his investors funding the monthly premiums would have gone broke.

In reality, it's all simply a form of gambling with the odds in favor of the house. Unless, of course, you know how to beat the house. And that was precisely what Petrenko planned to do.

The naïve among investors—and that's just about everyone— thought securities regulators jumped all over the CDS and CDO markets after the recession of 2008. But that didn't really happen. And Petrenko took advantage of the continued opportunities to leverage questionable debt. But he couldn't do it at the scale he wanted unless he could predict another recession. His plan, now that he had amassed one of the largest fortunes in the world, would let him do just that through pawns like White.

White went on. "Let's assume you're right, Mr. Cooper. The problem you have is that the monthly payments for the kind of volume of CDSs you'd need would be enormous. And if I use CDOs, I'd need enormous capital as well. Who has that kind of money?"

White knew how foolish his question was as soon as he asked it.

"Don't worry about that, Darren. And of course, Darren, you're right. That is why you are going to do this over a period of months. Each day, you will make moves in CDSs and CDOs all over the world. In varying amounts, but in the aggregate, in volumes never before seen. And you'll take other short positions in more targeted investments as a further hedge. You will get those instructions from me. By August 12, you will have a portfolio spread throughout our hedge fund network heavily invested in CDSs, CDOs, and short positions."

"And what might those shorts be, Mr. Cooper? Please don't leave me in suspense." His tone was filled with sarcasm that he could see was not appreciated by Cooper.

Cooper frowned, but let it pass, responding, "Nothing surprising. Stocks like Apple, Intel, Microsoft, IBM, and others. And perhaps long in others like Samsung. Pretty simple tech stuff."

"Fine, Mr. Cooper. You are going to bring the global markets to their knees and destroy the tech sector while you're at it. And you don't think that's crazy?"

"Oh no, Darren. It's not crazy. Trust me," responded Cooper.

Trust me. Right. Nothing like a criminal telling me to trust him.

"But why do you need me at this point? You can order these trades as well as I can," said White, hoping he might have a chance at getting out of Cooper's game. He knew better.

"Because, Darren, we pay you a lot of money and you'll make a lot more. Rather than asking me why we need you, perhaps you should be thanking me for such generosity when all we need you to do is follow orders."

Yeah, sure. That's probably what Heinrich Himmler told the SS murderers at the concentration camps. Just be grateful I pay you and do as ordered. Except in this deal, no one knows who Himmler is. So he'll never be caught. I'm the one whose ass is on the line.

"I'll be in touch," Cooper concluded as he put out his cigar, rose to his feet, and left.

White pushed his unfinished martini aside and ordered a Bloody Mary, his traditional cure for a hangover. He also asked the waitress to remove the ashtray and the remains of Cooper's disgusting, saliva-soaked cigar.

TWENTY-NINE

DAMASCUS

ABU AL-BADRI NEVER LOOKED FORWARD TO MEETING WITH COOPER. BUT SINCE COOPER—OR more accurately Cooper's benefactor—delivered the weapons and money al-Badri needed to make a difference in his war against the West, he put up with Cooper's arrogant Western ways.

The Four Seasons Hotel on Shukri al Quatli Street was the only five-star hotel in Damascus. Located in the central district, it remained a vital center for business, both legal and illegal, in the Middle East. While the war raging in Syria meant it was easy to get a reservation, the Canadian company that owned the hotel did not cut back on services. It was the kind of hotel Cooper liked. For al-Badri, it was just another example of capitalistic greed. As long as he wasn't paying for it, however, he was more than happy to enjoy the accommodations and hospitality.

As al-Badri walked into Kithara, the elegant living room lounge in the hotel, he saw Cooper sitting in the corner relaxing as he read the *Financial Times*. It was a small table apart from the rest of the room with two red cloth bucket chairs. The lighting, even though there was a bright sun outside, was dim. The deeply tinted windows allowed for privacy that al-Badri had no doubt Cooper preferred.

Cooper stood out like a sore thumb. The only white person in the room, he made no effort to disguise that he was clearly an American. Al-Badri assumed that the only reason Cooper could be so obvious was that he was under the protection of a very powerful man among the Syrians. Someone who had to either be on the right hand of Bashar al-Assad or a highly placed Russian. It was al-Badri's guess it was the latter. Al-Assad's regime was not known to permit freedom of movement to anyone remotely associated with the United States. They trusted no Americans. But al-Assad did trust the Russians and did as he was told. So al-Badri assumed only a Russian could offer Cooper the protection that allowed him to be so open in Damascus.

"Mr. Cooper, it is good to see you again," lied al-Badri as he sat down.

The waiter took no time getting there. Al-Badri ordered tea. At three o'clock in the afternoon, Cooper was already having a Chopin martini. Al-Badri never allowed himself to be seen in public consuming alcohol. He left that sinful practice to private places.

"And it's good to see you as well, Abu." Another liar. "Praise to Allah."

Such an infidel, thought al-Badri. *Meeting with you is hardly something I would praise to Allah.*

"Praise to Allah," responded al-Badri.

As Cooper folded his paper and dropped it to the floor on his right, the waiter delivered al-Badri's tea.

"The Western world may soon be facing tough economic times," began Cooper.

"Don't believe everything you read in the *Financial Times*, Mr. Cooper. Western journalists would not report the truth unless their lives depended on it. And most of them live in isolation from the real world where oppression, death, and bigotry live in every corner of our neighborhoods." Al-Badri had no respect for reporters.

"Yes, that may be true, my good friend."

You are not my friend. And someday you'll learn that.

Both Cooper and al-Badri believed that the Western world was at the beginning of one of the cyclical recessions that economists prematurely predict is coming, so most investors, even the smart ones, refuse to end their joy ride before it is too late. That is what Petrenko was gambling on. Take that lack of belief that the end was near, and then make it come faster than anyone could imagine, let alone react to in time to prevent the collapse of their portfolios. But not even Petrenko could predict when any bull market bubble would burst. For that reason he needed to speed up the process with terrorist attacks in cities previously thought safe. Al-Badri was just the catalyst he needed.

"My benefactor has some instructions for you. It is time to pay him back for his generosity."

"Pay him back? This is not about payback, Mr. Cooper. It is about ending the tyranny of Western capitalists and those who have fallen from Islam."

"Call it what you like, Abu, but his instructions are to be followed without question."

Cooper could see the disdain in al-Badri's eyes. But he also knew that al-Badri wanted the weapons and money Cooper delivered. An occasional "instruction" was a small price to pay.

Al-Badri expected the usual simple attack on some small targets. That seemed to be Cooper's norm. Easy to do but not particularly useful as far as al-Badri was concerned. A secondary attack in Stockholm outside its stock exchange, a suicide bomber at an HSBC bank in London, and a crazed driver in a Home Depot rental truck on the West Side of Manhattan financed by Petrenko were accountable for fewer than one hundred dead or injured. In contrast, al-Badri killed many more each month in Syria and Paris. So Cooper's previous "instructions" were more of a nuisance than a useful tool for Allah's jihad.

"Two dates—August 14 and September 11. Can you remember them?"

"Sure. Why those dates? And what task do you ask me to undertake?"

"Abu, do you see the irony of those dates?"

"Mr. Cooper, I don't give a damn about irony or history lessons. Get to the point. I have far better ways of changing history than you have in reminding me about irrelevant dates. Every day until Allah's victory is all that matters to me."

"While I know you are not a true student of history, August 14 is V-J Day and, of course, September 11 is a date that speaks for itself. But I will get to the point since you do not appear to be in the mood for any discussion."

Cooper waved to the waiter, motioning with his raised hand and acting as if he was signing a check. A Western way of asking for the bill that al-Badri saw as another example of impolite arrogance that offended his sensibilities. Al-Badri hadn't touched his tea. He had no intention of sharing any drink with Cooper.

The two sat silently, confusing al-Badri.

Are you going to get to the point or not, al-Badri wanted to ask.

When the check came, Cooper threw down twenty 2,000-pound Syrian notes, roughly eighty U.S. dollars. Al-Badri quickly calculated that to cover about five martinis.

With that, Cooper stood. "I know you're not a fan of the *Financial Times*, but there is a fascinating article on page fourteen."

As Cooper strolled off toward the lobby exit, he wished al-Badri a nice day.

Alone, al-Badri took his first sip of tea and picked up the copy of the *Times* that Cooper had discarded on the floor. He turned to page fourteen.

A small piece of paper, handwritten, was taped to the page.

August 14—Launch local cells and lone wolves. Small but numerous. Cause panic.

September 11—Put Lamont's weapons to their test. Dramatic.

The rest of the piece of paper outlined the specifics. Finally, thought al-Badri, targets rich with capitalist pigs, ripe for slaughter. Ironic indeed.

So, Mr. Cooper, your benefactor is raising the stakes.

Al-Badri peeled the piece of paper from the *Times*, put it in his pocket, folded the newspaper, and placed it neatly on the table.

This was what he'd been waiting for, and he could barely hold back his happiness. Not just for himself, but also for his newly returned comrade, Hashir Rashid.

After years in Guantanamo, Rashid was finally reunited with al-Badri. He was now one of al-Badri's key lieutenants. Al-Badri knew that Rashid never forgave himself for his failure in Florence as a teenager. Now al-Badri would offer Rashid redemption with Allah and let him lead the attack. Al-Badri kept the reunion from anyone associated with Cooper. He did not want to bring such scum into Rashid's life. Praise Allah.

Al-Badri calmly finished his tea as he plotted out the plan in his mind, seeing it as simple tasks and ones he would enjoy. From a safe distance.

THIRTY

NANKING, CHINA

YU YAN WAS ASLEEP WHEN THE DOOR OF HER HOME WAS KICKED OPEN BY OFFICERS OF THE Ministry of State Security, clad in bulletproof vests and armed with QBZ-95B assault rifles, their weapon of choice. Capable of 13 rounds per second, such carbines in the hands of a police force could annihilate a crowd in seconds. The officers looked like they were prepared for a riot.

Yu Yan's father was first out of bed and in the living room, meeting the butt of a QBZ-95B, breaking his jaw and sending him to the floor, bleeding and unconscious. Her mother followed, and now screaming, was shoved to the couch.

"Where is your daughter?" demanded the lead officer.

Her mother sat, weeping.

"Search the apartment. Find her," he ordered.

Yu Yan was terrified. She worried that her latest posts criticizing Xi Jinping and his henchmen might cause trouble. But she couldn't help herself. It was as if a secret hand was driving her.

Xi Jinping is a murderer. His government is suppressing free speech and subjugating all of us to a gulag. Rise and rebel. Bring back the memory and victory of Tiananmen Square, she posted on WeChat the day before.

In a panic, Yu Yan ran for the window, putting any concern for her parents behind her. She knew where she'd be going if caught. She could not bear that life.

She managed to get halfway through the window before she heard the crack of the QBZ-95B. It was the last sound she heard, dead before she reached freedom. Her final thoughts were whether she would be a martyr for her cause, a cause she now died for. Dead over a cause created for her by Petrenko's programmers.

Beautiful, thought Janković. *She did exactly what I wanted her to do.*

No one, not even China's secret police armed with the best technology in the world, could trace the demise of Yu Yan back to Janković. Dorda and Janković were safe in Montenegro and Petrenko was relaxing somewhere in Russia, thousands of miles from Nanking and the killing of Yu Yan, a mere pawn in Petrenko's game. Checkmate. *The Selfish Ledger* worked.

Dorda was elated by the success of Janković's work and expected accolades from Petrenko. Instead, Petrenko questioned whether one single example was anything more than luck. So he instructed Dorda to order Janković to show him more.

"Paula, we need to put Petrenko's paranoia to rest. I believe in you, but Petrenko wants more. What can you show him?"

"Do you know where he lives?" asked Janković.

"No. I'm told he's on the move a lot."

"Well, surely you must know some of his favorite places. Where have you met with him in Russia?"

"Both times we met was over breakfast at the Restaurant Catherine in St. Petersburg's Hermitage Museum," responded Dorda.

"And can you tell me what art Petrenko likes at the Hermitage?" asked Janković.

"Where are you going with this, Paula? Petrenko is a patron of Russia's art world. I imagine he loves lots of art. I doubt he has a favorite."

"I'm sure he is a devotee of art, Tad. All the more reason to use it as a way to teach our Comrade Petrenko that questioning my success has a price."

"Please, Paula, choose something not personal to Petrenko," pleaded Dorda.

"Just leave it to me, Tad."

THIRTY-ONE

HERMITAGE MUSEUM, ST. PETERSBURG

BORIS SOKOLOV WAS THE CHIEF CURATOR AT THE HERMITAGE MUSEUM, WHERE HE'D WORKED for the twenty-seven years since he'd graduated from the Russian Academy of Arts in Saint Petersburg. Everyone liked him.

But in Russian hierarchy, he remained a peasant who came from a family of apple and potato farmers in the outskirts of St. Petersburg. While he started at the bottom of the ladder at the Hermitage and rose to one of the most respected positions in Russia's art world, he never lost his resentment for the oligarchs that he believed plagued Mother Russia.

Janković also knew that Petrenko occasionally met Sokolov for breakfast at the Restaurant Catherine when he visited the Hermitage. That was simple for her to discover once she hacked into their reservation files. It was the only time Sokolov was allowed to dine at the restaurant. Employees of the museum were expected to leave such places to the rich and influential. Or to the tourists who liked to waste their money on mediocre Russian food.

Janković's algorithms, now more sophisticated than any in the world, took less than an hour to map Sokolov's triggers. By collecting data from his emails, social media posts, what others said about him, his subscriptions, his purchases, where he went on vacation, his home life, the home life of his friends, where he ate, what he ate, what he drank, every charge he made and every check he wrote, every traffic ticket he got and where he got them, when he cheated on his wife, what his girlfriend did, who she did it with, and on and on. Everything everyone does is recorded somewhere. And Janković's algorithms let loose in big data did Janković's bidding. With access to the world's largest computers, which collected data on millions of people every second, Janković's task was relatively easy provided she could get down to the visceral level of a person's psyche. Janković's talent came into play when she decided what she needed to do to motivate her target to do her bidding without the mark knowing they weren't doing it because they wanted to but because, subconsciously, they had no choice. Best of all, if caught, they would never be able to identify anyone but themselves for whatever deeds they committed. For Janković, it was the perfect crime.

Wednesday's text from Janković to one of Petrenko's safe numbers was simple. And Janković made sure Petrenko had no idea who it came from. Janković wanted to create as much confusion as possible around the lesson she was about to teach Petrenko.

Perhaps you'll be having breakfast again soon with Boris Sokolov. I suggest you do so before Friday, the message read.

Petrenko, remembering Sokolov, did not understand why anyone would send him such a message. After all, to Petrenko, while Sokolov was intellectually interesting with his knowledge of the Hermitage collection, he was hardly anyone who warranted an appointment for breakfast on such short notice. So Petrenko made a mental note of the intrusion and erased the message, as he did with all texts he received on any of his safe phones. The phones were safe because every call or text to every number anyone had was bounced through hundreds of connection points on the global telecommunications grid, where they were repeatedly encrypted until they reached one of a half dozen phones Petrenko used. As far as he was concerned, every call and text was untraceable. And that was true except when Janković wanted to see them. She had long ago hacked into all of Petrenko's communication network.

Petrenko was enjoying his breakfast in his apartment on Krestovsky Island, one of the many walled communities in the complex of rivers and canals that wind through St. Petersburg. Describing his home on Krestovsky Island as an apartment was a misnomer. With 4,500 square feet of living space, it was among the largest and most opulent in Russia. The security in the complex was state of the art, befitting one of the wealthiest men in the world.

Saturday morning's front-page headline in the *St. Petersburg Times* reported on a most unsettling development at the Hermitage.

Long Time Curator Shot Dead Defacing Michelangelo's Crouching Boy.

Yesterday at nine o'clock in the morning, Boris Sokolov, Chief Curator of our beloved Hermitage, was shot by security officers as he took a chisel to the Renaissance masterpiece—Michelangelo's Crouching Boy. Regrettably, significant damage was done before Sokolov could be stopped. Since he was Chief Curator, no one ever questioned where he went in the museum. Friday was no different a day than any other for Sokolov as he made his rounds. Witnesses say that as he passed the sculpture, he suddenly stopped, shouted slurs against Mother Russia, and began chipping away at the soft marble of the work. Museum officials said they were shocked by his behavior and would immediately investigate. Experts say that while the damage can be repaired, the Crouching Boy will never be the same. The iconic sculpture of a boy removing a thorn from his foot was brought to Russia by Catherine the Great as part of an extensive collection of antiquities she purchased from John Lye Browne, a London banker, in the 1700s.

Crouching Boy is the only work of Michelangelo in the Hermitage, and was one of Petrenko's favorites. Petrenko remembered a conversation he had with Sokolov about how lucky the Hermitage was to have acquired such a masterpiece.

The article stopped Petrenko cold, remembering the text he received.

His phone buzzed.

The new text read, "*Perhaps you can now appreciate how The Selfish Ledger works and no further examples will be necessary.*"

Petrenko's blood began to boil.

THIRTY-TWO

WASHINGTON, D.C.

TAFT NERVOUSLY SENT A TEXT ON THE PHONE HARRIS HAD GIVEN HER.

It rang back, and Taft answered.

"Hold on, Ms. Taft, I'll put you through."

"Rebecca, this is Richard Harris. I assume there is a reason you're reaching out."

Taft wasn't sure what to say and whether she could trust Harris. Isselin had told her to talk to him before she spoke to Harris or anyone else or used the phone, reminding her that her first loyalty was to *Axios*. Isselin made it clear that any news Taft had was to be reported to him before anyone else. But she couldn't get through to Isselin, and after leaving him two voicemails, she felt compelled to call Harris.

"Mr. Harris, I received an odd text on this phone. I'm not sure what it means. And you told me only you knew about this phone so I assume it's from you and you can explain."

"What does the text say, Rebecca? I never sent you any text."

"All it says is *NYC, August 14*."

"Interesting," responded Harris.

"Could this have something to do with Lori's list of dates?" she asked.

"Perhaps. Or it could be nothing more than a ruse. But the fact that someone texted the number concerns me. Only those of us with whom you have met know that number. Even you don't know it. Listen careful-ly, Rebecca. I want you to come to the FBI offices immediately and give the phone to Chandler Thompson. Do not use it or change anything on it. Whatever you do, do not discard the message. Don't tell anyone about it. Anyone, Rebecca. Bring it to Thompson now, and I'll meet you there. Do you understand?"

"Yes."

Harris hung up and immediately called Thompson.

"Chandler, Rebecca Taft received a message on the phone— *NYC, August 14.*"

"Jesus, Dick, how could that happen? No one but Grant and the two of us know the number. And I certainly didn't send the text," responded Thompson.

"And neither did I," answered Harris.

"Grant would have never sent it, either. So who sent it?" asked Thompson.

"I wish I knew. But it's a date on the list. So something is going to happen in New York on August 14."

On her way to the FBI, Isselin returned Taft's call on her personal phone. She didn't answer.

THIRTY-THREE

DAY'S INN, PHILADELPHIA

HASHIR RASHID HAD BEEN BOOKED INTO ROOM 211 AT THE DAY'S INN FOR A WEEK AWAITING word from al-Badri. At his last meeting with him a few weeks before, al-Badri had told him, "Rashid, my friend, I have an assignment for you that will give you the chance to atone for your failure in Florence."

"Praise Allah, Abu," Rashid responded.

The instructions were simple. Register at the Day's Inn and wait. Nothing more.

"Why tell me so little, Abu? What will my instruction be once I arrive? Please do not keep me in the dark. I'm prepared for whatever you order me to do," Rashid continued. "But not knowing will drive me crazy. And sitting around in Philadelphia is not something I want to do without knowing my fate."

"It's better that for now, you don't know, Hashir. You must trust me. Things are at work that will change the course of history. And you will be part of it. For the glory of Allah."

"I understand, Abu."

Rashid was given the papers he needed. A passport, credit cards, and cash. He flew into Dulles International outside Washington and took Amtrak to Philadelphia. He booked coach to be sure he didn't stand out.

The train station made sense. Security at America's train stations, including Union Station in the nation's capital, was abysmal. Apart from the dogs and occasional guards, one could easily pass through without notice, regardless of their intentions, however nefarious they might be. Terrorism experts had often warned Homeland Security of the risks, but Oliver Grant had only so many officers to cover airports and seaports. It was impossible to include every potential site a terrorist might strike. In the hierarchy of sensitive locations, train stations were just not the top priority.

The Day's Inn neighborhood on Race Street in Philadelphia was a mix of offices and residential apartments, no more than a half mile from Center City. Rashid assumed that Philadelphia was al-Badri's target and that whatever al-Badri had in mind, it would happen on either August 14 or September 11. After all, Philadelphia was the first capital of America and home of the Liberty Bell. It was where the Declaration of Independence was signed. What better target could there be?

Harris never told Rashid that Taft received a text about an event that would happen in New York City on August 14. Harris didn't know what, where, or when it would happen, so telling Rashid was not important to Harris. For all he knew, whatever al-Badri had in mind for Rashid might be elsewhere, including Philadelphia. So all he and Rashid could do was wait. Rashid had his phone with instructions to use it to text Harris through Signal once he learned what was going to happen. He was to use the phone for no other purpose, just as Taft was not to use her phone for any other purpose. Harris believed that's how he could keep communications secure.

Each morning, Rashid went for a walk to ease his tension, always wondering if someone was watching him. Rashid knew that al-Badri took no chances and that as much as al-Badri trusted him, Rashid could not be the only person involved in al-Badri's plans. So Rashid took his daily walks to watch and see if any faces became familiar, hoping to identify anyone who might be following him.

Rashid also made sure to eat breakfast every day at the hotel. It was free, and he actually came to enjoy the waffles. While the coffee was less than Rashid desired, he offset that disappointment by stopping by Starbucks for a cappuccino on each of his daily strolls. He marveled at how it seemed that the only places left in America to buy a good cup of coffee was a Starbucks. The little cafes he enjoyed in the Middle East and London had long succumbed to the avarice of chains like Starbucks.

He saw no one at the hotel who raised suspicions any more than he himself did on his walks.

THIRTY-FOUR

ST. PETERSBURG, RUSSIA

PETRENKO WAS ENJOYING HIS BREAKFAST AT THE RESTAURANT CATHERINE AS HE WAITED for Cooper to arrive. Petrenko made a point of strolling by the site of the Crouching Boy that morning, and saw that the masterpiece had been removed after Sokolov had damaged Petrenko's beloved work of Michelangelo. It troubled him deeply that Janković defaced such a masterpiece to prove her point. He resolved that Janković would pay for such transgression when she was no longer of use to him.

Cooper arrived at 10:00 a.m., as scheduled, and took a seat to the right of Petrenko. His breakfast arrived, and the waiter poured him a cup of coffee. He would have preferred a martini.

"Mr. Cooper, it appears our plans are well under way. I assume you can assure me of that." Petrenko seemed a little nervous, a demeanor unsettling to Cooper. While Petrenko was always short and to the point, he seemed distracted.

Cooper decided to address the tension.

"Constantine, you seem worried. I can assure you everything will go as planned. New York will feel the wrath of al-Badri on August 14. Then local attacks throughout the world will cause chaos in the markets. By September 11, the world will be on the verge of falling to its knees. Your holdings are in credit default swaps, collateralized debt obligations, and short on some stocks and long on others. You're also in some precious metals. The strategy will keep you in assets that will profit during the chaos and survive the economic collapse that will follow. You will be worth more than your wildest dreams. Most likely the richest man in the world. You can then convert enough into cash, gold, and silver, or into enough stock to control the largest companies in the world. Google, Apple, Amazon, you name it. They will be yours for the taking."

Cooper could see Petrenko relax.

"And the loose ends, Mr. Cooper? Are you taking care of them?" asked Petrenko.

"We've already begun, Constantine. Relax. You have nothing to worry about."

"I have everything to worry about, Mr. Cooper. So do you. This is not child's play."

"No, Constantine, it is not child's play. The plan is sound. We have complete control."

"Good. Your life depends on it."

Petrenko motioned to his attendant to bring him his coat and hat. Always a good dresser, Petrenko made sure his sycophants were readily at hand to see he looked his best wherever he went and whenever he left.

Petrenko stood while the attendant helped him with his coat.

Cooper began to stand.

"Sit, Mr. Cooper, and enjoy your breakfast. As if it were your last."

Cooper lost his appetite.

"Give me a Chopin martini. Three olives," he ordered, genuinely worried about his continued luck.

THIRTY-FIVE

SHENZHEN, CHINA

APPLE ASSEMBLES THE MAJORITY OF ITS IPHONES IN SHENZHEN, CHINA, THE EQUIVALENT OF Asia's Silicon Valley.

Instead of centralizing its technology operations in one location, China strategically established seventeen hubs, including Shenzhen, Shanghai, Beijing, and the Pearl River Delta, all handpicked by the State Council to encourage innovation zones throughout the nation.

Reminiscent of Apple's famous parody commercial satirizing George Orwell's book *1984*, China added full censorship of the cloud and online tools like Apple's Siri. In the Apple spot, a nonconformist, antiestablishment character took a sledgehammer to "Big Brother" to announce the arrival of the Macintosh computer. Ironically, Apple makes most of its devices in a country where Big Brother is a reality. China Telecom, the dominant state-owned communications giant in China, controls the data of over 130 million Chinese iPhone users. It's hard to get more "Big Brother" than that.

For Janković, this made China a ripe target for espionage and fit perfectly into Petrenko's design. If Janković could disrupt Apple's operations in Shenzhen, Petrenko could send Apple stock into a dive.

It wasn't a novel idea.

In 2017, Petrenko toyed with Samsung. Some simple moves by Janković produced flawed phones and mandated massive recalls. It cost Samsung millions in sales as its stock prices fell throughout the world.

But with Petrenko, one proven event is not enough. So Google fared no better with its operating system central to Samsung. The melting Android batteries of 2017 thought to be a manufacturing flaw were orchestrated by Janković's manipulation through her now growing cadre of *Selfish Ledger* minions. The plan worked.

Petrenko spared Samsung and Google further damage, using the events only as tests for Janković's programmers. Now, with so many dependent on Apple's operating system embedded in countless devices, it was too tempting to ignore a similar and more impactful move. And the juiciest part of all for Janković was that she'd be using what she learned from the maladies she perpetrated on Google and Samsung to bring Apple to its knees. Sweet revenge for Google and Samsung, even though they'd never know the favor Janković was doing for them.

Bianca Feng was Foxconn Technology Group's top manager in its Shenzhen plant, overseeing nearly a half million employees, including 300,000 who worked exclusively making Apple products.

It was a facility with its share of controversy. In 2010, following a series of suicides in the plant, Foxconn was targeted by labor activists, accusing the company of paying slave wages and making illegal overtime demands. Many of those suicides were unknowingly linked to Janković and her playing with destinies through *The Selfish Ledger*. But no one knew the connection. It was untraceable.

Feng was blamed for poor management and held responsible for employee discontent. She also was under orders to improve productivity at all costs. She knew that the lives of the workers who toiled at the plant were meaningless to her overseers. She had orders, and if she could not produce, her life would no longer be important. It was a matter of economic, if not personal, survival for her. A few lives here or there, or conventional rules of behavior broken, were the price to pay to feed the world's insatiable appetite for smartphones.

As Janković manipulated Feng's psyche, Feng grew increasingly disenchanted with her life at Foxconn. She became depressed for reasons she could not understand and began seeing Foxconn as her enemy. Feng's mounting paranoia made her consider revenge as the ticket out of her misery. She became obsessed with making Foxconn pay for its cruelty to workers. She was becoming irrational.

"Can you get Feng to do your bidding? Will she execute her part of the plan?" asked Dorda. "Petrenko is depending on us."

"She's proven easy to manipulate, Tad. She now sees villains in every shadow. With just a few more suggestions, I have no doubt I will get her to do whatever we want her to do. The suicides were child's play," Janković responded with confidence.

"You'd better be right, Paula. Neither of us can fail. Not if we want to stay alive."

Janković thought Dorda was overly dramatic with his fears. The two were too crucial to Petrenko. At least Janković felt that way about herself. She'd made sure no one else understood *The Selfish Ledger*. Dorda thought he understood, but Janković knew better. Petrenko's limited knowledge was worthless without Janković's algorithms and codes. And only she knew those. Whatever big bangs Petrenko had planned needed loyal pawns to pick up the pieces. Janković knew that Petrenko's routine stock manipulation scams were sideshows to his bigger plan to bring the global economy to a halt. The arbitrage Janković could oversee in the aftermath would make Petrenko billions more. But not without Janković's master strokes. That was something Dorda did not understand. As far as Janković was concerned, Dorda's doubt about her abilities was a liability. And Janković's *Selfish Ledger* on Dorda made sure Janković was always a few steps ahead of him.

THIRTY-SIX

HAMPTONS, LONG ISLAND

DARREN WHITE LOVED THE SUNRISE FROM THE SECOND-FLOOR DECK OF HIS BEACHSIDE HOME in the Hamptons. The deck had an unobstructed view of the ocean; a view that today was marvelous. But then a phone call from Cooper interrupted the serene moment.

"So, Darren, where are we now?"

"Seriously, Mr. Cooper? You get my reports. Read the fucking things."

"Darren, I don't want to read anything. I want to hear it from you. I want to know you are on top of it. I want to hear in your spoken words that you understand and follow orders. Do not make me ask twice."

"Fine. We're—no you—are now paying $25 million a month for CDSs in hedge funds in fifty-one countries. And your millions in shorts are two months out in Apple, IBM, and the other tech stocks you told me to buy. We've got millions in CDOs and are long in a few other nontech stocks, mostly energy. And you're long in Samsung, as instructed. All this without what I think is a true hedge. So you or whoever it is you work for better be right, Mr. Cooper, or you are about to lose billions. I doubt even your mystery benefactor has that much money. But I guess it is his to lose. Just make sure I get paid."

"Darren, why do you insult me? Have we not lived up to our end of the bargain? Have we not paid you millions in the past two years?"

"The money's been there, but at what price, Mr. Cooper? Where do I go when the shit hits the fan?"

"My, my, Darren. Do I detect a conscience lurking in your larcenous mind? I think it's a little too late for that, Darren."

"Fuck a conscience. I just don't want to spend my money behind bars," responded White. "You can read my reports. That is all you need. You know every deal, every dollar, and every hedge in your friend's empire. And to hell with him and you when it doesn't work."

White disconnected, expecting an immediate call back from Cooper with yet another threat. No call came. He felt relieved and satisfied that he'd finally put Cooper in his place.

As he continued to take in the view, enjoying a morning Bloody Mary to rid himself of the hangover from too much enjoyment the night before, he saw Geraghty approaching, wearing only the robe White had given. His mood improved.

"Morning Sheila. This is my favorite time of the day. Don't you agree?"

He had met Geraghty the night before at 75 Main in South Hampton, both a restaurant in the evening and a favorite after-hours club that attracted some of the most beautiful women summering in the Hamptons. White was a regular and very successful at picking up one-night stands from the bevy of talented young women looking for someone rich with whom they could pass the night.

Geraghty caught his eye early. A stunning brunette at just over five feet five, she had a body any man would fantasize over.

When he approached her at the bar, she was at first standoffish. White liked that. It made the hunt all the more exciting. He refused to give up.

"Please, miss, I mean no offense. Let me buy you a drink. That's the least you can let me do."

"If you must."

"And what will you have?" White asked.

"A Black Russian," she responded.

Waving to the bartender, White ordered, "Please bring this lovely lady a Black Russian with Stolichnaya vodka."

He turned to Geraghty. "After all, if you're going to have a Black Russian, you have to go Russian all the way. Don't you agree?"

"And what will you have, Mr. White?" asked the bartender.

"My usual, Anthony. A Macallan 25, neat."

"I guess you're a regular here," observed Geraghty.

"I'm a regular at just about every bar in the Hamptons. My place is just a mile or two away on the beach. It has a wonderful view."

"No doubt," responded Geraghty. "And I bet you drive there in your Ferrari."

"No, I drive a BMW 760i," responded White.

White assumed from her response that she was impressed. Most women in the Hamptons were. If Geraghty knew anything about BMWs, she knew the 760i was the most expensive model built by the company. Its sticker price was north of $175,000.

By midnight, White had her name and her employer, Deutsche Bank. He learned that she lived alone in Manhattan. She liked summering in South Hampton, regularly taking the Jitney on Fridays and staying at the Surf Club Resort.

It did not take much to get her to go home with him and enjoy his bed. Always thinking of himself as a great lover, White thought Geraghty seemed very pleased at his prowess and techniques. When they finished the next morning with a third round, he donned a robe and left her to see the sunrise from his deck. Geraghty joined him shortly after he made his first Bloody Mary. She had gone to the kitchen and poured herself a cup of coffee as she walked onto the deck, wearing one of his terry robes. And nothing else.

When she appeared, White could barely hold back from pulling on her robe's cord for one more look at her gorgeous body, but decided he would first enjoy the sunrise before he enjoyed her one more time.

Geraghty moved quickly. The butcher knife from the kitchen was handled swiftly and expertly as it slit White's throat. She was well trained.

Gagging, he briefly stared at her in disbelief, blood pouring over his white terry-cloth robe as he dropped his Bloody Mary to the deck.

"Greetings from Mr. Cooper," offered Geraghty with a smile.

White died in less than a minute, never rising from his chair.

Sheila Geraghty, who had never before been to the Hamptons, gathered her clothes, dressed, and after reporting by phone to Cooper, swept the place for prints and left, leisurely walking the two miles to downtown and the Jitney back to Manhattan. While she couldn't wait to get the brown dye out of her natural red hair and remove the contacts that changed the color of her eyes, she didn't want any record of a taxi ride. As always, she made sure no one would ever learn her real name. That worked well for her in the well-paying line of work she chose.

THIRTY-SEVEN

KEY WEST, FLORIDA

SCOTTY WEINREB WAS ENJOYING THE EVENING WITH SOME NACHOS AND BEER AT THE GREEN Parrot, his favorite hangout.

He barely noticed the man who sat at the stool next to him at the bar, except for the ink on his arms and neck. Weinreb figured he was just another biker who spent time in Key West.

When the man spilled his own drink into Weinreb's nachos, Weinreb instinctively grabbed his beer.

"What the fuck, asshole! You're going to have to buy me another drink!" demanded the biker.

"Hey, man. I didn't spill your drink. You did. And all over my nachos. So I'm not the asshole," responded Weinreb, immediately regretting his response once he took a closer look at the biker, all too stereotypical of a badass who no doubt was with the Hell's Angels or some other gang.

"You callin' me a liar?" asked the biker.

Now scared, Weinreb thought it best to back off.

"Sorry, I'm not calling you anything. If you'd like me to buy you a beer, fine. Just let me enjoy what's left of my nachos."

"No one calls me a liar."

With those words, the biker grabbed Weinreb by the shoulders, twisted him around, and put his arms in the front and back of Weinreb's head. The rest happened quickly as Weinreb's neck was broken and his ability to breathe vanished. As Weinreb fell to the floor for the last time in his life, the biker quickly ran out of the bar amid the chaos.

THIRTY-EIGHT

PENINSULA HOTEL, HONG KONG

THE BOY WAS NO MORE THAN TWELVE YEARS OLD WITH BARELY A HAIR ON HIS BODY EXCEPT for his head. Exactly what Pak Heir Zhang liked.

Having enjoyed the child's body most of the night, Zhang grabbed the boy's head and pushed him to his crotch, forcing the boy to take his penis into his mouth. The boy put up little resistance. Just as he had put up no resistance for hours before while Zhang had his way with him.

Enjoying the moment as the child satisfied Zhang's fantasy, Zhang noticed that the boy was gently biting him. He enjoyed it until the door was kicked open and the Hong Kong police stormed in. As they did, the boy bit hard, tearing into Zhang.

Zhang screamed and pushed the child off him, blood spewing from his erection. In shock, an officer drew his gun and fired one round into Zhang. It was all that was needed to end the last night of fantasy Zhang would experience.

Loose ends. Cooper made sure they were being taken care of. Petrenko's plans were on schedule.

THIRTY-NINE

DAY'S INN, PHILADELPHIA
AUGUST 13

AS RASHID TOOK HIS DAILY WALK, HE NOTICED A BLUE VAN PARKED NEAR THE STARBUCKS. The blacked-out windows gave it an ominous look. Although suspicious, he decided not to change his routine and continued on to get his coffee.

As he walked out of the Starbucks, coffee in hand, a woman approached him.

"Come with me, Hashir. Abu al-Badri sends his regards."

Knowing he had no choice, he followed her to the van, discarding his coffee in the trashcan in front of the Starbucks. A man opened the passenger door to greet him.

"Praise Allah, Hashir," he said.

"Praise Allah," Rashid responded.

The woman motioned for Rashid to get in. He complied, concluding that if they intended to kill him, he would be dead by now.

Once in the van, Rashid noticed that another man was driving, making it four of them.

As the van pulled from the curb, the woman spoke again.

"Hashir, we have instructions for you from Abu."

Finally, I will know the target in Philadelphia. He assumed Harris had someone watching.

The driver was very good, darting in and out of traffic and turning onto a number of streets, one after another. He was obviously making sure no one was able to follow them.

The woman sensed that Rashid was nervous.

"Don't worry Hashir. We're just being careful." She was telling the truth.

After a half hour of maneuvering, the driver said, "We're good."

Shit, if Harris had me followed, they are long gone. Rashid was right.

"Good," said the other man.

The woman resumed the conversation.

"My name is Adara Bousaid. My friends—our friends—are Kareem Nejem and Tahir Zaman."

"I'm Tahir," announced the driver as he turned onto the Benjamin Franklin Bridge en route to New Jersey.

It meant they were leaving Philadelphia.

"OK," responded Rashid. "Now that we have introductions out of the way, would you mind telling me where we're going?"

"We're on our way to New York City," Bousaid responded. "The Big Apple, as they like to say here in America. The big rotten apple."

Nejem and Zaman laughed.

Rashid did all he could to remain calm.

"And what are we going to do in New York?" Rashid asked, wishing he could press the panic button on his phone to alert Harris. But there was no way he could reach in his pocket for it without raising suspicion.

"We're going to blow up the headquarters of Citibank," Bousaid calmly answered

"And kill as many bankers as we can," added Nejem in laughter.

"Citibank? Are you idiots?" responded Rashid. "Security in New York is the best in the world. Has al-Badri lost his mind?"

Bousaid ignored Rashid's question and said, "Hashir, give me your phone."

"Why do you want my phone?" replied Rashid, now worrying about being discovered.

"Abu's instructions. No one is to have any phones."

Rashid reached into his pocket and handed the phone to Bousaid, pressing the panic button as he did so.

Bousaid took a glance at the phone, but Rashid saw no reaction from her. She handed it to Nejem, who promptly produced a hammer and crushed it, calmly throwing the remains out the window. Rashid's hope of being tracked was smashed as well. He needed to know more. "Citibank?" he asked. "And how do you propose we get in? Security there is solid as a rock. None of us can possibly get through it. Don't you think they might notice us wearing explosives or carrying weapons? I'm all for killing the bastards, but I don't want to be stupid," Rashid insisted.

"No one said we're going inside the bank, Rashid. We won't need to."

Zaman pulled onto the Atlantic City Expressway.

FORTY

PODGORICA, REPUBLIC OF MONTENEGRO
AUGUST 13

JANKOVIĆ SAT AT HER COMPUTER, FEELING THAT THE WORLD'S DESTINY WAS IN HER HANDS. For two years, she had been preparing for this day. The day she would show Petrenko and the world that her theories from *The Selfish Ledger* transcended any previous attempts at terrorism. She wanted to prove that she, not Abu al-Badri, knew that real change did not come through the Will of Allah or any other god. It came through technology and pliant minds.

"The fourteenth is tomorrow, Paula. Are you ready?" asked Dorda.

"Tad, you always question my ability. You must stop doing so and become a believer."

"All I believe in now, Paula, is that I don't want to disappoint Petrenko. Not because I care about what he wants but because I care about what he will do to you and me if we fail. I wish I'd never met him."

If you only knew…

"Relax, Tad, we will not fail."

"Show me again. I want to see your plan again."

Janković pulled a chair over to her computer terminal and motioned Dorda to sit down. It was a chair with wheels, so it was easy for him to get close to the monitor.

A map of the world appeared with some countries highlighted in red, including the United States, France, Italy, Germany, Great Britain, Poland, Russia, Finland, Brazil, Chile, Argentina, New Zealand, India, China, Japan, South Korea, Israel, Syria, Saudi Arabia, and South Africa.

Janković moved the mouse so the arrow hovered over the United States. With a click, the map zoomed in, showing a myriad of dots in cities throughout the States. Janković clicked on Charleston, South Carolina. A picture of a woman appeared with data below it.

"This is Juanita Chavez. She is an illegal immigrant from Honduras and a chambermaid at the Planters Inn next to Charleston's old market square. She has been addicted to social media since she arrived and uses it to keep her relatives in Tegucigalpa informed of her activities. Foolish. She should have been discovered by ICE years ago."

"Tegucigalpa?" asked Dorda.

"Tad, Tegucigalpa is the capital of Honduras. Chavez illegally entered the United States through Mexico in one of the caravans," responded Janković.

Janković clicked open another icon in Chavez's file. "But our friends at the CIA are not focused on illegal aliens from Honduras or Mexico. They foolishly think they are not enemies of the state. Poor Juanita cleans up the mess rich American tourists leave her every day. Few ever tip her. At first, she was just disappointed. But now she is irate. I've made sure of that. Tomorrow, she will act. So will dozens of others around the world. It will be a marvelous day."

"What will she do?" asked Dorda.

"Her task is a simple one. She will go postal, as they like to say in America, and stab as many people in the lobby—tourists and co-work-ers—as she can until she is stopped. I figure she will kill at least a half dozen and wound some others. Hopefully including children and women. It will be a bloodbath. Then she'll either be killed herself or subdued. Either way is fine with me. It will awaken the prejudice Americans have for illegal immigrants and the failure of ICE and Homeland Security to do something about them. The reaction will be immediate as authorities round up undocumented workers throughout the country. And when they find out she had false papers legitimizing her right to be there, just like the killers in San Francisco and Brooklyn, Iowa, the country's anger will cascade into panic."

"Like the killers of Kate Steinle and Mollie Tibbetts?"

"Exactly, Tad. I'm impressed. While you don't know geography and world capitals, at least you remember the news of killings in America. And all I need to do is hit 'enter' on my keyboard. The chaos will begin."

FORTY-ONE

SHENZHEN, CHINA
AUGUST 13

JANKOVIĆ REGARDED HER PROGRAMMING OF FENG AS HER MASTERPIECE. FOR MONTHS, SHE filled Feng's mind with anger and paranoia about Foxconn. Feng was programmed like a computer, thinking that Foxconn was directly responsible for the rash of suicides in the plant. She was convinced that the peasants that worked there were merely pawns in Foxconn's obsession with making profits at any cost. For Feng, this was the worst part. Profits were fine, but not at the expense of the people. All her life Feng was taught the doctrines of communist rule in the Moa Zedong way. The people and their well-being were the responsibility of the State. Foxconn was the evil State in Feng's mind.

"Secret memos found in Foxconn's files revealing their role in the death of assembly line workers" was an early social media post on WeChat, seen only by Feng.

"Children and mothers left homeless under the Foxconn rule" read another sent exclusively to Feng.

Janković followed those with special videos of starving families forced to survive only on rice. It reminded Feng of the potato famine and the infamous battles between the Catholics ruling Great Britain and the farmers in Ireland. Starvation is a slow and painful way to die.

Pictures of malnourished babies with bloated stomachs appeared regularly on Feng's social feeds. Crying mothers and dying children were standard fare. When it first started, Feng would forward them to friends and then try to talk to them. But whenever she spoke about it, her friends denied ever seeing the posts or photos, warning her that the State may have intercepted them. And if that was true, they told Feng, she could get into a lot of trouble.

Janković knew every person Feng contacted via email, social media posts, or even in conversations. Manipulating Feng's *Selfish Ledger* connected one dot to another, mining the big data so easily accessed through Janković's digital spiders freely roaming China's Sunway computer network.

Heeding her friend's warnings, Feng eventually stopped forwarding any of the posts. As her paranoia grew, Feng became convinced she could no longer even talk about them, believing that anyone, no matter how close a friend Feng thought they might be, could be an informant, ready to turn her over to authorities for a ceremonial trial and swift execution. Just like the executions posted on her feeds every week.

When Feng's second in command, Jian Heng, took his own life one evening after work, also killing his wife, Nadia, and only child, Peigi, Feng became desperately distraught. She had spoken to him that day—August 3—asking if he had seen any of the posted headlines about Foxconn and the deaths its appetite for profits fed.

"Bianca, you must stop asking me such things. I have seen no such headlines," insisted Heng. "I've told you many times that I don't want any of your trouble. Please stop."

"But Jian, we need to care about our workers. Don't you see they are dying? They are being worked hour after hour with ever-increasing quotas. They're at a breaking point, and the masters at Foxconn want more. How can we possibly satisfy them?"

"The Americans want more phones. Every one they buy is paving the way for a greater China for all of us. Why not feed the capitalist pigs as much as they can eat, Bianca?"

"But it's not just the Americans, Jian. Our own people now have millions of phones, including children. And we make the phones here. We're turning people—our people—into digital zombies." Feng got the expression—digital zombies—from a Janković post. Increasingly, Feng spouted Janković's words as if they were gospel.

Two days after Heng's suicide, Janković knew Feng was ready.

Click here to learn how to let loose a deadly virus. Not one that kills people. One that kills computers, the cyborgs of the future, before they kill us.

Feng followed the programming instructions, and within minutes, the virus was in place, ready to launch on August 14. Janković could have done it herself, but it was all the sweeter for Janković to force others to do her bidding. She was in control and took comfort in knowing that Feng assured her that Apple would soon lose its ability to sell iPhones, iPads, and Macs as its supply of chips vanished.

FORTY-TWO

CHARLESTON, CERNOBBIO, AND RIO DE JANEIRO
AUGUST 14

CHARLESTON, SOUTH CAROLINA

Juanita Chavez was cleaning rooms at the Planters Inn as she did every day.

Her phone vibrated. She was prohibited from having it set to ring. A management rule.

Twenty-eight immigrants killed at the border by ICE agents.

Of course, it wasn't true. Her Selfish Ledger was at work.

It was 1:00 and her shift ended. As she prepared to go home, leaving through the lobby, another text message appeared. Chavez didn't recognize the sender's name but didn't care.

How long before the oppressed aliens avenge the murder of their Latino brothers and sisters trying to find new lives? When will Americans realize that the wall has spawned a killing field?

Her emotions, already on edge, took a new turn. She was confused.

The next text set her into her programmed assignment.

Some names of those killed have been released. Jose Luis Gonzalez, age 24. Juan Sanchez, age 16, Miguel Hernandez, age 12, Maria Lopez, age 15, Veronica Martinez, age 22, Margarita Chavez, age 16.

Margarita Chavez was the name of her sister.

Of course, none of it was true.

Her Selfish Ledger at work.

The final text read, *Kill or be killed.*

As Chavez entered the lobby, crowded with white people she hated, she was overcome with emotion. She reached into her handbag and took out the pocketknife she carried for protection. And then she began.

Her first victim was a middle-aged woman sitting in the lobby. Chavez stabbed her in the neck, hitting her carotid artery as if Chavez were a surgeon. It was a lucky blow but good enough to send the woman's blood all over the lobby floor.

It took her seconds to strike the second person, a bellman pushing a luggage cart. He tried to fend off the knife, but he was too late. Chavez sunk her knife into his eye. He fell, screaming in pain.

In those few moments, chaos ensued as others in the lobby ran. No one tried to stop Chavez.

Chavez lunged at a young boy as he stood confused when his mother tried to grab him and protect him from harm. The mother, her instincts overcoming her, needed to stop Chavez. While the swipe of the knife from Chavez missed the boy's arm, the result was a gash across the mother's throat. As her son ran in confusion, his mother bled to death.

The hotel guard finally drew his revolver and shot Chavez. As she fell, she screamed, "For my brothers and sisters killed by America."

In minutes, it was picked up on social media complete with a video conveniently hacked off the hotel security CCTV cameras. Janković made sure of that. It spawned a Twitter frenzy.

CERNOBBIO, ITALY

Harry's Bar was a favorite watering hole on the Piazza Risorgimento. It overlooked the ferry dock on Lake Como, one of the posh Italian resort cities and just blocks from the Villa d'Este, a sanctuary for the rich and famous. George Clooney and Richard Branson had mansions on the lake.

Lake Como was a preferred location for many of the refugees from Syria and North Africa. Beggars were everywhere, spoiling the serenity and panhandling for change from the wealthy tourists enjoying the early evening calm. It was the only complaint tourists had of the otherwise blissful enclave.

Peter Raymond was enjoying a glass of Champagne with his wife, Elizabeth. They were celebrating their twenty-fifth wedding anniversary. Joining them were their longtime friends Dave and Sally Kasper.

The four were among fifty or so in the courtyard bar. At least a hundred were milling about the piazza, some on strolls, and others waiting for the next ferry.

It was target-rich.

Syrian Osama Abadi had prepared for his moment since he had arrived a month before. A member of al-Badri's legion of jihadists, he yearned for the day to die in the glory of Allah. Today was his day.

He dressed smartly to blend in with the rich tourists. Getting the money needed for expensive clothes was no longer a problem now that Petrenko was financing al-Badri. Looking right made it all the easier to blend in and not be identified as a threat.

Abadi was strapped in explosives and ball bearings, a bomb that was relatively typical. But with Lamont's help, it also included capsules of sarin, a deadly gas hundreds of times more toxic than cyanide. On detonation, it assured a substantially increased kill zone, particularly for first responders or anyone else who chose to be a hero and attempt to rescue someone. It was a cool day, so his coat did not seem bulky, although it was unlikely he'd look unusual in any circumstances given his slight stature.

Abadi walked into Harry's Bar and sat at a table next to the Raymonds and Kaspers.

"Are you vacationing here?" he asked.

"Yes," replied Peter Raymond in a tone he hoped would convey the message that they were not particularly interested in being interrupted.

"Where are you from?" Abadi asked. He wanted to toy a little with someone he was about to murder.

"The States," replied Raymond's wife, feeling that her husband's brush-off was rude. After all, the man seemed perfectly polite and well dressed.

"I've always wanted to go to the States," replied Abadi. "But never had the chance."

"And where are you from?" asked Raymond's wife, deciding to show some respect for someone who seemed perfectly nice.

"Syria," Abadi replied.

Dave Kasper decided to join the conversation. "Really? So what do you think of all the refugees here in Lake Como? I was surprised to see so many in such an expensive resort."

"Yes, there are many people abandoning their homes in fear of dying in the civil war."

Kasper's curiosity pushed him further, "I assume you are not a refugee yourself. You appear to be far better off than most we see."

The waiter came to Abadi's table and asked if he'd like something to drink. Abadi dismissively waved him away and turned his chair to face Kasper.

"We are all refugees. Refugees who have lost their God, Allah, and who must make a choice to profess our faith and return or die trying."

Abadi stood, yelled "Glory to Allah," and pressed the button on the detonator he held in his hand.

The ensuing explosion instantly killed dozens, while the sarin began to take its deadly effect on scores more. The Raymonds and Kaspers, along with Abadi, were virtually vaporized, parts of their bodies more than fifty feet away from their table. Dozens of others were wounded, many severely. Many more would later die.

Janković added the incident to the social media stream. More video.

RIO DE JANEIRO, BRAZIL

Copacabana Beach, a popular haunt for locals and tourists alike, was crowded, as it was every day. The shops along Av. Vieira Souto were bustling with people enjoying the afternoon. Couples arm in arm gawked at the half-naked bathers on the beach.

Target-rich.

Hanifa Almasi, whose first name meant "true believer" in Arabic, turned her van onto Av. Vieira Souto.

As she gunned the engine, Hanifa thought of al-Badri and the many nights they had spent together. She thought of the love she had for him and his cause. Most of all, she thought of her love for Allah and hatred for infidels. While she had no bomb, or any weapon for that matter, the van was all she needed.

She ran over one pedestrian after another, sending bodies into the air as if they were twigs tossed in the wind. Within minutes, dozens were dead as she sped down the road and drove off into the distance. Caught an hour later, she was shot dead by a local police officer, but not before uttering her last words: "For the glory of Allah."

More grist for social media. More video for *YouTube*.

As other terrorist attacks occurred in at Pomeranian Dukes Castle in Szczecin, Poland, the Mannerheimintie in Helsinki, Finland, and the Dongdaemun Design Plaza in Seoul, South Korea, some using weapons, explosives, and gases supplied by Lamont and others not, Facebook and Peephole were overwhelmed with posts. Instagram, YouTube, and Images were inundated with gruesome photographs and videos, most pre-orchestrated by Janković. Twitter crashed as people around the world were tweeting in confusion and fear. The panic Janković planned was working like a charm.

FORTY-THREE

WASHINGTON, D.C.
AUGUST 14

"PLEASE ANSWER MY CALL," TAFT SAID AS SHE USED THE SECURE PHONE HARRIS GAVE HER, disobeying his instructions. But since he had called her earlier in response to a text, the memory had his number. She had to leave a voicemail.

In what seemed to Taft like an eternity, Richard Harris finally called back.

"Are you seeing this?" Taft asked Harris. "Terrorist attacks are happening all over the world. That can't be a coincidence."

"We know, Rebecca. We're trying to get a hold on this. I told you not to call us again. Someone probably has the number."

"But I don't understand," she replied. "I want to know what you're doing about it."

"Then come down to the FBI. Just don't tell anyone you're doing so. I'll have you cleared at reception."

Harris hung up.

FORTY-FOUR

SANTIAGO, CHILE
AUGUST 14

SANTIAGO DE CHILE AIRPORT

Avianca flight number 115 was on autopilot, approaching the Santiago de Chile airport for its scheduled 3:31 arrival. With 121 passengers flying in from Bogota, Colombia, the plane was nearly full.

Assad Antar, Mohammed Shadid, and Layal Moghadam were ready. Shadid and Moghadam were in row 10, each in an aisle seat. Antar was in row 22 in his own aisle seat.

In the final approach, minutes from landing and while all the passengers and flight attendants were dutifully strapped in their seats, Shadid and Moghadam stormed the cockpit. The plastic guns supplied by Phillippe Lamont were easily smuggled aboard at Bogota's El Dorado International Airport, where security was as third rate as the third world country Colombia had become.

First shooting two flight attendants, they peppered the cockpit door with more shots, managing to get it open as the pilot desperately tried to radio ahead that they were under attack, taking the plane off autopilot and turning away from the airport. Moghadam, another woman who, like Hanifa Almasi, lived to do al-Badri's bidding, shot the pilot in his head, killing him instantly.

Shadid made sure the same fate befell the co-pilot as the plane began to dive.

Antar, now running down the aisle, made his way to the front of the plane, randomly shooting passengers along the way, creating sheer panic. No one knew what to do, petrified for their lives.

Shadid tore the dead pilot out of his seat and took over the controls. Like the terrorists of 9/11, who had received flight training in the United States. As hard as Homeland Security tried, it was never able to identify every would-be terrorist trained in the United States. So it took Shadid less than a minute to regain control. His flight instructors and hours in a simulator had prepared him well.

Once Antar made it to the front of the plane, he stood guard, shooting two more passengers as they tried to rush him. By then, all four of the flight attendants sitting in the front of the plane were dead, still strapped into their seats.

Shadid grabbed the headphones as he called to the tower, "Praise be to Allah" and aimed the Airbus A300 at the main terminal, remembering the visits he had made to the building weeks before as they planned the attack.

The conflagration shook the ground as though there was an earthquake, and hundreds perished.

Rich in targets, and more posts and prearranged videos by Janković.

FORTY-FIVE

WASHINGTON, D.C.
AUGUST 14

HARRIS, THOMPSON, GRANT, AND THEIR TEAMS WERE ASSEMBLED IN A SITUATION ROOM AT FBI headquarters. To an outside observer, it would have resembled a family argument at Thanksgiving, everyone speaking over one another, pointing at maps and graphs. They all seemed clueless and on the edge of desperation.

Taft raised her hand and called out to Harris.

"Rebecca, please don't interrupt," responded Harris. "We have enough on our hands."

"I know, but I'm getting more odd text messages on my phone."

"What kinds of texts?"

"Locations. Cities and places."

"Show me."

Harris took the phone from Taft. On the screen, a message read *The Recoleta Cemetery, Argentina. The Capital Center for the Arts, Concord, New Hampshire. The Umayyad Mosque, Syria.*

"I don't understand what they mean," observed Taft.

"Who are they from?" asked Harris.

"Someone with the handle #russianrevenge," responded Taft.

"Russian revenge?" asked Thompson.

"Yes, just like Lori Torchia warned us," replied Taft.

"Read me those locations, Rebecca," demanded Harris.

Harris wrote them down and ordered Dave Connelly, one of his aides, to immediately contact authorities at each location and tell them they were about to be attacked.

FORTY-SIX

BUENOS AIRES, CONCORD, AND DAMASCUS
AUGUST 14

RECOLETA CEMETERY, BUENOS AIRES, ARGENTINA

The warning was too late for the twenty murdered at the Recoleta Cemetery, where the remains of Eva Perón attracts thousands of curiosity seekers every year. While guards were able to subdue the terrorist before he killed more, his praise to Allah rang clear to all who were witnesses. A worthy disciple of al-Badri.

CAPITAL CENTER FOR THE ARTS, CONCORD, NEW HAMPSHIRE

The roadies on the crew for that night's appearance of country star Roy Peters, the latest winner of *The Voice*, were busy setting up the stage and checking the acoustics at the Capital Center for the Arts in Concord, New Hampshire, a sleepy, bucolic New England town where crime was petty, and people were trusting.

When Chief of Police John DePalma got the call from Connelly that Concord was a target for a radical Islamic attack, DePalma immediately relayed the information to three squad cars and dispatched them to the center. He then called the center's director to evacuate the building. The director complied, and by the time the first squad car arrived, a crowd of people had assembled in front of the center, joined by the curious passing by.

On arriving, thirty-year veteran Detective Mike Santangelo took notice of the crowd of more than thirty and was immediately concerned. If there were suspects in the crowd, they would be hard to spot. Worse, thought Santangelo, they could use any one of the innocent people as a hostage and human bulletproof vest.

Racial profiling ran through Santangelo's mind. New Hampshire, let alone Concord, is not an ethnically diverse place. In the sixties and seventies, the state was a bastion of Republican conservatives led by William Loeb, publisher of the right-wing *Manchester Union Leader*, and Governor Meldrim Thomson, a man whose racial prejudice was rarely subdued. While an occasional Democrat got into office, much of the state was clearly bright red and not overly hospitable to anyone who did not look like a descendant from the Mayflower. Much of that prejudice had been lost over the years as the state elected Democrats as often as Republicans, but some folks in Concord still held the older views.

Santangelo had been trained not to fall prey to local prejudice. But no one denied that as politically unpopular as racial profiling might be, it was a tool police often used to identify suspects. Particularly when ethnicity might be a distinguishing difference from those around them and a motivation for a crime.

As Santangelo walked toward the crowd, he kept scanning the people. He was immediately able to eliminate most of those gathered because he knew or recognized them. That was an advantage for police in small towns.

"Everyone freeze right where you are!" Santangelo ordered in a loud, commanding voice. He needed to get the attention of the crowd and gauge their reaction, possibly identifying a suspect by their movement. While Santangelo worried that a response might be to grab a hostage, that was a risk he chose to take.

"All of you, down on the ground! Now!" Santangelo was trying to keep the eyes of everyone in the crowd on him, watching to see if anyone looked away or at someone else.

The crowd began to obey.

Good, thought Santangelo, *if they all get down, we can control the situation. If any of them don't get down, then they're our likely suspects and an easier target with everyone else on the ground.*

As Santangelo drew closer, he noticed a furtive reaction from a dark-skinned man who was slow in getting down. Suspect number one for Santangelo.

The suspect's expression struck Santangelo as if he were looking for someone else to tell him what to do. Following where the suspect was looking, Santangelo caught the eye of a second man about ten feet away. Suspect two for Santangelo. The connection between the two suspects was clear.

As he raised his pistol, a Sig Sauer P320, the weapon local police adopted as their service weapon in 2017, Santangelo could feel his pulse beating on his temples. In his thirty years on the force, he had never fired his weapon except at the firing range. Something told him this day might put an end to that streak.

His partner, rookie Barbara Kolesaire, was immediately behind him, her P320 in hand. Chief DePalma sent her out with Santangelo that morning, hoping she would learn a thing or two from the veteran.

What ensued happened in seconds. Santangelo and Kolesaire were no more than fifteen feet from the crowd when Santangelo thought he saw a gun in suspect two's hands. As the man began to turn his head toward Santangelo, Santangelo opened fire, instantly taking the man down with one bullet in the side of the suspect's head and the other in his chest.

"Stay down," Santangelo screamed as some in the crowd started to rise in panic. They obeyed.

The other man, the one who seemed to want instructions, stood, put his hand in a pocket and began to take something out. Kolesaire, as if on cue, wasted no time shooting him, emptying four rounds from her P320 into the chest of the suspect. He fell like a rock, dead before he hit the ground or his hand left his pocket.

"No one move. Not an inch." Santangelo ordered. No one moved.

With two men now lying dead, some in the crowd were weeping while others were craning their necks to get a peek at what happened. Nothing attracted attention like bloodied corpses.

"Kolesaire, keep an eye on the crowd," ordered Santangelo.

Santangelo approached the man he shot, asking those around him to move away. Slowly. They complied but kept their eyes on Santangelo.

Upon inspecting the corpse, Santangelo confirmed that the man he shot held a Heckler & Koch 9 millimeter luger. Santangelo immediately recognized the German-made pistol and knew that its ten-round capacity magazine, along with the extra ones he was sure he would find in the suspect's pockets, held more than enough bullets to put down dozens. He was surprised to see such an expensive weapon in the hands of a terrorist and mentally noted he'd have to include that in his report.

"Kolesaire, start moving the people to the street," ordered Santangelo.

"Everyone, please get up slowly and come toward me. Put your hands in the air as you walk," instructed Kolesaire.

Requiring everyone to put their hands in the air was protocol to reduce the chance of someone among them drawing a weapon and engaging an officer. Or worse, moving their arms in a fashion that alarmed an officer and caused them to shoot. Everyone remained a suspect until proven otherwise. Kolesaire remembered that basic training well.

Santangelo moved to the other body. While the man had held no weapon, a grenade lay beside his body. Santangelo found three more in his jacket pockets. Nice toys from Lamont. The one beside the suspect's body still had its pin in it. Kolesaire's shot had made sure he did not have time to pull it. Her decisive action saved dozens of people.

While not an expert in grenades, Santangelo had seen enough in his career to be familiar with them. He thought the ones with the suspect were unusual. He was right.

On later inspection, the grenades were identified as ET-MPs (Enhanced Tactical Multi-Purpose grenades) developed by the U.S. Army in 2016. No bigger than a tennis ball, the grenade fit in the palm of a hand and could be thrown easily. The breakthrough in design over grenades used since World War I was the lever on top of the grenade that could be flipped, turning the bomb into either a concussion grenade or a fragmentation grenade. A concussion grenade kills merely by its blast. The concussion setting is used when a soldier cannot get to cover before using the weapon. In concussion mode, the kill radius is relatively small and the weapon can be used in a more tactical environment where the soldier can throw it far enough away that he is not in danger. In contrast, when a fragmentation grenade is detonated, it sends ball bearings in all directions and has a kill zone of nearly fifty feet in diameter. So a solder can only safely use it when he has cover. The ET-MP gave a user the choice and made it the most lethal grenade in the world. Lamont was believed to be one of only a few arms dealers who had access to them. How he got them was one of the most sought-after answers the CIA wanted to have and was why Lamont was so dangerous.

Of course, surveillance cameras at the center recorded it all by CCTV cameras that were easily hacked by Janković. She made sure it was posted on social media for all to see. It took seconds for the footage to go viral, inciting more fear and panic.

UMAYYAD MOSQUE, DAMASCUS, SYRIA

One of the most sacred sites in the Islamic world, the Umayyad Mosque had been mostly razed by al-Badri and his ISIS compatriots in an earlier scorched-earth campaign to establish a new Caliphate for his Muslim way of life. Yet despite the rubble that lay around the mosque, devout, peaceful worshipers continued to pray there. For them, the grounds remained sacred.

In the aftermath of a bitter civil war, despot Bashar al-Assad had no patience for any further rebellion from any sect of the Muslim world. Ruthless in his cleansing of Syria, with support from Russia and the indirect help of the United States, ISIS and other opponents to his rule were crushed while he stayed in power. Throughout the civil war, al-Assad claimed that his defense of Syria was against radical Islamists. Yet many charged him with far greater atrocities than committed by ISIS, Jabhat al-Nusra, and other elements in opposition to his rule. While he publicly deplored the destruction ISIS left behind, in private he had no remorse. As far as al-Assad was concerned, any opposition to his rule was better off dead. Few appreciated how he let surrogates in the United States and Russia fund the fight against ISIS while he lay in the wings watching and consolidating his power.

When the war ended with more bloodshed than anyone could possibly imagine, the United States eventually withdrew and turned its attention to Iran, now rumored to be back in the business of building nuclear bombs despite promises to the contrary. With forces in Iraq, the United States felt it could leave Syria.

Diplomatic relations between Syria and Washington remained severed and Harris had no sympathy for the plight of Syria or al-Assad. When Connelly asked Harris who to call in Syria, Harris sarcastically suggested Connelly call the Kremlin. Understanding sarcasm and how Harris held no sympathy for Syria or its plight, Connelly never made a call.

For lack of a warning that should have come, fifty-eight devout Muslims praying at the ruins of the Umayyad Mosque were gunned down by al-Badri's henchmen. The carnage at the mosque could have been prevented. But no one who could have stopped it cared to make a simple phone call.

FORTY-SEVEN

PORTLAND, OREGON
AUGUST 14

JANKOVIĆ WAS PARTICULARLY FASCINATED WITH THE PREPPERS, A GROWING MOVEMENT OF conservative thinkers who believe that the United States government, as they know it, is about to collapse. To survive the coming apocalypse, preppers became entirely self-sufficient and went off the grid. Or so they thought. In today's world, few self-described survivalists are willing to entirely disconnect from the world. They continue to keep their mobile phones close by. The excuse they use is that the phones are needed to warn fellow preppers when the end arrives. In reality, particularly among the younger preppers, the phones are used for texting, games, and following right-wing news, most of which is fake but is what they want to hear and read. And much of that fake news is planted by Janković and her programmers.

The preppers movement, despite often being filled with conservative alt-right thinkers, rejected the neo-Nazi thinking of the skinheads in Portland, Oregon, and elsewhere in the Northwestern United States. Although preppers were not as readily prone to violence as skinheads, Janković believed that preppers offered a rich environment of disillusioned people ready to be influenced not by the truth but by radical change and ideas. A prepper's decision to resort to violence was not to attack the establishment, as would a skinhead, but to defend against those who would attack them when the government collapses. Janković had come to learn that while it's possible to program anyone over time, the most natural prey for her were people who embraced violence as a means to preserve what they considered their God-given freedoms when anarchy arrives. On the other hand, skinheads embraced anarchy as a solution, not a threat. Oregon was filled with preppers and skinheads. A volatile combination. The preppers just needed some gentle persuasion to go from talk to action.

Janković called in Dorda to watch her next move, one she was particularly proud to share.

"Tad, come see this," Janković said with a big smile.

"Now what, Paula? Another highlight reel?" responded Dorda.

Dorda had come to love watching clips and photos on Janković's computer screen while she wreaked havoc. Since Janković seemed to have no limits on the atrocities she was willing to unleash for her personal entertainment, Dorda was happy to watch every train wreck she offered.

"No, Tad. This one's live. In the skinhead capital of America. Portland, Oregon."

"Portland? I always thought it was a very liberal city. Since when was it known for skinheads?" asked Dorda.

"It always has been, Tad. It's just that the liberal media doesn't like to highlight it. They prefer to report on left-wing causes and largely ignore the far more volatile right-wingers. They do so at their peril. There is nothing like unleashing a paranoid conservative on a naïve liberal. It's no contest."

"And that is what you're going to do now, Paula?"

"Exactly. And this time, we'll watch it live."

Dorda pulled up a chair as Janković feverishly typed on her keyboard as the six numbered screens on the wall came to life with clear live feeds from CCTV cameras in Portland, all now controlled by Janković. His only wish was that he had some popcorn to enjoy while he watched the show.

"Last night, there was a brief altercation between a group of skinheads and preppers," started Janković.

"You've told me about the preppers, Paula. And let me guess, you orchestrated the altercation," responded Dorda.

"Not directly. I've been planting dissension between the two groups for months. It's been a lot of fun. The two are like the Hatfields and McCoys, the legendary feud between a couple of backward hillbilly families in West Virginia and Kentucky. Real short on brains and quick on brawn. Macho shit all the way."

"But you were involved indirectly?" asked Dorda.

"Tad, that's the beauty of what we're doing. We create hatred and tension where it lay suppressed for generations. Suggestion by suggestion, we bring back extremist thinking and behavior. At some point, it reaches a flashpoint. All we've done is set that evolution in motion. To keep it interesting, we occasionally add some gas to the fire."

"And you're adding gas now?"

"Look at the screen two," directed Janković.

"OK, but I see nothing."

"Wait. See the crowds on screens four and five?"

"Yeah. What am I looking at?"

"Did you ever watch *West Side Story*, Tad?"

"Sure. The Sharks and the Jets. Is that what I'm seeing?"

"Better. On screen four, you're watching very angry preppers who believe, thanks to some social media placements and texts, that the skinheads are about to attack their enclave outside Portland. On screen five is an armed group of skinheads who believe the preppers are arming against them and planning their own attack once the government falls. Of course, none of that is true, but the two groups sure believe it is. I saw to that. Soon they'll meet on screen two, and all hell will break loose."

"Why would they attack one another, Paula? I'm not sure I understand why the two groups would be so opposed to one another. Both are anti-government and want to bring down the establishment. So what's the problem between them?"

"It's the same problem you saw in *West Side Story*, Tad. It's about who will be in control at the end of the day. The Sharks or the Jets. And these idiots know of only one way to resolve it. Violence."

"OK, but I don't see how this advances Petrenko's agenda. We're supposed to be orchestrating terrorist attacks, not skirmishes between anarchists and survivalists."

"That's where you're missing the point of the game, Tad. Once the shooting starts, the police will quickly arrive, and the violence will turn against them. The Sharks and Jets will unite against a common enemy— law and order. And that, Tad, is as much a terrorist moment as anything orchestrated by al-Badri. He has to kill his supporters to achieve his goal. We simply manipulate a few expendable people here and there and let the terror unfold. We're far more efficient and decidedly cheaper than al-Badri. Our weapon of mass destruction is a mouse and keyboard, Tad. And no one can stop us."

As Tad continued to watch, Janković's prediction came to life. First there was shouting, then some pushing and the first gunshot. It had already turned into a shoot-out when the police arrived. As if orchestrated in a script, the attempted intervention by the police only served to unite the otherwise feuding sides, just as Janković predicted. When tear gas was unleashed against the crowd, it triggered a bloodlust for revenge and didn't slow down a single prepper or skinhead. Tad watched with morbid fascination as dozens were killed and chaos reigned. When it was over, the police had won, but at the expense of six lives from their ranks. That was a small loss, however, compared to the scene in the street as dozens of misguided dupes in Janković's game lay dead and bleeding. In the end, forty-seven people died. Portland would soon be in a shutdown, every citizen afraid to venture out of their homes.

"Be sure to send the video to Petrenko. He'll enjoy it," instructed Dorda.

"I don't need to send him anything, Tad. It's already posted on Facebook, Google, Peephole, Images, and Instagram. It won't take long for it to be pulled down, but by then thousands will have downloaded it, and many more millions will have seen it. In no time, it will be reposted by someone. All the poor souls will be scared to death and run to put whatever money they have under their mattresses," Janković said, laughing.

FORTY-EIGHT

WASHINGTON, D.C.
AUGUST 14

FBI HEADQUARTERS REMAINED IN A FRENZY WITH NO IDEA WHAT MIGHT COME NEXT.

Three more messages arrived on Taft's phone.

Wellington Cable Car, Wellington, New Zealand. Museum of Islamic Art, Doha, Qatar. Fraunces Tavern, New York City.

Harris had Connelly sent word to local authorities.

But Janković knew none of those locations would be attacked. No terrorists would be found. That did not stop Janković from posting photographs of dead bodies strewn in each location. Photoshop at its best. For Janković, even fake news was an effective weapon. Panic did not always need real dead bodies. Once the spreading panic began, any story, true or not, contributed to the chaos.

By 3:00 that afternoon, news outlets and social media reported a global terrorist conspiracy hitting dozens of locations worldwide.

Exactly as Janković had planned.

FORTY-NINE

PARIS, TOKYO, AND MANCHESTER
AUGUST 14

BUDDHA BAR, PARIS, FRANCE

Another text message to Taft. *Buddha Bar, Paris.*

Connelly called, but his warning was too late for patrons of the popular Paris nightspot no more than 100 yards from the United States Embassy. Just off Rue Saint-Honore, the Paris version of Beverly Hills' Rodeo Drive, security was as tight as it could get. No vehicle could approach the bar without getting through virtually impenetrable barriers guarded by the armed gendarmerie. No one believed any terrorist would dare try to target the location, even for the glory of Allah.

They were wrong. Despite the rising alt-right movement in France and growing discontent with a liberal immigration policy that allowed radical Islamic supporters to run free in Paris streets, attacks continued. On this day, twenty-one people died in the Buddha Bar before the terrorists were subdued.

More to post on social media.

The irony that the bar was directly across the street from the Sofitel Paris le Faubourg hotel where Cooper made Petrenko's deal with Lamont was not lost on Janković. She was disappointed that al-Badri, and not she, had orchestrated the carnage.

PLAZA OMOTESANDO HARAJUKU, TOKYO, JAPAN

Teeming with pedestrians, the Plaza Omotesando Harajuku was a terrorist's dream. Particularly a terrorist who was a pawn for Janković.

Janković had programmed Aiko Takahashi for nearly two years. An artist, Takahashi was poor. Her art even more so. She sold some, but not enough to earn a living. So she worked at a local McDonald's.

Janković had convinced Takahashi that she was the victim of a conspiracy by wealthy art collectors who were buying her works cheap, waiting for her to die so they could then turn her into a legend and reap profits over her carcass.

So when Janković told her she would find famed collector Hideyo Suzuki at a restaurant off the plaza, Takahashi did not hesitate to plot her revenge. She intended to confront the conspirator, call him out for his crimes, and slit his miserable throat. All according to the plan Janković had planted in Takahashi's Selfish Ledger.

But when Takahashi entered the restaurant where Suzuki was enjoying dinner with his wife and children, she lost her courage. Killing someone in front of children was simply unacceptable to her. While the cowardice disappointed Janković, she knew that not all of her minions would go through with the plans she had for them. It did not matter. The panic Janković was spreading only needed a few to carry out her orders. And she could add to the panic by inventing attacks that never actually occurred, knowing full well that it would take days to reveal the truth. So those who failed to follow orders were inconsequential to the global panic.

This was the beauty of her plan. Janković only needed some of her disciples to carry out their tasks. She could simply lie about the success of those who failed. She could invent others. It did not take much online chatter, grotesque videos, and conspiracy theories to panic millions of people, all of them addicted to their social media feeds. Zombies ready for Janković to slaughter.

"Disappointing," noted Janković, dismissing the failure as an unfortunate misstep in Takahashi's Selfish Ledger. Janković resolved to review the program later.

Takahashi was never found by authorities. After Dorda gave Cooper Takahashi's location, Cooper saw to it that loose ends with Takahashi were addressed as well.

SANFORD QUAYS, MANCHESTER, ENGLAND

Nick Swimer, the Manchester chief of police, took Connelly's warning seriously. Remembering the 2017 carnage at the Manchester Arena bombing during the Ariana Grande concert, he was quick to act. Swimer swore he would never again let an Islamic terrorist detonate a shrapnel-laden homemade bomb like the one used at the arena. He would never again be described as a failure in protecting innocent Brits.

His officers arrived en masse, thirty-strong, accompanied by a SWAT team ready for whatever might happen.

It did not take them long to spot al-Badri's henchman, Jamel Nazari. He was too obvious. Sweating and clearly nervous, he was gunned down well short of accomplishing his mission.

Swimer, now believing himself a hero, was satisfied that he stopped Nazari and saved dozens of lives. For al-Badri, Nazari's death for the glory of Allah was all he needed, and a success. As far as Janković was concerned, al-Badri had failed because his operative was discovered before his sacrifice was complete. Death of a failed terrorist was not something Janković saw as success.

FIFTY

WASHINGTON, D.C.
AUGUST 14

"I CAN'T TELL WHAT'S TRUE AND WHAT ISN'T," REMARKED HARRIS, ANGRY AT HOW FAR they were in the dark. With a hopeless feeling, he had no idea what might happen next.

"There is no pattern," Chandler agreed. "The attacks seem random. And while some are clearly the work of Islamic terrorists, others are not. Some are real. Some are fake. Yet they're all happening today. It cannot be a coincidence," he added. "There has to be a connection."

"It's Russia. It has to be," suggested Taft. "That's what Lori Torchia told us was going to happen."

"Rebecca, we've monitored every communication coming from Russian sources capable of this kind of coordination. We've found nothing. And without a name, we're entirely in the dark. When this nightmare is over, the world may melt down. Investors are already talking about a crash worse than 2008."

"Then do something to settle them down."

"Do what, Rebecca?" replied Harris. "We cannot fight something we cannot see. Someone is pulling strings and weaponizing social media."

"Then shut it down."

Harris responded, shaking his head, "We can't just shut down social media, Rebecca. No one can. It would create even more panic. And even if we did decide to shut down the Internet, we can't be fast enough to stem the panic."

"Richard, have you heard from Rashid?" interjected Grant.

"Who's Rashid?" asked Taft.

"Never mind," replied Harris, angry that Grant would disclose a CI's name to a civilian. "And, no, Oliver, we have not heard from Rashid. But we have eyes on him."

"Why can't I know who Rashid is? Maybe I can help," suggested Taft.

"Rebecca, please. Let us do our job. When we need your help, we'll ask," said Harris.

"What has he told us, Dick?" Grant was relentless and didn't give a damn about what Taft knew or didn't know about Harris's precious CI.

Harris resigned himself to ignore protocol if for no other reason than to shut up Grant as well as Taft.

"We know he's in New York. He arrived last night. Earlier yesterday we got the panic signal from his phone, and then it went dead somewhere on the Atlantic City Expressway. We haven't heard from him since."

Taft's phone vibrated.

Is your iPhone working today?

FIFTY-ONE

FOXCONN, EVER FEARFUL OF DISRUPTION IN ITS SHENZHEN PLANT, CALLED BIANCA FENG TO be sure the facility was secure. They trusted Feng.

"Bianca, is security in place?"

Feng could barely disguise her feelings. The overseers were scared. Just as they should be. Just as Janković programmed Feng to think.

"I don't see any threats," she lied. "No one is outside the plant, and everyone is accounted for. Why are you concerned?" asked Feng with a smile that those on the other end of the call could not see.

"Good. But please double check. Social media is in a meltdown. Terrorist attacks are happening all over the world. We have to assume we could be a target. There are also reports of viruses being launched all over the place. Make sure we are not vulnerable, Bianca. Be certain of it."

"I will," responded Feng, with no intention of checking on anything.

Feng hung up, leaned back in her chair, and continued watching her computer screen.

When the masked face of the infamous hacker group Anonymous appeared with its sinister grin covering her screen, Feng smiled. She knew that all the computers at Foxconn were watching the same image, including the overseers she'd just spoken to on the phone with an assurance that all was in order. She knew all of Foxconn was beginning to feel the kind of panic Feng wanted to inflict. Feng assumed that she'd one day be caught, but that was of no concern to her now. She stopped the killers she worked for. And that was all worth whatever consequences she might next face.

Apple be damned flashed on the screen. Simple but certainly to the point.

In an instant, tens of thousands of chips in the factory were wiped clean and infected with a virus that made them worthless and impossible to program. Ruined. Then, as the virus took control, clean rooms were filled with dust and contaminants, rendering them unusable to produce the sensitive silicon connections needed for new chips.

All over the world, iPhone, iPod, and Mac users were being automatically updated while owners of many of the remaining devices were authorizing manual updates after receiving notice that an important update needed to be programmed immediately to prevent cyber attacks. That update destroyed every device it touched. Petrenko knew that many users, too lazy to review updates before they were installed, had their iPhones, iPads, and computers set to operate automatically as preset times. He also knew that millions more would dutifully follow what appeared to be an important notice from Apple. Like the lemmings they were, people throughout the world did as instructed.

The plant's cooling system then failed. The heat rose quickly, further disabling the plant.

Then the electricity cut out. The cell towers that allowed mobile phones to operate immediately went offline. No one within a hundred miles of Shenzhen could make a call.

Thousands of employees panicked, rushing out of the countless buildings that covered the landscape, trampling whatever lay in their way to escape, including bodies of their fellow workers.

As they ran to exits, the fire control system throughout the facility started raining water and foam fire retardants everywhere, contaminating or destroying everything it touched. It turned the floor into a slippery mess, causing people to fall over one another like rag dolls.

The virus Feng had launched at Janković's command was working perfectly.

It would take months to get Foxconn operations running again.

Feng smiled, only saddened for those who got hurt and her inability to call her overseers to gloat over their misery.

Apple was brought to its knees, a victim of its avarice to build chips in inexpensive, sweatshop-laden Asian plants.

Janković typed on her keyboard, thousands of miles away.

Apple plant destroyed by a super virus. Chips for new phones gone for months. Millions of iPhones now inoperable. Opportunity for Google and its Androids?

Janković could barely wait to see the tech giant's stock go into free fall. And she wanted to ensure the panic, so she kept typing, feeding Facebook, Peephole, and Twitter.

Apple stockholders in a panic. Historical sell-off under way. Too late for Apple to respond.

But Janković was not done with China. Not by a long shot.

FIFTY-TWO

SHANGHAI
AUGUST 14

STATE-OWNED SHANGHAI ELECTRIC GROUP COMPANY LIMITED IS RESPONSIBLE FOR THE power management for millions and essential to China's economy. SEG is the electrical utility that powers the Shanghai Stock Exchange, one of two exchanges operating in China. The other is in Shenzhen, a city already brought to its knees by Feng's virus.

Responsible for a market capitalization of more than $5.5 trillion, SEG is the fifth-largest stock exchange in the world. Without it humming, China's economy could collapse. At the least, going offline for any period of time pushed global markets into a selling panic.

It was child's play for Janković. She no longer needed anyone on the ground. Pak Heir Zhang was redundant, in more ways than Janković knew.

In China's rush to automate its electrical grid, it was entirely dependent on a network of digital terminals that routed traffic and monitored demand. While China installed state-of-the-art protection throughout the Sunway TaihuLight Supercomputer, they missed smaller and far more critical details. In making sure they protected the total system, they failed to watch hacking that opened doors to local grids. They remained vulnerable. That was the key Zhang gave Janković. It was all she needed.

Most security threats are believed to come straight at a server, attempting to break through firewalls with the right passwords. It's how movies like to portray the hacker. But that is an amateur's folly.

Janković found her way into systems through the least suspected entry point. To enter into the Sunway core, she did precisely what she did in 2018, when she hacked into the Trump Casino through a thermostat in an aquarium in the lobby. The thermostat was controlled by the hotel's computer network through an Internet connection, making it a perfect door into a system. Janković quietly withdrew thousands from the casino before the break-in was discovered. And while Janković hadn't taken much, it pleased her that she took it from Donald Trump.

Just like the casino, the Sunway computer control room had Internet-connected thermostats. So in a few simple keystrokes, Janković was in. It took her no time to create a massive, fictional demand in Shanghai, far more than SEG could satisfy, triggering doomsday safeties as if China were under nuclear attack. The programmed defense was to shut down any part of the grid not essential to military and hospital operations. Business assets, including the exchange, were deemed secondary. After all, why would anyone want to trade stocks in a nuclear holocaust?

As the Shanghai Stock Exchange grid obeyed Janković's order, it fell dark and panic heightened. All trading stopped. Worse, the key Zhang gave Janković insured that none of the backup generators at the exchange kicked in. Batteries were quickly drained, and millions of transactions lost to the ether. Millions more were without power and flooding Shanghai's streets in panic, all of which was posted by Janković on YouTube.

FIFTY-THREE

NEW YORK CITY
AUGUST 14

AFTER A NIGHT AT THE KIMBERLY HOTEL ON 50TH STREET, THE FOURSOME AWOKE TO A sunny New York day. Bousaid shared a room with Rashid, checking in as Mr. and Mrs. Robert Phillips. When they had arrived at eleven o'clock the night before, the desk clerk took no notice that the pair looked nothing like someone named "Phillips." Bousaid gave him a credit card and driver's license that matched her fictitious name. The front desk clerk could not have cared less about knowing a guest's true identity. It was nothing new to have people check in with false IDs. There wasn't a hotel in New York City that didn't experience trysts under aliases every now and again.

Bousaid made no advances toward Rashid as they caught some sleep in their room. Rashid didn't expect that she would, but was relieved nonetheless. What concerned him most was his inability to get to a phone or find a way to communicate with Harris. It lay heavy on his conscious that if he could not get to Harris soon, many innocent people would die. He knew he needed to stop Bousaid and her gang before they executed their plan.

"Where is Tahir?" asked Rashid as he and Bousaid met Nejem in the lobby that morning. Rashid had already seen the news of some attacks in Europe with deepening concern that a terrorist Armageddon was beginning.

"He's already in the van," responded Nejem. "He and I prepared it last night while you lovebirds got some sleep," continued Nejem with a smile.

"That will be enough, Kareem," snapped Bousaid.

"My apologies, Adara. A woman of your honor should never be insulted by a heathen like me," responded Nejem with as sarcastic a tone as he could muster. Rashid wondered if he would be freed from trying to stop the attack if the two of them tried to kill one another. It was clear that Nejem did not like taking orders from a woman.

"Just go to the van, Kareem. Wait there. We will be along soon enough. And make sure Zaman doesn't do anything stupid. Go!" ordered Bousaid. Nejem obeyed with a wave of his arm in front of his face while rolling his hand in the traditional gesture of respect among Arabs.

"We have some time, Hashir, and I'm hungry." Bousaid began to make her way to the restaurant. Rashid obediently followed, confused that Bousaid would find time to relax for breakfast when she was about to die. All he wanted to do was find a phone.

After being shown a table, Bousaid ordered oatmeal with a banana and a cup of tea. Rashid ordered coffee.

"So tell me, Hashir, how long have you known Abu?"

"Since training. He and I grew up together in the cause. Why do you ask?"

"You'll know soon enough, Hashir. I just wondered how someone could get so close to Abu. He speaks of you like you are his brother."

"I am his brother. As I am your brother and you are my sister. And Abu's sister."

"Sure, Hashir. But some brothers and sisters are closer to one another than others are. Don't you agree?"

Where is she going with this?

"We are all equal brothers and sisters before Allah, Adara," responded Rashid.

"OK, Hashir, I'll give you that."

Her oatmeal arrived.

"Adara, I have to go to the bathroom. Please excuse me for a couple of minutes. I'll be right back."

"I'd prefer that you didn't leave me just now. I'm sure you can wait a few minutes. You'll have plenty of time to relieve yourself later."

"Very well, Adara, but I really have to go." Rashid feigned discomfort.

Bousaid smiled and silently cut her banana into the oatmeal and added a few scoops of brown sugar. To Rashid, it looked like a disgusting pile of mud. He never did understand the way people ate oatmeal.

As Bousaid mixed her little concoction with a spoon, she asked, "Hashir, are you ready to die for Allah?"

"What kind of question is that, Adara? You know the answer."

"Perhaps, Hashir, but I'd like you to say so. Please indulge me." Bousaid put a spoonful of her mud in her mouth.

Hashir knew he needed to play along. "Yes, Adara, I am prepared to die for Allah. No one doubts that. Why do you insult me with such a question?"

"Forgive me for doubting you, Hashir. I just wanted to know since today is not the day you are to die for the glory of Allah."

"What are you talking about, Adara? That is why we are all here. To finish a job we were given by Abu. No one is to question his orders."

"Exactly, Hashir." She reached into her handbag and gave Rashid an envelope.

"Open it, Hashir. It is from Abu. And since you've been brothers for so long, you'll recognize his handwriting."

Rashid opened the envelope and read the letter.

Hashir, my brother, I know you want revenge for Florence so many years ago. We all want revenge. But I need you beside me, not a martyr in the glory of Allah. Not yet. Our sister Adara and brothers Kareem and Tahir will teach a lesson today. You will come home to fight another time. I await you with thankful arms. Abu.

"I don't understand. Why?" asked Rashid.

"I don't know either, Hashir. But as you said, we do not question Abu's orders." She took another spoonful of oatmeal and gently dabbed her mouth.

"I'll let you pick up the check, Hashir. Like I said, you'd have plenty of time to relieve your bladder. May the glory of Allah be with you."

Bousaid rose and calmly walked out of the restaurant.

Rashid was now on the edge of panic. He knew their target was just blocks away but did not know where the van was waiting for Bousaid to arrive. He had no idea when they were going to strike.

As he rose from his chair to find a phone, the waiter stopped him.

"I'm sorry sir, but do you want to charge breakfast to your room?"

Rashid was in no mood for delay.

"Yes." He continued to walk away. The waiter stopped him again.

"My apologies again, sir. Can you give me the name and room number, please?"

Name and room number! I have no idea what name Bousaid used. And I am running out of time.

"Never mind. I'll pay cash. How much?"

"I'll get the check."

Rashid took out his wallet and gave the waiter a $100 bill.

"This should cover it. I'm sorry, but I'm in a hurry." He turned and rushed away, barely hearing the profuse thank-you from the waiter.

FIFTY-FOUR

WASHINGTON, DC
AUGUST 14

HARRIS IMMEDIATELY TOOK THE CALL. THE CALLER ID READ "KIMBERLY." HARRIS HAD NO idea who Kimberly was, assuming it was someone's name and not the name of the hotel where Rashid was waiting.

"Hashir, where are you?"

"There's no time to worry about that, Harris. The target is the Citicorp building on Lexington in New York. They have a van that I assume is loaded with explosives."

"Who has a van, Hashir? How many are there?"

"What the hell difference does that make, Harris?" Rashid was frustrated and desperate, inclined to hang up and run the four blocks and personally stop them. There would undoubtedly be some police in the area.

"OK, Hashir, calm down. You're right, now is not the time. It's just that we've been dealing with one crisis after another here and my head is spinning. I'm sorry."

That calmed Rashid down, but he knew little time remained.

"Call whoever you can, Harris. I'll get there in a few minutes and see if I can help."

"No, Hashir, we can't afford to lose you. You are the only person we have left who might lead us to the people behind all of this. We can mobilize more than enough police to stop them or at least keep casualties to a minimum."

As he spoke to Rashid, Harris wrote on a piece of paper.

Van. Citicorp Building. New York. Bomb.

He handed it to Connelly.

Casualties to a minimum! thought Rashid.

"Hashir, describe the van."

"Blue. Darkened window. Three people. Two men and a woman. Adara Bousaid, Kareem Nejem, and Tahir Zaman."

"OK. Stay where you are, Hashir. I'll keep this line open. Don't hang up."

Rashid could hear the phone hit the table as Harris put it down. He could only listen as Harris barked orders. It sounded as though there was sheer chaos on the other end of the line, everyone shouting over one another.

What kind of a command center does Harris run? wondered Rashid.

FIFTY-FIVE

NEW YORK
AUGUST 14

MARTY PFEIFFER, CHIEF OF THE NYPD COUNTERTERRORISM BUREAU AND ITS CRITICAL Response Command, headed an elite squad ready to respond to terrorist and active-shooter attacks.

When he received the warning about Fraunces Tavern, he sent three of his elite units to the scene. As soon as they reported that there was nothing to be found and no active threat, Pfeiffer knew it was a diversion. If there was going to be an attack, it would be somewhere else in the city, not near the tavern. His training taught Pfeiffer to predict the patterns of deceit and tactics used by terrorists to move attention away from their targets through ruses like the threat at the tavern.

"Bill, move your units north. If there's going to be a strike it will be uptown," Pfeiffer ordered. Bill Duggan, one of Pfeiffer's commanders, relayed the order to the three teams he led to the tavern. They proceeded up Broadway.

"Marty, where are we going?" Duggan radioed back to Pfeiffer.

"I don't know yet, Bill. All I know is whatever might happen, it will not be downtown. Just start going north. When you get to 23rd Street, split up. You stay on Broadway and send the other two units to 6th and 3rd Avenues. I'll let you know the targets as soon as I can."

Pfeiffer mobilized seven other units to position themselves between a grid from 42nd Street and 68th Street to the south and north and First and Ninth Avenue to the east and west. He called Connelly to report.

"Mr. Connelly, I have units moving north now," Pfeiffer told him.

"Why? Your units should all go to the Citicorp Center. That's where the attack is happening," responded Connolly with a tone of growing panic. Connelly, like everyone at the FBI situation room, was frustrated and short on nerves.

"Mr. Connelly, I've been at this a long time. I'll have a unit at Citicorp in minutes before I hang up this phone. This is New York City, Mr. Connelly, not Washington. We know what we're doing here. The warning about Fraunces Tavern was a diversion intended to get our assets out of the way. So no attack will be near there. And we—and you—have no reason to believe Citicorp is the only target. So I need units dispersed around the city. Let me do my job, Mr. Connelly."

Pfeiffer hung up the phone.

Tahir Zaman turned left off Third Avenue onto 55th Street as Bousaid and Nejem prepared the detonators.

"Harris, have you told the police?" screamed Rashid in the phone. All he could hear was orders being yelled.

Zaman turned left onto Lexington Avenue, two blocks from the Citicorp Building. He stopped behind a car at the red light at 54th Street, looking directly at his target.

In front of the building, he saw an NYPD van pull up and about a half-dozen police officers in riot gear exit onto the street and down the stairs into the building. As the terrorists' vehicle sat at the light, another NYPD van pulled up. Pfeiffer had decided to send backup after Connolly's hysteria.

"Adara, we have a problem!"

"What?" Bousaid made her way to the front of the van for her own look.

"What should I do, Adara? The police are in the way. I can't get the van into the courtyard."

The light changed.

"Drive into the building to the south on the left side. If we can't take down the Citicorp building, the one next door will have to do."

Zaman gunned the engine.

The Critical Response team, trained to spot unusual movement, immediately saw the threat and opened fire. But it was too late.

Zaman drove the van into 599 Lexington Avenue, an easy target with virtually no external protection except a few three-foot-high stanchions intended to thwart an attack. They did little good, particularly for the dozens of commuters entering and leaving the corner's subway station stairway, which sat outside the protection of the stanchions. It also didn't help that the building was designed with an overhang into the courtyard in front of the lobby entrance. While the overhang was a nice design, it also made the building more vulnerable to collapse with the right explosive.

Zaman's van was laden with Semtex, a favorite of terrorists. It was primarily used in commercial blasting and demolition, and was the same explosive that downed Pan American Flight 103 on December 21, 1988. Known as the Lockerbie bombing, that attack killed 243 passengers and 16 crew. Semtex was generally available on the market, relatively inexpensive, and easy for Lamont to source. He had to be careful not to raise eyebrows with the volume his shell company was buying, but there were countless construction projects in New York City to provide him the cover he needed.

With more than 200 pounds of Semtex in Zaman's van, it made Lockerbie child's play.

When the explosion occurred, much of the impact was felt above the blast zone, and the windows on the entire side of the building shattered. Nearly forty stories of glass and metal of the building's front façade came cascading down on scores of people walking in front of the building. While the collapse was not nearly as dramatic as that of the Twin Towers on 9/11, the casualties were in the hundreds.

Rashid didn't just hear the explosion. Only three blocks away, he felt it as the windows of the buildings around him shook and many shattered. The rancid odors of death and destruction consumed the area.

PHASE FOUR

CLEARING THE FIELD

FIFTY-SIX

ST. PETERSBURG, RUSSIA

FOR PETRENKO, AUGUST WAS A MARVELOUS MONTH. AUGUST 14 PRECIPITATED THE PANIC HE planned. The markets were in chaos. Tech stocks were in the cellar. Within days, Apple was trading at half the market price it had on August 13. And it kept falling. Without a supply of any chips and its millions of phones inoperable, Apple's customer base shifted to Google and its Android operating system devices. By August 25, trading in Apple stock was suspended. Petrenko's short on Apple and options on Samsung reaped millions. But his profits on the CDSs and CDOs exceeded even his wildest dreams. In all, he made billions in just two weeks. The fools who took the wrong side of Petrenko's bets lay in ruins. Goldman Sachs. Deutsche Bank. Bank of America. AIG. Their greed got the best of them. IRAs, pension plans, institutional and individual investors fell bankrupt. The government intervened on the Tuesday after Labor Day and suspended trading on the stock exchanges. But it was too little, too late. And to al-Badri's glee, thousands of infidels lay dead in the streets, with many more to come as September 11 loomed on the horizon.

Petrenko, sitting in a leather chair in front of his fireplace, poured himself a Macallan, his usual brand. But this time it wasn't just any Macallan.

The Macallan Valerio Adami was one of twelve bottled in 1926 and auctioned in 2018. The bidder paid $1.1 million for the bottle, a record for one of the rarities. The unnamed collector was rumored to be from Asia and participated in the auction by phone. In truth, the bidder was a shill for Petrenko.

Petrenko also eschewed his usual cigar and opted for one of his rare sikars. Sikars (not cigars) were made by Mayans in the twelfth century and discovered by Christopher Columbus in the fifteenth century, crediting him for bringing tobacco to Europe. In 2012, a collection of Mayan sikars was discovered in Guatemala. They were in perfect condition and were considered the oldest in the world. Petrenko bought them at auction for over half a million dollars. Any regular collector would have never lit one up. But today was special, and the cost of smoking one from the collection was a mere drop in the bucket for Petrenko, now the wealthiest man in the world.

It was time to celebrate.

As Petrenko was thoroughly enjoying the moment, Cooper arrived as ordered, and was escorted by the butler to a bright red leather chair beside Petrenko.

"Will you have anything to drink, Mr. Cooper?" asked Petrenko's butler.

"Chopin on the rocks please."

"My, my, Mr. Cooper," interjected Petrenko. "You come to Russia, and you drink Polish vodka?"

"Constantine, *you* don't even drink Russian vodka."

"True. So would you like a cigar? I can offer you your favorite, a Padron 1964 number 4. I'd offer you what I'm smoking, but you'll never earn that privilege," Petrenko said with the usual sarcastic tone Cooper had come to expect. Petrenko had no intention of offering any of his Macallan either.

"I'll pass. I'm trying to cut back."

In truth, Cooper wanted to spend as little time as he could with Petrenko. Smoking a cigar would mean he'd be stuck with him for more than an hour.

"Very well," responded Petrenko as he took another drag on his sikar and a sip of the Macallan. "Mr. Cooper, I think it's time to celebrate. Wouldn't you agree?" asked Petrenko.

"Celebrate?" Cooper responded with surprise. "Constantine, we still have loose ends. I hardly think now is the time to celebrate."

"And what would those loose ends be, Mr. Cooper?"

"What are we going to do about the reporter, Rebecca Taft, and her editor? Or agents Harris and Thompson?"

"We'll deal with them in due time, Mr. Cooper. But they've been very useful to us in chasing ghosts and missing what we are doing. So they're still valuable alive."

"But sooner or later, Constantine, they'll figure it out. They are not stupid. We're less than three weeks away from the final move."

"No, they're not stupid. And when they wake up on September 12, it will be too late. That will be a wonderful moment, Mr. Cooper. What I wouldn't give to be a fly on the wall when they face reality!"

"Why take that risk, Constantine? Why not eliminate them now?"

"Eliminate them? No. No. We'll do that in due time after the 11th, Mr. Cooper. But not before they understand the failure of what they've done. I want them to suffer defeat. I want them to feel the pain."

"As you wish," responded Cooper, once again taken aback by Petrenko's vengeful nature, something Cooper believed would one day be Petrenko's doom.

"And while you're making a list of loose ends, Mr. Cooper, add Paula Janković, Tad's lackey. What she did to Michelangelo's Crouching Boy is inexcusable."

"But who will replace her? Isn't she critical to operating the Selfish Ledger?"

"I'm sure Tad has a backup, Mr. Cooper. Just take care of her a week or two after September 11. That should give us plenty of time to enjoy our victory." Cooper wondered when he would be a loose end as well.

"And Mr. Cooper, let's plan a little get-together. I think it is time for some of our friends to finally meet me. And I would like to meet them, too. Get al-Badri and his right-hand guy up here so we can all enjoy some fine wine and think ahead about September 11. I'll bet even devout Muslims like al-Badri occasionally have a drink to celebrate dead infidels!" laughed Petrenko.

"I think this idea is a very bad one, Constantine, but if it's a party you want, then it's a party you'll get. Is there anyone else you'd like me to invite?"

"Yes, invite Dorda and Janković, too."

The butler brought Cooper his Chopin.

"Janković? I thought you wanted me to eliminate her. Why bring her to a party?"

"Because I always find it enjoyable to spend some time with a doomed person, particularly a woman who makes the mistake to cross me. I'll have some fun. I understand she's quite good looking."

Cooper decided to try one more time to bring Petrenko back to reason.

"Constantine, do you really think that's a smart idea? You have always depended upon me to keep your identity a secret. It keeps you outside the spotlight. The fewer people who know you, the better."

"Yes, Mr. Cooper, you have done just that. In a very expert way. I appreciate it. And you will continue in that role for as long as you wish to. Please allow me this one indulgence. This one time. I really want to celebrate."

Cooper wasn't ready to give up.

"Then why not wait until after September 11? We can't afford leaks or mistakes before then."

"You worry too much. As long as you clean up the loose ends we talked about, there will be no leaks or mistakes."

"Very well," Cooper responded.

"Oh, and Mr. Cooper, I want you there, too. You're part of the celebration."

So, Petrenko, I guess I'm not a loose end until you have your little party.

"Thank you, Constantine," Cooper responded with as much of a positive tone as he could muster. "And if you're inviting the team, do you want me to include Lamont?"

Why not also show Lamont the asshole I work for? After all, he has been asking.

"Great idea. Just make sure he doesn't bring any guns!" Petrenko grinned and took another drag on his sikar.

"Now sit back and relax, Mr. Cooper. And tell me all about your plans for our loose ends."

FIFTY-SEVEN

WASHINGTON, DC
AUGUST 28

"SO WHERE ARE WE?" ASKED HARRIS WITH NO BELIEF HE WOULD GET AN ACCEPTABLE answer.

"Pretty much nowhere," responded Thompson. "We still don't know the source that coordinated all the attacks on the 14th. And September 11 is only two weeks away. God only knows what's going to happen next."

"I don't understand," added Taft. "We were warned that it was a Russian. With all the technology you have at hand, how can you not know who is pulling the strings? I thought you had informants. People on the inside."

"We do, Rebecca. But they're as much in the dark as we are," Thompson said.

"OK, let's go over what we do know," concluded Harris.

On the whiteboard on the wall, Thompson listed the facts they knew:

- Al-Badri was behind some of the terrorist plots.
- Rashid, their inside man, is watching al-Badri and has provided intel on al-Badri's operations.
- Al-Badri is not the brains behind the operation. He's not that smart.
- Lamont was believed to be responsible for the sale of some of the weapons. But who is paying him?
- David White was found murdered in the Hamptons with no suspects on any list.
- Someone is feeding Taft hints. But why are some true and others false?

- China is in chaos and markets throughout the world are in freefall. Someone is profiting from it, but who?
- Thousands are dead.
- What is planned for September 11?

More hours of analysis and debate. No progress.

FIFTY-EIGHT

PODGORICA, REPUBLIC OF MONTENEGRO
AUGUST 31

"YOU WANT ME AND JANKOVIĆ IN ST. PETERSBURG TO PARTY WITH PETRENKO? ARE YOU serious, Cooper?" asked Dorda.

Invitations had already been conveyed to al-Badri and Lamont.

"Tad, I follow orders. So do you. Just be there. I'll send you the location once I have it." He hung up.

"Now that's interesting," observed Janković. "Petrenko wants to celebrate and spend some of the billions we've helped him earn. You think he'll share any of it with us?"

"Paula, be careful what you wish for. Petrenko doesn't share anything. I don't know what he's up to, but you're not coming. I want you here, watching my back. Can you hack into wherever we are?"

"Probably, but how is that going to help you?"

"I don't know. But you're the only person I trust."

The only person you trust. Such a fool.

"OK. I'll give you a secure phone without a ringer. It will only silently vibrate. We'll work out a code that you can press on the buttons, so I'll know if there is a problem. I can watch the streets and maybe even get into cameras at the site. No doubt he has them. It will depend upon how far in advance I know where you'll be."

"Won't Petrenko know I have the phone? What makes you think he'll let me bring one?"

"Good point. But there is always vulnerability in every security system. Just keep the phone until Petrenko takes it from you. That will give me a location. I'll think of more to do by tomorrow. Just let me know where you're going to be as soon as you can."

FIFTY-NINE

WASHINGTON, D.C.
SEPTEMBER 4

"WE HAVE ONLY SEVEN DAYS," OBSERVED THOMPSON.

"I know that, Chandler. I don't need a countdown!"

Nerves were on edge.

Gathered at the table were Richard Harris, Chandler Thompson, Oliver Grant, Rebecca Taft, and Hashir Rashid. Dave Connelly and a half dozen other agents sat in chairs along the wall. The whiteboard was now filled with questions with no answers in sight.

"Hashir, I don't know what to say. I'm so sorry about New York," offered Thompson with genuine sincerity in his voice.

"Sorry? I don't care if you're sorry. I should have done something. But you made me sit there. Now hundreds are dead because I did nothing."

Harris called everyone together before Rashid returned to Syria. Al-Badri was waiting for him, according to his letter, "with open arms." The idea sickened Rashid and he'd made one excuse after another to avoid returning. He doubted al-Badri would accept any more.

In previous days, Harris, Thompson, and Rashid spent hours debriefing about the New York attack and how communications failed. Rashid took it particularly hard, feeling he should have done more. It bothered him even more now that he might soon return to Damascus, a hero in al-Badri's eyes.

"Dick, I think Hashir being ordered back to Syria by al-Badri may be a breakthrough," observed Grant.

Rashid was about to explode. *A breakthrough? For who? The innocent people who died while all of you sat in your comfortable offices in Washington?*

"Mr. Grant, whatever is happening, why is it a breakthrough that Mr. Rashid is being ordered back to Syria?" asked Taft.

Harris interceded in the conversation. "We don't know for sure, Rebecca, but it may be a chance to find out who is leading all of this. Sooner or later, people will start talking. They're going to want to crow about their success. So whoever it is, we may be close. This may be the only opportunity left before September 11."

"We also know that Cooper and Lamont are in Russia. That can't be a coincidence," added Grant.

"Look, everyone, we're at a loss. This is all we have," concluded Harris, turning to Rashid.

"What will you have me do?" Rashid asked, resigned to the reality that since he had no plan, he'd have to play whatever game others had in mind.

"We're going to give you a phone we can track and a transponder like the necklace Rebecca is wearing. Do Muslim men ever wear jewelry, Hashir?" asked Harris.

"Men cannot wear chains. That is not permitted because it imitates women. We cannot wear anything on our wrists, neck, or ears. That is something that is only for women. But men can wear rings. There is a long tradition of Muslim men and the only jewelry we're permitted to wear," responded Rashid.

"Oliver, can we put a transponder in a ring?" asked Harris.

"We can put a transponder in anything, Dick. But why not put one under Hashir's skin in his shoulder? Unless they have a metal detector or other sophisticated device, it will never be found."

"No, that will not work," interjected Rashid. "Al-Badri will check. He always does."

"Then it will be a ring," responded Harris.

Thompson rose and left the room, a sign that the meeting was over. As others likewise rose, Harris said, "Please stay with me for a moment longer, Hashir."

SIXTY

DAMASCUS
SEPTEMBER 8

WHEN RASHID ARRIVED IN SYRIA, AL-BADRI GREETED HIM WITH OPEN ARMS, JUST AS HE had promised.

"My brother, it is good to have you back. Allah be praised." His hug was genuine. Rashid's was not.

"Allah be praised, Abu." The greeting sickened Rashid.

The two got into al-Badri's car for the ride to the hotel where al-Badri would drop off Rashid.

Al-Badri could hardly keep his excitement in control during the ride. "It is time to celebrate, Hashir. Tomorrow we fly to Russia to meet the man behind it all. He is someone I've waited to meet for years. The time has finally come. We can all celebrate what will happen in just three days!" declared al-Badri.

"Where in Russia?" asked Rashid.

"I don't know. I've only been told we're to fly to Russia on a jet that will meet us at the airport. A private jet, Hashir! We'll travel in luxury."

"Abu, I need some sleep. What time do we leave?"

"I understand, brother. You must be exhausted. We take off at nine tomorrow morning. You won't need a visa," al-Badri responded with a laugh.

Once on the street of his hotel, Rashid took the assigned detour to a café.

He immediately saw his contact. The description of him that had been given to Rashid left no doubt.

"May I join you?" Rashid asked.

"Please do," was the response.

Rashid reported what he had been told and left. The truth was he did need to get some sleep.

In his room, he bathed and did his prayers in the traditional way, praying to Allah for forgiveness. While he had come to understand that a true God abhorred the violence that men like al-Badri spread throughout the world, he still desired in his heart to believe that his Allah was a fair God and would find a way to bring Rashid to redemption.

SIXTY-ONE

KRESTOVSKY ISLAND
SEPTEMBER 9

WHEN AL-BADRI AND RASHID ARRIVED, COOPER GREETED THEM AT THE GATE OF THE Krestovsky complex.

"Thank you for coming, gentlemen." Cooper looked at Rashid. "You must be Hashir Rashid. It is a pleasure to meet you. My name is Frank Cooper."

"I know who you are, Mr. Cooper. Abu told me all about you."

"No doubt he did. But you have the advantage, Mr. Rashid. He has told me very little about you. And I'm anxious to learn more. Please follow me."

The three walked along a long path leading to the main building. Two armed guards were at the door. An x-ray machine with a conveyor belt and a walk-through metal detector was positioned behind them. It was the same setup most airports used.

"Forgive the security, gentlemen," Cooper commented. "It's routine. I'm sure you understand. After you."

A security guard greeted them. He handed each of them a small plastic bowl.

"Please put everything you're carrying in the bowl and on the conveyor belt please."

Al-Badri placed his phone in a bowl and walked through. Rashid followed, putting his phone in the bowl.

"Your ring, too, please," the guard politely ordered.

"I can't do that," responded Rashid. "I am a devout Muslim, and I do not remove my ring. It would be a sin to Allah."

Al-Badri gave Rashid an odd look but said nothing. He had never heard of such a sacred rule, but Rashid was far more devout than he was, so he let it pass. This was not the time to argue about interpretations of the Quran.

Without waiting for the guard to respond, he walked through the metal detector. It remained silent.

Cooper followed.

"Now that wasn't so bad, was it?" laughed Cooper.

Al-Badri reached for his phone.

"I'm sorry, sir. You cannot take your phone with you. Please turn it off and leave it with me. You can have it back when you leave."

"Do you not trust us, Mr. Cooper?" asked al-Badri with a menacing tone.

Before Cooper could reply, Rashid interjected, "Don't worry Abu, no one will need to make any calls." His comment drew another odd look from al-Badri.

Rashid did not bother to reach for his phone, knowing that even if turned off, it continued to transmit. His concerns heightened, however, when the guard put the two phones in what appeared to be a metal-lined case, most likely to prevent any detection. Rashid worried that his ring might not be enough.

Once through security, a man Rashid correctly assumed was one of the servants greeted them.

As he walked with al-Badri, his brother in arms remarked, "Hashir, I didn't know you were so devout. When did you start wearing a ring?"

"Abu, I've always worn it. You just never noticed," replied Rashid as calmly as he could.

"Really? Well, you'll have to tell me all about it when we get back to Damascus."

Indeed I will, Abu. Indeed I will.

The apartment was as ornate as anything Rashid had ever seen. Artwork was on every wall. Rashid assumed much of it was priceless.

Cooper escorted them into a room with a fireplace and red leather chairs in a semicircle in front of it. As they entered, the three men sitting in the chairs rose.

"Greetings, my friends. I'm thrilled you're all here. My name is Constantine Petrenko." He extended his hand to al-Badri.

Rashid had heard of Petrenko but not from Harris or anyone else in the FBI, CIA, or Homeland Security. He had seen his name in occasional articles about Russian oligarchs who became billionaires after the fall of the Soviet Union.

So much for America's intelligence operations, thought Rashid.

"Let me introduce you to our comrades. This is Thaddeus Dorda from Montenegro. He goes by Tad." Dorda acknowledged the introduction with a nod. "Unfortunately, his associate Paula Janković was unable to make it. Much to my disappointment." Petrenko's look at Dorda made the depth of his disappointment clear. "Mr. Dorda and the missing Ms. Janković run my social media efforts," added Petrenko.

"And my name is Philippe Lamont," interjected Lamont, rising and extending his hand to al-Badri.

"Yes. This is Philippe Lamont," repeated Petrenko. "Philippe has been instrumental in providing you with the many toys you so love to use on the infidels you hate," added Petrenko with a smile.

As al-Badri shook Lamont's hand, he commented, "Thank you, Mr. Lamont. Your toys, as Mr. Petrenko likes to describe them, are most appreciated."

Looking at Rashid, Petrenko asked, "And you are?"

"I am Hashir Rashid, Mr. Petrenko."

"Hashir is my brother," interjected al-Badri. "Without him, our cause would have never succeeded."

"Indeed," replied Petrenko. "Please, everyone, sit down. We have so much to talk about."

The butler asked Rashid and al-Badri if they would like a drink. Both declined.

"And I guess neither of you will join us for a cigar either," joked Petrenko. Neither al-Badri nor Rashid thought it was funny.

Once everyone was comfortable, Petrenko continued.

"My friend, Mr. Cooper, tells me he thought this celebration was a mistake until after September 11. Didn't you, Mr. Cooper?"

"Yes, Constantine, I did. And to be frank, I'm still not sure why you insisted when we're only two days away from putting your final plans in place."

"And what plans are those, Mr. Cooper?" asked Petrenko.

"To be honest, Constantine, I don't know. You've been very secretive about them," responded Cooper.

"Indeed I have. Would you like to know why?"

Cooper looked confused and could only think, *what kind of game is he playing now? Does he take us all for fools?*

"I'd certainly like to know," observed Lamont. "After all, you haven't given me a hint. And you haven't asked me to provide any new 'toys,' as you like to call them. So what is your plan, Constantine?"

"Today, I've made billions. I crushed China's markets. I killed Apple. Goldman Sachs, Bank of America, and UBS are on the edge of collapse. What more could I ask for or want? I feel as if it is Christmas for a Christian like me." Petrenko looked pleased with himself.

Petrenko took another sip of his drink while the smile on his face created a tension everyone in the room could feel.

"It may be Christmas for you, Mr. Petrenko, but for us, it is too soon to celebrate. Our victory is yet to be achieved. What are your plans for the 11th?" asked al-Badri.

Petrenko put his glass on the table in front of them and turned to al-Badri.

"What I'm saying, Abu, is that we're done. There is no plan for September 11. There never was. We all have what we wanted. I have my money, and you have a new life in your jihad. Nothing stops you from continuing your battles, although I'm not sure if you'll ever achieve what you see as victory. We can all affect the world order in the short term, but we cannot change it in the long run. That's how markets work, Abu. They rise, and they fall. The victors know when to ride the waves. The losers think they can outlast the ups and downs, always preaching that it's a long game. It's not. True fortunes are made on taking advantage of short-term fluctuations."

"I don't understand," replied al-Badri. "I thought we had a plan."

"We did, Abu. And our plan has worked. That is all the reward we need. Another attack will only bring unneeded instability. We crushed China, but we need the United States. Without it, there will be no viable markets. For now, we need to return to some degree of normalcy. Perhaps in the future, we can create the chaos again. But not now. What we need to do now is step back and enjoy our spoils. Let the world adjust, never knowing when we will strike again. We should start enjoying our victory!" declared Petrenko. With a grin, he took a drag on his cigar.

Al-Badri was speechless.

"That is not what we understood, Mr. Petrenko." Rashid spoke evenly, hoping to keep the conversation under control. He could sense the anger building in al-Badri. The others sat in silence, trying to absorb Petrenko's words.

Al-Badri refused to be calm. "We had a deal, and September 11 was to be a day of reckoning. A day of revenge. Are you saying that we're going to be denied that glory?" asked al-Badri, his tone clearly on edge.

"Abu, don't you see? You don't need to kill anyone right now. We can get them all to kill one another," replied Petrenko with a chilling laugh. "Many of the attacks over the past month were orchestrated by my operatives, not just yours. Learn from our success, Abu. Don't get greedy. You'll have more than enough opportunities in the future. I promise you I will continue to see that Mr. Lamont gives you what you need. But what you do with it will depend upon what I tell you to do and when I tell you to do it." Petrenko's comments were orders, not suggestions.

Rashid knew he needed to speak. "Yes, Mr. Petrenko, you have your money. Abu, you have your collection of dead people in the name of Allah. I'm not sure what you won out of this, Mr. Dorda. And as for you, Mr. Lamont, no doubt you're happy to know Abu has enough money to buy all the toys he wants." Rashid spoke his words in a calm, deliberate manner. He was not confrontational.

"What are you saying, Hashir? Petrenko has betrayed us! Don't you see that?" implored al-Badri, confused by Rashid's compliant tone.

"Abu, whatever betrayal Mr. Petrenko may have done to you, you betrayed Allah. You are as much a sinner among us as the rest of those in the room. The others just wanted money. You wanted to destroy our religion. For that, I cannot forgive you. As for the rest of you, I'll see you in hell."

Petrenko rose, sensing the ominous nature of what Rashid was saying, and shouted for his guards.

Those were his last words.

The cruise missile launched from the CIA ship in Helsinki harbor, just 186 miles from St. Petersburg, hit the compound with a force few had ever seen. Loaded with more conventional explosives than ever before used, it leveled the building and everything around it, instantly killing everyone inside. Priceless art up in smoke. Dozens of souls off to meet their God, whoever that God was.

Rashid's last thought was how much he would have liked to tell Harris not to worry about September 11.

SIXTY-TWO

WASHINGTON D.C.
SEPTEMBER 10

RICHARD HARRIS, CHANDLER THOMPSON, AND MICHAEL HELLRIEGEL GATHERED IN THE OVAL Office for a meeting with President Samantha Harrison.

While waiting for the president to arrive, Harris observed, "Hashir died a hero," recalling his last conversation with Rashid, just six days before, when the two of them remained in the room after Thompson went to requisition the ring Rashid wore to his death.

—

"Hashir, we're asking a lot of you. You can say no. You have already sacrificed enough. I won't order you to put your life in further danger."

"That is not your choice to make, Mr. Harris. I chose this way, and I will see it through. We all know what needs to be done."

"Hashir, we will get you out before we do anything. Just pinpoint the location and let us know that our mystery man is there. Then get out. We can take it from there."

"No, Mr. Harris. I am not coming back. Wherever al-Badri is taking me, your target will be there. You can be assured of that. You will strike and turn us all into cinders," Rashid calmly replied.

Harris, shocked, asked, "Why, Hashir? I don't understand. Why do you need to die?"

"I've already died, Mr. Harris. I died in Florence when I was prepared to die for al-Badri. I died in New York when I couldn't stop the slaughter of hundreds of innocent people."

"That was not your fault, Hashir. There was nothing you could do," implored Harris.

Showing no emotion, Rashid continued, "Mr. Harris, do you remember when we talked about God, and you told me that if I believed in God, then that God had to be a just God? A God of peace, not violence. Do you remember that?"

"Of course I do, Hashir. But I don't understand what that has to do with delivering you to a death sentence. I never told you that you had to die for that God. We do not have to do that, Hashir."

Still showing no emotion, Rashid calmly replied, "It is not about what you have to do. It is about what I have to do. It is about the salvation of my people and the glory of Allah—my God, Mr. Harris. A good God. It is exactly what I must do."

—

The president entered the room and brought Harris back to attention.

After Harris debriefed President Harrison, Thompson asked, "And what of the Russians, Madam President? We have never struck so deep in their territory."

"There will be objections and speeches at the U.N. I promised Putin he could have his moment. That is all he wanted. He is as happy as we are that Petrenko is dead. His only regret was that his intelligence operation was no better than ours in discovering Petrenko's plot. It hurt Russia as much as it hurt all of us."

The president stood and walked to the window.

"Mr. Hellriegel," she continued as she stared at the White House gardens, "you and I are going to have a long talk about why no one, not the CIA or the KGB, could identify Petrenko."

"Yes, Madam President. Whenever that is convenient for you," replied Hellriegel.

"Mr. Harris, what can we expect tomorrow, September 11? That is the next day of reckoning on the list."

"We don't know. We're not picking up any chatter. It seems without Petrenko and al-Badri, there is no leadership left. It's certainly premature to say we can be comfortable, but we may have caught a lucky break."

"Let's hope that luck holds, Mr. Harris. The world depends on it," concluded the president.

SIXTY-THREE

PODGORICA, REPUBLIC OF MONTENEGRO
SEPTEMBER 11

PAULA JANKOVIĆ TOOK ANOTHER SIP OF WINE, CONFIDENT IN HER VICTORY. SHE NOW SAT alone. The survivor with her entire army of programmers safe.

She didn't need to know where Dorda was going. She knew it from the phone that the CIA gave to Rashid. She'd hacked into it just as she hacked into Taft's phone. She was smart enough to keep that information to herself, laughing at the thought that anyone believed they could keep secrets from her and her network of spiders, cookies, algorithms, and bots. No one could hide from Paula Janković.

She pressed "enter" on her keyboard and sent her latest command to a Selfish Ledger at www.whitehouse.gov.

AUTHOR'S NOTE

IT IS NO SECRET THAT CYBERWARS ARE THE POLITICAL AND IDEOLOGICAL CONFLICTS OF THE future. Indeed, the United States has long been in a cyberwar with the likes of China, Russia, and North Korea. Terrorists like ISIS, Hamas, and others are becoming experts in cyber terrorism as well. While not a "hot" war, the economic impact of an all-out cyberwar far exceeds anything experienced in WWI and WWII combined.

The underpinning of traditional terrorism is its radical, primarily fundamentalist Islamic followers intent on killing those with whom they ideologically disagree. While their motivation is not financial profit, they are astute enough to know they need money to finance their jihads. ISIS is a classic example of such a structured group—ideologues with an appreciation for finance.

Financial terrorism takes a different twist. Unlike radical Islamic terrorists, the goal of a financial terrorist is to kill no one. Rather, a financial terrorist wants to keep as many fools alive as possible from whom he or she can take money. When they do kill, it is to silence a witness, not to promote any ideology. Combined, radical and financial terrorists are a lethal mixture of those who could not care less about dying for their cause and people who put a price on everything and anything as long as it brings in a profit.

Established law enforcement cannot do much in the fight, restrained by rules that work to the advantage of terrorists. While they try to combat the scourge, they know their limitations and fervently want to find a way around them if they ever hope to win—even when that means crossing the line. A line that grows ever vaguer every day.

This is a story about a potent combination of financial and radical terrorists with a new twist they bring to their unholy alliance. The prospect of such a pairing in today's world of technology is not fiction. It is already happening.

To my readers, this story may seem implausible. But it is not. One cannot imagine what a well-funded alliance between a billionaire financial terrorist and a dedicated Islamic fundamentalist can accomplish. What I have described is not wild speculation. It is all possible. Perhaps probable. *The Selfish Ledger* is real. It is not some wild fiction. Just do a web search for it if you doubt my thesis. And search on Google for the plans that IBM's Watson has in store for you with artificial intelligence, or the warnings of Dr. Zeynep Tufekci. It's all easy to find on the Internet.

Social media's manipulation of our minds; machine-learning replacing our decisions; and advances in artificial intelligence are happening with alarming speed. It is doubtful that any of it can be stopped. It is the price we are willing to pay for the convenience we ask of the Internet and our insatiable desire for fifteen minutes of fame as we post what we think and what we want, foolishly believing that anyone really cares what we think or want. Ask yourself some simple questions. Where will you and your children be when artificial intelligence and rogue algorithms make all this a reality? Is your future security dependent upon the luck of reporters, the CIA, the FBI, Interpol, and Homeland Security? Will your luck run out and the destiny I predict be unavoidable? If you still doubt me, read George Dvorsky's essay, *How We Can Prepare for Catastrophically Dangerous AI—and Why We Can't Wait*. Then think about it all when you next log on to a computer and click your mouse, send a text, search the Internet, call for an Uber, make a reservation on Open Table, or post your thoughts and pictures on Facebook and Instagram.

ACKNOWLEDGEMENTS

I HAVE A LOT OF PEOPLE TO THANK IN MAKING THIS BOOK POSSIBLE. A BIG THANK YOU GOES to my wife, Carol Ann, not only for her comments on the book but also for her patience with my often interruptive and sometimes annoying writing habits. Gerry Weston and Gerry Lauro for their help with securities trading. Both are Wall Street retirees and know the games the Bulls and Bears play. Mike Santangelo for his expertise in firearms. Mike is a collector and enthusiast of safe gun ownership and one of my cigar buddies. I've spent hours with him enjoying a smoke and learning about guns. Felix Hofer, who lives in Florence, Italy, for his help in making sure my scenes in that country were accurate. There is nothing quite like having Felix as my personal tour guide to one of the most beautiful countries in the world. Mitch Becker for his always insightful thoughts on my prose and storyline. Mitch has helped me with all of my books. My assistant, Nancy Schulein, for keeping the ball rolling with schedules as well as helpful suggestions. Lauren Harvey for her great jacket design. Lauren has created most of my covers. Brent Jostad, a narcotics and money-laundering prosecutor, for his advice on the preferred communication methods used by criminals. To my publicist, Keely Flanagan, for putting together the marketing and publicity plans around the book. Thanks also go to Jeremy Townsend, my editor, and Kate Petrella, my copyeditor, for their contributions with polishing up the book. However good my writing may be, the two of them make it better. And last, but certainly not least, to my publisher, Claire McKinney. This is my second book that her company, Plum Bay Publishing, has steered to readers around the world.

CAST OF CHARACTERS

NAME	DESCRIPTION	FIRST APPEARANCE (BY CHAPTER)
Abadi, Osama	Terrorist	42
Abazo, Omar	Terrorist	26
al-Assad, Bashar	President of Syria	46
al-Badri, Abu	Terrorist	8
Alighieri, Dante	Artist	1
Allah	God	1
Allman Brothers	Band	22
Almasi, Hanifa	Terrorist	42
Ansis, Fredric	Alias	7
Antar, Assad	Terrorist	44
Anthony	Bartender, 75 Main, South Hampton, Long Island	36
Bernstein, Carol	Reporter	15

Boston Red Sox	Hated Baseball Team	28
Bousaid, Adara	Terrorist	39
Branson, Richard	Investor	42
Breen, Nick	Lawyer	15
Browne, John Lye	London Banker	31
Brunelleschi, Filippo	Artist	1
Burry, Michael	Visionary	28
Castro, Fidel	Prime Minister of Cuba	6
Catherine the Great	Empress of Russia	31
Chavez, Juanita	Illegal Alien	40
Chavez, Margarita	Pawn	42
Chevalier de Lamarck, Jean Baptiste Pierre Antoine de Monet	Evolutionist	20
Chiang, Yu Yan	Revolutionist	24
Chicago Cubs	Beloved Baseball Team	28
Christ, Jesus	Son of God	18
Clooney, George	Actor	42
Connelly, Dave	Agent, United States Central Intelligence Agency	45

Cooper, Francis	Attorney	5
da Vinci, Leonardo	Artist	1
Dawkins, Richard	1970s Evolutionary Biologist	20
de' Frescobaldi, Marchesi	Vintner	2
DePalma, John	Concord, New Hampshire Chief of Police	46
Dorda, Tad	Hacker	19
Dracula	Fictional Character	14
Drew, Nancy	Fictional Character	17
Duarte de Perón, Eva	First Lady of Argentina	46
Duggan, Bill	NYPD Commander	55
	Hacker	17
Dvorsky, George	Writer	Author's Note
Feng, Bianca	Manager, Foxconn Technology	35
Gandhi, Mahatma	Man of Peace	27
Geraghty, Sheila	Murderer	36
God	Himself(s)	1
Gonzalez, Jose Luis	Pawn	42

Gordon, Jason	Reporter	15
Grande, Ariana	Singer	49
Grant, Oliver	Homeland Security	11
Hamilton, William	Twentieth-Century Evolutionist	20
Harris, Richard	Special Agent, United States Central Intelligence Agency	3
Harrison, Samantha	President of the United States	25
Hellriegel, Michael	Director, United States Central Intelligence Agency	25
Heng, Jian	Bianca Feng's second in command	41
Heng, Nadia	Wife of Jian Heng	41
Heng, Peigi	Daughter of Jian Heng	41
Hernandez, Miguel	Pawn	42
Himmler, Heinrich	Nazi	28
Hoover, J. Edgar	Former Director of the Federal Bureau of Investigation	3
Hue, Beatrice	United States Congresswomen, Chair of the House Intelligence Committee	3

Humayun, Farid	Terrorist	1
Isselin, Michael	Editor	13
Janković, Paula	Hacker	19
Jinping, XI	General Secretary of China's Communist Party and Chairman of the CPC Central Military Commission	24
Kadar, Daniel	Agent, France's Direction Générale de la Sécurité Extérieure	26
Kasper, Dave	Victim	42
Kasper, Sally	Victim	42
King, Dr. Martin Luther	Man of Peace	27
Kolesaire, Barbara	Concord, New Hampshire Police Officer	46
Kouachi, Chérif	Terrorist	26
Kouachi, Saïd	Terrorist	26
Lamont, Philippe	Arms Dealer	8
Lewis, Michael	Author, The Big Short: Inside the Doomsday Machine	28
Loeb, William	Publisher, Manchester Union Leader	46

Lopez, Maria	Pawn	42
Marcus, Joyce	Assistant to the President of the United States	25
Martinez, Veronica	Pawn	42
Michelangelo di Lodovico Buonarroti Simoni	Artist	1
Moghadam, Layal	Terrorist	44
Monet, Jean-Baptiste Pierre Antoine	Nineteenth-century evolutionist	20
N.Y. Mets	Hapless Baseball Team	28
Nazari, Jamel	Terrorist	49
Nejem, Kareem	Terrorist	39
Orwell, George	Author	35
Peters, Roy	Winner of The Voice	46
Petrenko, Constantine	Russian Oligarch	5
Pfeiffer, Marty	NYPD Chief of the Counterterrorism Bureau and Critical Response Command	55
Putin, Vladimir	President of the Russian Federation	6
Rashid, Hashir	Terrorist	1

Rashid, Osama	Father of Hashir Rashid	1
Raymond, Elizabeth	Victim	42
Raymond, Peter	Victim	42
Sanchez, Juan	Pawn	42
Santangelo, Mike	Concord, New Hampshire Police Detective	46
Scott, James	Senior Fellow, Institute for Critical Infrastructure Technology	Preface
Shadid, Mohammed	Terrorist	44
Simpson, Horace	United States Senator, Chair of the Intelligence Oversight Committee	3
Sokolov, Boris	Chief Curator, Hermitage Museum	31
Spock, Mr.	Lieutenant Commander, U.S.S. Enterprise	26
Steele, Raymond	Broker	6
Steinle, Kate	Victim	40
Stevens, Christopher	U.S. Ambassador to Libya	13
Suzuki, Hideyo	Art Collector	49

Swimer, Nick	Manchester, England, Chief of Police	49
Taft, Rebecca	Reporter	12
Takahashi, Aiko	Artist	49
Thompson, Chandler	Agent, Federal Bureau of Investigation	11
Thomson, Meldrim	Governor, State of New Hampshire	46
Tibbetts, Mollie	Victim	40
Torchia, Lori	Hacker	12
Trump, Donald	Investor	52
Tufekci, Zeynep	Professor	20
Watson	Computer	20
Weinreb, Scotty	Hacker	22
White, Darren	Broker	6
Yuanzhang, Mochou	Friend of Yu Yan Chiang	24
Zaman, Tahir	Terrorist	39
Zedong, Mao	Chairman of the Communist Party of China	24
Zhang, Pak Heir	Computer Scientist	21

CPSIA information can be obtained
at www.ICGtesting.com
Printed in the USA
LVHW090959170919
631340LV00001B/46/P